JONATHA

PETER BREAKSPEAR

To my wife, always there for me.

Jonathan Brown is a work of fiction: all characters and events are the result of the author's imagination and bear no relation to events or people either living or dead.

1.

Jonathan Brown didn't attract much attention; just over six feet tall with an athletic build and short greying hair; he looked like many of his age group who looked after themselves. In his early forties, a man who came across as serious and not prone to wasting time in idle chitchat. Today, he was just another man walking with the flow of people that filled the streets at this time of day in this part of Nottingham; the shoppers were out in force; many with children in tow because of the school holiday that had started the day before. The crowds had swelled by many office workers that had come out to get a takeaway lunch or to sit for forty minutes with their friends in one of the many cafeterias and eateries on every street corner in big cities these days.

He slowed his pace; he didn't want to arrive at the meeting a second too soon; someone hanging around would attract attention. The target would be on the corner of Tolbert Street and Goldsmith's Street just outside the large shopping complex that occupied a whole city block. He would wait for someone who had asked him over to this part of the city for lunch. Jonathan didn't know the person he was to kill and had only the briefest idea of whom or what they were; a Doctor but not a medical Doctor but some scientist. It didn't matter to Jonathan the only information he ever wanted was enough to do the job. Jonathan was at the crossing and there was no sign of the man who was to die.

Jonathan stopped at the crossing that led to the shopping centre; he saw him across the road looking down the length of the street; he was looking for someone; *shame he would never meet them. Jonathan pondered why he hadn't seen him before; perhaps the crowd had hidden him from view as the angle changed when Jonathan had approached the crossing.*

Standing in the second rank of people waiting for the lights to change, Jonathan made a final assessment of the man; he was wearing a light blue, long sleeve shirt over which he had an open leather jacket; the shirt sleeves peeping out of the cuffs. Excellent, Jonathan thought as the lights changed. Jonathan closed with the man about to die. Jonathan moved to one side as he walked towards him; he could see inside the targets jacket and his shirt that had a packet of cigarettes or something similar sticking out of it; might be a phone so he would avoid that.

Going well so far, Jonathan said under his breath as the distance closed. He would pass to the left of the target on his right side and then continue into the shopping centre.

The man was startled as Jonathan brushed past him, caught off balance he was about to say something but found the world closing in on him as he suddenly could not remain standing. He was dead as he hit the floor; a tiny wound to his chest that went into his heart just to the left of the object in his pocket. The blade, Jonathan's own design, had a sharp edge at the forward end that would pivot round if it met anything that resisted such as a rib. As the blade came out the same pivot caused the edge to move sideways slicing a large hole in the heart.

The blood there was from the puncture site was hidden by the jacket; blood pressure down to zero so no more blood would arrive at the wound. The target appeared to have fainted.

Jonathan was inside the shopping centre and heading for the elevators to the car park, the blade well-hidden up his sleeve. Some people outside stopped to assist the man on the ground but many didn't; walking past, into or out of the shops; *they were in a hurry don't forget*. An off-duty nurse started CPR whilst a half dozen people used their phone to call an ambulance many more used their phones to record the drama and upload the images for the world to see; it would add to the confusion at the emergency response switchboard. The nurse found the wound and soon realised that this chap was well beyond what she could achieve.

“He’s been stabbed!” Panic in the crowd spread; people running in all directions. *What if the person with the knife was intending to stab again?*

Jonathan took the elevator down to the bottom level of the car park; a small Ford was in the parking space as he had expected; the keys in the ignition and the exit ticket was on the dash; it was all going well; soon he would be on his way to the airport and away to Spain for some well-earned rest. "What about the target?" Jonathan had put the whole job out of his mind; he would soon work on another; the Tolbert Street job was history.

As Jonathan exited the car park a figure in the shadows was speaking into a mobile phone. "Yes, he has gone; no problems." The figure took the card out of the phone, broke it in half and dropped one half down a small drain by the entrance to the ramp, he would dispose of the other half and the phone in the street. The supermarket pay-as-you go had only made one call in its entire life. Bit of a waste.

Jonathan parked at the rear of the long stay car park at the East Midlands airport, just over an hour before his flight to the sunshine. He left the key in the ignition and threw the ticket into the bin as he went through the exit that led to departures; the car would be there for months before anyone became suspicious; it might even be stolen when some chancer noticed it was unlocked and the key left. It didn't matter either way; the car was untraceable, taxed, insured and registered through a myriad of different companies. If it was chased down, the trail would take them to conclude that the car was owned by the local Police, tracks well and truly covered. The blade, without the pivot end, went into the bushes on the way into the main building. The business end thrown into the undergrowth on the way to the airport; gloves into a bin just inside the entrance.

Within twenty minutes Jonathan was in the departure lounge having a coffee, watching the stream of people that out from the duty-free section of the lounge. The departures filled with the usual groups; families getting away for the annual break, some businessmen all typing away on their laptops and the inevitable stag party waiting to go somewhere to get drunk over two days.

This time the groom dressed as a chicken; Jonathan couldn't see the relevance but hey ho. Jonathan sipped his coffee and waited for the gate to open.

Back at the entrance to the shopping centre the Police had cordoned off the area and closed the adjacent shops; a serious incident declared as soon as the stabbing had been confirmed. Professor Alan Swift, the well-known bio chemist was on his way to the morgue having died at the scene; the team he led would miss him.

2.

Across the Atlantic in an apartment halfway up one of the many buildings in Lower Manhattan a figure moved away from the phone.

"It seems Professor Swift is no longer with us Hector."

Hector was a very large man who looked like he was about to have a heart attack; he wasn't, but always looked on the brink. Under six feet tall but more than twice his ideal weight he did not cut the image of a fit athletic man, not even close. He had lost count of how many times people had asked him if he was all right. It still amused him. Years of a bad diet and little exercise had taken its toll, but he didn’t care much; *when He decides it’s time to go, then I will go.*

"The Professor was only a distraction at this stage; it is fortunate that we were alerted to his operation early on and could lure him to Nottingham so he could be dealt with; we shouldn't have to intervene again if the plan stays on schedule. Do we know of any others who might be a problem?"

"No Hector, but the female Doctor who is the number two in France may get suspicious." The man talking and had the manner of someone who was always thinking of what will happen next; someone who could not relax, even when he seemed to others to be relaxing. He was less than a third the size of Hector but slowed his pace to conform with Hector’s lumbering.

"No matter, we will get our man from Spain again if she gets too close, in the meantime she will be distracted by the good Professors demise. I feel it is time for a coffee and something to eat don't you think?"

The two men took their time as they descended to the ground level; both men had little need for speed and the larger man could hardly have gone any faster. Once out in the open air they turned and walked north, neither man saying anything; the journey was a well-practised one, and they soon arrived at their usual eating place on the corner of Christie and Broome; a small coffee house but one that had excellent sandwiches and the best coffee in town. Well both men would say that but neither of them had been anywhere else in this city in recent years. One reason was that it would require walking a longer distance or getting onto the public transport, an idea neither of the men would entertain.

Both men sat in the corner with a view to the outside; here they had a good view of the busy traffic that always seemed to be there, day or night in this part of town.

"Who looks after our security these days? The big man asked, looking at a figure that stood on the corner opposite the coffee house; almost out of view from their position but not quite.

"Why do you ask? Have you concerns?

"See him over there? Well he is our man for the day and I spotted him straight away; if I can see him, then the opposition can see him. I think we should have a security review as soon as we get back to the office."

The two men were being monitored as was the security provision that they were talking about. The opposition, as the big man referred to them, were not far away and had been recording the movements of not only the two men but also the team of men assigned to protect them. The single man across the road was part of a three-man setup; the other two were further down the street at opposite ends of the block. The team were playing the usual deception game.

Two large coffee cups were delivered to the table; neither man had said a word to the proprietor but their visit was a well-practised one; the only variation was the cakes or sandwiches that the men sometimes requested. This time they both asked for a small slice of Madera.

"Will the project remain on track?" The smaller of the two asked.

"At the moment, the plan is going almost as expected, aside from the Professor and the job that had to be done over there." The big man waved his hand in the air as if showing the direction where the Professor met his end. Professor Swift had been dealt with because he had tried to contact a journalist not realising that his efforts had been intercepted by the organisation; the professor thought he had arranged to meet someone in Nottingham to discuss what he had found out but there was no journalist and no real contact had been made, instead he was lured to the corner in the city to await his death.

"What we must find out is why and how the Professor deviated from what he was doing; he seemed to be focused and very determined in the research. What prompted him to dig into the background is, at the moment, a mystery." The two men sat and drank their coffee, the big man picked up his cake and ate it in two bites; the smaller of the two cut his into small cubes and ate, taking sips from his coffee in between. Both enjoying the quiet that compared to the hustle and bustle of the street outside where everyone seemed to be in a hurry.

"We should get a report later today if the team has been successful in the lab; we will give a few days off to mourn the Professor. Who shall we appoint in his place? I thought that the team leader from the mirror project could step up."

The teams the small man was talking about were two funded groups chasing the same target. Both teams knew of the other but there was no cross contamination of information or ideas. It had been decided a long time ago to duplicate the work just in case there was an incident that compromised the research; the Professor was such an incident but he was dealt with in time.

"Will the lead from the UK team to be up to speed at team one?" The big man knew the answer but asked, anyway.

“Yes, he should be able to fit in straight away; both teams are on track and very close to each other’s findings.”

Although both teams had been working in isolation, the discoveries they had made and the conclusions they had reached were similar but the group in France was ahead. The work had been monitored at several stages to determine if there had been cross contamination of work but there was no evidence this had happened.

“With the amount of money that has been invested in this project we need to keep a constant watch on things.” The two men sat in silence, both watching the man across the street. Now they both knew he was there he seemed to stick out like a sore thumb.

“They are still sitting in the coffee house drinking coffee and talking and looking at me.” The man was answering the team leader on the two-way communication they used. A hidden ear piece and a small microphone taped to his neck under his shirt; even a low voice would be picked up and transmitted. Sometimes it seemed like he wasn’t talking at all but at the other end the sound would be clear and sharp.

"They have seen you then?" The voice in his ear said.

"Hardly could have missed me, stood here like a lemon." He had worked with these two gentlemen for two years now; they had never seen him, or at least he didn't think so. They knew that the security team was looking out for them but if the team was doing their job, they would go unnoticed. Today was different; he was stood bare arsed in the street and feeling exposed; something he would never do by choice.

A car stopped in the road outside with the car radio turned right up; Dexy's Midnight Runners singing Come on Eileen.

"Who buys that stuff and who is Irene supposed to be?" The smaller of the two asked to nobody, referring to the music that had started outside the coffee shop.

"It's Eileen and not of your time." Hector stirred and attempted to rise. The small man didn't offer to help; he had learnt that lesson some time before. The big man struggled but made it to his feet.

"Moving." The man across the road said.

"Don't follow; stay on the corner as if you have not seen them go." A voice said.

It would have been difficult not to see the two men leave the coffee shop and wander back the way they had arrived an hour before but it would all add to the confusion. Someone watching might regard him as either short sighted or inept.

The two men arrived back at the door to the apartment block without incident; their security team was with them throughout the walk.

"Did you see the fellow across the street? He never even noticed we had left; I will get a hold of the security manager and suggest a change of the team for the future."

"I'm sure we were not in any danger but it might be a good idea to shake things up; people get complacent and this little routine has been going on with little change for some time now."

"The Lodge meets on Friday." The big man was out of breath again.

"We will all need to be there."

"I will be there; we have some serious things to consider so it will be a closed meeting at a higher level than usual."

The two men settled back into the apartment and worked on a pile of paperwork stacked over two desks that sat in the middle of the room.

"We need to get some of this into the shredder when we can; not a good idea to keep this thing in here despite the security we have."

The team, watching the two men and their security had gathered enough information to plan; it would be put into place the next day when the two went for their coffee at the same time. The control of this one went right up to the Director, so it had to go to plan or they would all be investigating livestock thefts in Alaska.

3.

Jonathan Brown was getting off the aircraft at Alicante, feeling the warm air on his face; he liked Spain, not too hot but pleasantly warm even at this time of year.

"I wonder how long I will have." It had been almost a year since the organisation had tasked him with such a short notice job as this one in Nottingham. The money was exceptionally good though. He passed through immigration and the customs area without incident. The car, left by a third party, was in the car park with the keys hidden inside, within ten minutes he was on the way home. *A swim and later a few beers will go down nicely.*

"He is on his way." The man in the doorway would probably have gone unnoticed by any other than Jonathan.

"Alternate plan we think." Jonathan said to himself; working out the new route he was to take to the safe house and away from the man in the doorway.

To the observer, it seemed that Jonathan was indeed going home to his small house perched on the side of the hill with a stunning view across the coast. This wasn't the first time he had been contacted close to his home, but it had not happened in Spain before; he wondered what was going on. It was not a hit because they would have had a go by now; they have had plenty of opportunity. No, they were after a chance to speak to him and from experience he knew that might not be all that pleasant.

He drove straight past the entrance to his house and made a sharp turn down a track that ran at right angles to the main road; after a hundred yards, he re-joined the tarmac and sped down towards the coast. He made the hidden turn in ten minutes and entered an underground garage that was almost invisible from the road; at the far end were two other cars. He got out and retrieved a handgun that was hidden in the wall. Everything was quiet outside but he could just hear the approach of a vehicle, coming fast up the road. It was a medium sized Mercedes with three men in it. The car didn't stop or even slow down but sped past the entrance to the garage and disappeared down the road.

Jonathan replaced the weapon into the hiding place; it wasn't a good idea to be picked up by the police and be found to have a gun; besides, he didn't need it at this particular moment. He retrieved his bag and put it into one of the other cars. His new ride was a different model, bigger engine and a different colour; the registration plate was Portuguese not Spanish. He made sure the chase car was gone, pulled on a black baseball cap, eased out of the garage and went back the way he had come.

"House number two it is then." Jonathan was about an hour from his other place; the house that he was going to have a swim at would never see him again. Travel light and always be ready to abandon anything and everything; that way he would stay alive for some time longer. First thing he had to do was find out who was chasing him and why; perhaps he had been rumbled in Nottingham; unlikely but possible. More careful from now on; he may even have to get out of Europe and go east. He must get a message to his contact and tell them to find out how he was traced.

"We lost him; he is very good and gave us the slip very easily."

"Doesn't matter now; we have the connection to the latest killing in the UK. Our man was only a small player and will probably not know as much about the project as we do. Let him go." The man in Spain sitting in the Mercedes was a little disappointed; the target was obviously very professional, and he was looking forward to getting after him. That was not to be; perhaps sometime in the future.

"OK boys we are done here, let's go home." The big car drove back down the round and headed towards the airport; *nice day for a drive.*

4.

Doctor Helen Dudman, an experienced research scientist, was sitting in her office at the facility in France; she was reading the transcript of a message that had been sent securely by the people who paid her wages. She had got it about two hours before and had read it a dozen times. She was in shock; Professor Swift who she had worked with for two years was dead! What was he doing in Nottingham? He was supposed to be having a short break on the coast in the South of France not getting stabbed in Nottingham. She had been on the internet the whole time looking for news items that might give her some more information about his death; strangely the message she held in her hand had more information than the news channels. It was a random attack, and the Professor was in the wrong place at the wrong time; the wrong place alright. Did her friend have some secret liaison going on? She doubted it but wouldn't have bet any money either way. What had he said to her the other day? "Helen, I think we are going in a direction that we shouldn't." She had asked what he meant, but he changed the subject and the conversation took a turn back to the job in hand.

Her computer beeped at the arrival of several emails; she put the paper down and looked at the screen. Usual work stuff but the last one was from the director of the project; she thought this was perhaps only the third mail she had ever received from him.

Dr Dudman, due to the departure of Professor Swift I am appointing Professor David Catchpole to the lead of the project; you will remain as second to assist him in the catch-up process he will have to undertake. The profesor has been leading the unit in the United Kingdom.

"That's nice." She had a small wish at the back of her mind that perhaps, maybe she would become the lead but hey ho, crack on regardless. She had never heard of this Professor Catchpole so it would be interesting to see where the project would go from here. She made a note to check on this Catchpole. *Forewarned is forearmed.* Doctor Helen Dudman had been a scientist for the whole of her working life that's if you didn't count the time as a waitress which part funded her time at the university. At just over six feet tall she struck an imposing figure when she wanted to; she had learned long ago that it was beneficial to be able to fade into the background as the situation required but it was also useful to assert herself to get what she wanted. Many a colleague had been taken by surprise by her forthright nature when pushed.

Catchpole was already on his way; he had been told about the move a very short time after the news of Swift. That caught him a little by surprise; obviously, the project cannot afford any undue delays. For Professor Catchpole, it was all a bit quick; he had been doing well, or so he thought, with the team he had been leading in Wales. He wondered what differences he would find with the research; from the paperwork, he had at the briefing the two projects appeared to be very similar except this new one was a little behind but not by much. The general direction was the same, and the conclusions reached by both teams so far were the same.

He thought about what he was going to say at the team briefing when he arrived in the morning. A shame he had to move to France; he had gotten used to the countryside in Wales. He arrived at the facility just after ten at night; after showing his passes he was shown to the accommodation block that was used by most but not all the staff; this setup was in the middle of nowhere.

First things first, he thought as he put his suitcase on the single bed that was against the side wall under the one window that looked out onto a grassed area. "There might be a nice view in the morning." He said to himself.

The view in the morning was disappointing; a large, well-kept lawn area that filled the space between the accommodation block and the perimeter wall; what was behind the wall was hidden. David estimated that the wall was probably in excess of ten feet in height with anti climb fixtures on the top. "Perhaps there are some security problems here."

He made himself a coffee from the machine that sat just inside the room door; David was never a man to have breakfast, but he found that he would get irritable without a coffee first thing. After the second cup, he quickly read through the briefing notes; ten minutes later he was walking over to the admin building that was about fifty metres away; couldn't miss it, a large brightly coloured sign was at the entrance to the building. As he walked towards the entrance he was surprised to notice that the layout of the facility was identical to the one in Wales; all except the perimeter wall; the one in Wales had a mesh fence that you could see through; this place was built more like a prison than a research facility.

Doctor Helen Dudman was at the door to meet the Professor; she had been alerted that he had arrived the evening before and had guessed that he would be on time in the morning, so here she was. She thought that it may have looked like she knew exactly when he would turn up but it was just an educated guess; it did make it look like she was completely on the ball though.

“Good morning Doctor Dudman.” Catchpole offered his hand.

Helen Dudman was surprised he recognised her; she was sure they had not met before.

“Professor Catchpole, the team are in the conference ready for the catch-up meeting.”

The two scientists walked side by side towards the large conference room that was used for all the major briefings and conferences on the site; neither spoke for the half a minute it took to complete the journey.

The conference room held about thirty people; mainly men but there were a few women, all were very qualified in the area of bio sciences and it had taken some time and a lot of resources to assemble them. The offer of much more money and better working conditions had swayed the majority and the promise of a generous end of project bonus kept them here.

The room fell silent as Professor Catchpole strode to the front and positioned himself just left of the lectern.

"Colleagues." He had used the generic form of address and not ladies and gentlemen or Doctors, etc. He had got into the habit some time ago on a project that was not nearly as important as this one.

His eyes swept the room making sure that all present were paying attention; he needn't have worried because everyone in the room was hoping for more information regarding Professor Swift, a man all in the room had liked.

"As you all know I am to take up the position of team leader after the most unfortunate death of Professor Swift; it is still not clear why he was murdered or even why he was in Nottingham. As far as we can determine his visit was not connected to the project; at which point I would like to remind you all that all of our work and anything associated with it is to be kept within this facility. There is a lot at stake here."

"Are you suggesting that the Professor's death was anything to do with the project?" A small man at the back was on his feet, his manner indicating that he was a bit annoyed with the last comment.

"Not at all Doctor James; Professor Swift did not declare where he was going; quite the contrary he informed the unit that he would be south of here on the coast for a couple of days, not in Nottingham waiting outside a shopping centre for heaven knows what. So, I remind you all; obey the rules and follow the procedure;

if that is a problem please let me know and you can get a better job somewhere else."

Doctor James was wrong footed by being addressed by name; he was sure that he had never worked with Professor Catchpole before. *So, the new professor has done extensive homework.*

"We will continue as before; the team has done sterling work, and the project is going to plan. Professor Swift and all of you have produced some quite remarkable results." As far as he was aware this team did know of the other one in the UK but no more detail than that. When he had heard about Professor Swift, he thought that Swift had been contacting someone from the UK setup, perhaps he was. But why would he do that? There had been zero contact or discussion of any kind between the two teams; everyone involved had agreed that was the only way to progress.

"As soon as any more information comes regarding Professor Swift, I will let you all know, until then let's get to work. I will conduct a review to get myself completely up to speed." He indicated that the meeting was ended and one by one the scientific team filed past him and left the room.

"Doctor Dudman, I would like you to go through Professors Swift's paperwork with me; can we make a start now?"

"Of course, Professor, his office is just down the corridor next to the main research room." She led the way to a small office at the end of the corridor. The door label said Professor Swift in yellow letters on a black background.

"A strange combination of colours for a door name board; it draws your attention however." Catchpole thought.

The office was very neat and tidy with a small desk with two chairs in the middle of the room; all around the edges of the room against the walls were filing cabinets with a sequential numerical index stuck to each draw. There was no computer terminal.

"Your man Swift seems to have been a very tidy man."

"Only following protocol Professor; we all follow the clear desk policy; even though we are in a secure and controlled workspace, we all put everything away and in the right place, nothing is left on the soft except category two information; all category one stuff is here as hard copy; we do not have routine access to soft copy once it has been uploaded at the end of each working day. All the work you require should be easily found."

"The work plan will be in here." Helen opened a filing cabinet marked 80 to 100. She pulled a thick file marked GO from the middle of the drawer and placed it on the desk.

Catchpole sat, opened the file and started reading; most of the contents were printed in an oversize font, probably 14 or 16 and most pages had hand written notes at the margin.

Helen pulled another file and sat next to Catchpole; she left the second file unopened.

Catchpole worked steadily through the information, asking Helen to confirm some items that were not obvious to him; mainly the hand-written annotations that Swift had made. He was quite surprised that this team was so far ahead of his own; they had gone astray with their conclusions but were now almost looking at the end game and the publication of their findings, beating his own group by several months at least. The briefing he had received when he was told he would be doing this had been misleading to say the least; *perhaps they didn't know the true extent of the work that had been completed here in France.*

The second file presented several problems; Professor Swift had often used what appeared to be a set of codes. Almost on every page he had written a series of numbers and letters in the margin.

"What is this all about?" He asked after a quick leaf through.

"I don't know, Professor Swift only used this annotation in this file, he never used it anywhere else." The file contained most of the conclusions that had come from the research; it wasn't obvious why he had made the entries next to some paragraphs and not others that dealt with very similar things.

5.

Just under four thousand miles to the West the big man was looking at a piece of paper that had just come out of the printer.

"Something going on here I think."

"What is that?" the smaller of the two asked, not really interested, thinking that Hector was just reading aloud as he often did.

"We have been under surveillance as have our team outside this morning; the man we saw across the street was ours and he was there to be noticed so I take back my comments earlier; perhaps they do know what they are doing after all. Our man in Spain was also contacted and followed so it seems someone is on to us."

"Perhaps not Hector, maybe they have stumbled onto something that has taken their interest." The small man was deeply concerned about this; things had to be tied down very quickly, the project couldn't be allowed to fail at this late stage. Besides, he didn't fancy spending the rest of his life in a government facility out in the middle of nowhere surrounded by nut jobs.

"Our team here is on the case and have closed down the options; we will move from here to the place in LA, much nicer weather and better beaches. Our chap in Spain has become invisible so we don't need to worry about him. The Lodge meeting can be done remotely."

The plan now being put in action was well rehearsed but had only been carried out once before; it had worked well then so there should be little difficulty now. The two men would leave immediately and relocate to the West Coast; the rooms they occupied in New York would be sanitised so not even the experts would gain information from them.

Hector picked up a small briefcase and went over to the far end of the room by the ornamental chimney breast, the smaller man pressed a button on his phone and a door opened silently in the wall. It had not been apparent before and would not be noticed once it was closed again. The two men went through the opening which led into a small room with an elevator on one side; this would take them to the car park in the basement of the building. Their driver would already be in the car with the engine started. The door closed silently behind them.

As the hidden door closed the main door to the apartment opened and the clean-up team arrived; they would remove everything that connected the two men to these rooms. Once finished the apartment would offer no clues to who had been living there these past months.

The last man in checked again that all had been done correctly then made for the door. "Everything done." It had taken only fifty-five minutes; the man was pleased with the team; the apartment would probably not be used again in the near future.

Hector and the small man had reached the helicopter park quite quickly; only took thirty minutes from leaving the apartment to getting on to the aircraft. "Good going!" The small man thought to himself as he climbed aboard. It would only be a short hop to JFK.

The man standing at the edge of the apron spoke into the microphone. "They have gone, so we will have to assess where and for what purpose they have moved. I don't think they are on to us but we will take a step back for the time being; I recommend that the raid tomorrow be cancelled; I suspect the apartment will be clean by now.

A thousand kilometres away the Director was standing on the edge of the ocean watching the sun go down; he was always calmed by this experience, it must be something from his childhood. He was in Canada at a fairly well-known tourist spot; a lighthouse sitting on the point at Peggy's Cove, Nova Scotia. Although no longer a working lighthouse the place had become a picture postcard sort of place that was visited by thousands each year. He preferred this time of day, as the light faded, because the crowds had gone and only a few people with cameras remained to capture the quite stunning sunset. It would get a little busier in a few hours as groups turned up to use the restaurant.

"What do we know James?" A man had appeared at the Director's side.

"The two have moved to their secondary location on the West Coast, they should be there in a couple of hours but we still have a sight of them; they may well think that they have given us the slip, but all is in hand. We can now link them to the assassin in the UK but the motive for the hit is still not clear."

The Director remained staring at the receding sun; he had to formulate the next response and brief the players on his team once he returned to the house.

"Did we get a hold of the shooter?"

"No Director, he is very good and we are trying to determine where he has come from; he is not one of the known groups and does not appear to have been in operation before, at least not on our turf any way. We think that he is British, or at least pretending to be British; our friends over there should be able to give us a detailed history of him."

"Keep digging James, we need to know what the two from New York are up to. Have the two research teams that they control done anything different recently?"

"No, Director, the research they are both involved in continues to take the same route; one is a little further down the road to a conclusion but the research appears to be the same. The outcome is apparently to discover ways of identifying genetic traits in disease and how best they can be countered."

The Director knew that there would be vast profits connected with the research the two men were overseeing but he was a little puzzled by the steps they were taking to safeguard the work. Many multinational companies had similar operations that had to be protected but these two were acting like spies working for a foreign power.

“Let me know if anything else turns up and keep an eye out for the assassin; if he turns up again, we may have to do something; we can’t have individuals killing people without our say so can we.”

“Goodbye James.” The Director remained looking at the point where the sun had disappeared; what clouds there were still reflected the sun’s rays from over the horizon.

James turned on his heel and walked over to the large black Ford with blacked out windows that was waiting on the access road in front of the restaurant. As he approached a very large man in a suit opened the rear door. James sat in the back and started to plan what he was going to do with the two men in California and how he would deal with the man in Spain should he ever turn up in the game again. The security got into the front next to the driver and the car was gone. It would take them several hours to get back into the States but this had been a typical meeting with the director why they couldn’t sit around a table somewhere nice was a mystery. They were in Canada, James wasn’t that keen on Canadians; they were far too relaxed and didn’t seem to take anything seriously.

“We should go, director; your evening session is waiting.” The man speaking was the director’s personal aid; the session he was talking about was the therapy the Director had to undergo each evening if he wanted to survive the next couple of years.

The "Affliction", as the Director always referred to it, was a small genetic problem he had inherited from his father who had not lasted as long as he had; not by a long way. The advances in the medical world had seen to that. There was no easy answer; he would likely die within two or three years if medical science didn't come up with anything new. Still it would end with him; he and Margaret had decided very early on that it would be reckless for them to have children even though the problem would not be encountered with girls. He had chosen to oversee this project in Europe because he had an interest in all matters concerning genetic research. The Director had become, not an expert, but a very informed amateur in the subject over the last ten years. When this project was flagged as unusual at the agency he immediately found himself interested. They were doing something with genetic diseases but he was very curious as to why all the secrecy and it now seems that they are involved in assassination. Might be soon time to call a halt to whatever they were up to.

The journey to the house at Prospect only took thirty minutes; small winding roads along the coast. He and Margaret had been this way many times; they both had this area as their favourite place on Earth; not for the scenery, which was stunning, but the feel of the place; like going back to an earlier, more relaxed time. Not a care in the world in a place that took you for what you were and didn't expect anything extra from anybody.

Prospect probably wasn't even a town, but a large village. Several times bigger than Peggy's Cove but small all the same. Largely built from wood, the houses gave the impression of a film set that was built to represent the Americas two hundred years ago, not a set but real with real people; a fascinating place; the Director thought so anyway.

Once in the house he thanked his driver and watched as his security team gave the rooms a once over; they never did find anything; normal routine had to be followed.
Margaret had triggered a device that had been meant for him nearly two years ago now. Something as simple as turning on the bedroom light; the bomb in the wall had been small and directed to anyone stood next to the switch. It had not been in the wall long but had been very well hidden. The investigation deduced that Margaret was killed by a small shaped charge of the type that was used in cluster munitions against armoured vehicles; an odd but effective choice of the weapon. Aside from the blast the charge had focused a molten penetrator that had cut her in half. No chance at all of survival, even if she had been wearing state-of-the-art body armour, which she wasn't of course. Who and why the attack had been made remained a mystery; they all expected another but none had materialised. He knew that there were many out there ranged against him. He missed Margaret more than people thought, always appearing to be the ultimate professional. One day he might find out who did it and why but for now he would have to wait and concentrate on the job in hand. "*Make*

sure that you are shooting the Alligator that is closest to the canoe."

The Director opened a small bag and removed a silver photo frame that had a picture of Margaret and him sat on a rock at Peggy's Cove; both were smiling, not a care in the world. He placed it on the table next to the bed and ran his finger around the silver edge; a ritual he did every time he set it down. The view from the window was quite impressive in the daylight; dark now with a flash every twenty seconds or so of the Peggy's Cove lighthouse up the coast. It was previously much brighter but was now only a token light to comply with the image tourists have of light houses.

The phone is his briefcase rang once; there was no internet connection here but his phone was directly linked to one of the many satellites that moved over head; he was always contactable, even here.

"Yes?"

"Just to let you know Director, the two are now ensconced on the West Coast and are to attend the meeting later on tomorrow, about midday your time." The voice was female and was probably not even in the United States; *Very clever this communications stuff.* The Director thought.

"Thank you." The director put the phone down; there would soon be a knock on the door from the medical technician with his treatment.

The Director woke with a start as he always did; he would be in the room watching Margaret being blown to bits, it was always the same. He had not been anywhere near at the time but his mind had placed him there and he couldn't get out of it. It was not something he would ever get used to.

Getting out of bed he looked out of the unshielded window; there was no one here that would be looking into windows. A large hand-written sign across the road had been placed on the side of a wooden shed like structure, "SLOW DOWN! - DONT BE A BONEHEAD!" A sign for the many Brits and US tourists that came this way and couldn't get out of the habit of driving everywhere like there was no tomorrow. If you were in a collision with a pedestrian in this part of the world it was your fault, simple. Drive more slowly, everything can wait.

He watched a medium sized SUV go past and park at the end of the track that led away from the main road. A man emerged and let two large and very energetic dogs out to walk away from Prospect onto the rocky coastline. The Director's team had seen this man many times before and had deduced that he was indeed just walking his dogs; come rain, snow or shine he was always there, sometimes there would be others with him but usually he was on his own. The Director had often thought about going the same way and talk with him; to move into another world away from all this nonsense he was involved in. To wander down the coast with the dogs and be normal, whatever that was. His team would never allow that of course; protocols to be followed, someday his life may depend on it.

The secure phone that was on the table rang once. "What is it?"

"Director, our man inside the operation is still not able to determine what they are up to. Do you wish to be kept informed at level one?" The voice had been a matter of fact indicating that this little operation was not a high priority and should not be at level one; the team had way more important things to be getting on with. This was, in the opinion of the team, an industrial espionage type set up and shouldn't concern the Director and the agency to this extent.

The Director thought for a moment. "No, we will put it at level two for now but I still need to be informed if anything new comes out of our man inside."

"Thank you, Director." The connection was ended.

The "Man inside" was a colloquialism of course; it may be a woman, several people or even a device of some sort; always referred to as a "Man"; a catch all.

The Director would be leaving this tranquil place in the morning; back to the West Coast, better weather but way too busy for his tastes these days.

6.

"How is our friend in Canada getting along; is he still interested in us?" Hector was on the phone to the security team. They had been in Nova Scotia the whole time the Director had been there; two teams of spies watching each other except in this case Hector believed that the team looking after the Director was completely unaware that they were all under surveillance.

"Excellent! Let me know when the Director gets home." Hector put the phone down and watched the lights on the base flash as it shut down the sequence that had connected the secure line.

"We have had a modicum of success!" Hector was speaking to the small man who was hunched over his laptop in the corner of the room. "We have been downgraded to level two so we should be in the clear from now on; no need to let the team know, of course, we do not want them losing sight of the ball do we."

"That is good news Hector; are we still looking for the second mole in France?"

"Yes, of course, but I'm sure we will be given direction on what to do about that this evening." Hector had his eyes shut.

"Don't forget we have the Lodge link tomorrow; the Principal will want to know all that we have in place to prevent any further delays."

"Already programmed and ready to go." The small man said. Our man in Spain has been warned off for another job."

The two men began organising the briefing that they would give the next day. After several hours, they had completed and double checked each other's work.

"I think we are ready and still have time for a coffee; what do you think?" Hector was already over by the coffee machine and was starting to pour two quite large mugs of coffee.

"That is an excellent idea Hector." The small man said, moving over to take the oversized mug.

The next day the two men sat in silence and waited for the top of the hour. Exactly as the clock showed six the telephone rang on the secure phone.

The big man let the phone ring three times before picking it up. "Hector." The big man said. "Switching now." The large TV screen on the wall illuminated; six men in suits sat at a desk looking into the room at the two men. All but one of the six looked to be in their late sixties or early seventies but the last one looked much younger, maybe thirty at most.

Hector checked the sound level from the TV and put the phone down.

"We have been reading your report gentlemen." It was the youngest of the six that was speaking. Neither of them liked this young chap very much; in their opinion he was way too young to hold such a high position, but he had been elected into this by a large majority of the members. He didn't even look his age never mind appear to be old enough for the post he now held. He was about six feet tall and very well built; the type who never missed a gym session if he could help it. He had a strange attraction; the type of man who could talk to anyone and appear, within minutes, to be their friend. Some remarked that he bore a resemblance to the Actor Brad Pitt but Hector was slowly coming to detest him. "Too young and cannot be trusted." Hector remarked when it was announced that the youngest Principal ever had been elected.

"As the progress at the site in France has moved ahead, do we still require the other one in the UK? It seems we may be wasting resources at this point; we do agree that two sites at the onset was the right way but now it seems we are duplicating work for no real benefit."

The silence was an indication that Hector should say something; all six seemed to be staring straight at Hector and he felt that something unplanned by him was about to happen.

Hector cleared his throat. "We have always thought that the two sites working in isolation was the best bet for success; both sites were aware that the other existed but did not share work or results." Hector paused. "Where was this leading?" he thought.

“We all know the reasoning behind the option of two sites and we all now know that one of the sites had a leak; we have dealt with that and we are now moving on. Our new man in France has indicated that they are ahead in the research but are still some way from a successful conclusion. If we close down the second site, we will have to secure the information gained. To stop this team in mid flow might cause problems; they are all dedicated professional people and will be highly suspicious if the project were to fold at this stage in the project.

The youngest of the six was speaking again. “We feel that the two sites are about to become unaffordable, at least in the way they are currently configured. We propose that the two should now share information to move the project on. We also think that once the site in France is clearly moving towards a conclusion, the second site should close. This office will coordinate the sharing of any information that will be of use to the team in France.”

Hector was extremely irritated that he had not been part of the discussion that had reached this deviation from the plan; a plan that had been years in the making. “Are the financial constraints suddenly too tight to have the two sites working along a duel path? We did fund this project very generously from the start; financial worries have not entered into the project until now. May I ask what has changed?”

“Of course, Hector you can ask questions; you are a senior member just like the six of us here." The young man was still the only one of the six saying anything; to

Hector he was looking younger by the minute and he was feeling like he was being lectured to by a schoolboy. “We all have to watch budgets and ensure that there is no waste in the financial area of the project; we feel that the time has come to take a step back from the race as the end is now firmly in sight. The extra planning that now has to take place will require considerable cash input.”

Hector was getting annoyed and was starting to think that he was being marginalised for reasons that he couldn’t fathom.

“What has happened to the great master plan? It appears to me that the master plan is no longer in place.”

“The plan is proceeding according to expectations, but we have decided that it needs a little tweaking to enable a small test before we move on.” One of the other men sat at the table was now speaking; he was an old acquaintance of Hectors and they had both known each other for quite a number of years.

“The decision has been made and steps have been taken to close one site and to proceed with the next step once the information is shared. If the test goes according plan, then we will close the second site. This project has been some years in the making but now we can envisage the outcome. You must remember, Hector that the whole project was, by necessity, kept to a need to know regime; there are things that you do not need to know; I’m sure you will understand this.”

The six men sat and stared at Hector from the TV screen. "Of course, I know that but it would have been nice for the two of us to have an inkling that the project was as close to conclusion as it is."

"It matters not." The child was speaking again. "We will shortly send you a list of personnel that we want you to deal with by your man in Spain; time is getting tight so you will need to expedite the process as soon as you get the instructions."

"Can I ask what the small trial you speak of will entail?" Hector was watching his influence and authority evaporate before his eyes and he wasn't expecting an answer.

"I would like to thank you both for your dedicated work with this project and have it recorded in the minutes that without the work you both have contributed the project would not be anywhere near the conclusion that is now in sight. Subject to confirmation our next conference will be in twenty days from now on the twenty second." The schoolboy leaned forward, and the screen went blank as the link was cut.

"What do you make of that then?" Hector was very unhappy; he had never been side-lined like this before. What was going on?

The small man was also a little bemused by the last twenty minutes; nothing like this had happened in his experience. He wasn't asked to contribute to the meeting at all. "I think that, perhaps, things have been moving in a direction that we have not been a party to. Maybe "The

Project" is not what we think it is. We can only do as we are asked; they are not going to change direction now so we had better get on with it."

"Who do they want rid of now? I thought that there was only one, maybe two, leaks from the site in France. This is getting a little uncomfortable my friend." Hector sat down and stared at the now blank TV screen.

He remembered when he was elected to the position that the schoolboy now occupied; a good twenty years ago, but even then, he was not even close to the present incumbent's youthful age; how things have changed. He had a brief notion that he would put himself forward for a second term as Principal but immediately put the thought out of his mind; he would never get the support from the ruling committee. The young man was firmly in the chair and would likely be replaced, when the time came, by another boy. The whole empire seemed to be moving in a younger, more aggressive direction. It would soon be time for him to bow out; perhaps then he could indulge himself on the coast. He was concerned that he was not told the detail of the "small trial" when he had asked directly.

7.

Jonathan Brown was relaxing outside one of the many small eateries that had appeared in the small Portuguese town over the last ten years. The establishment could probably hold twelve people at best but was never very busy; just a continual flow of patrons in and out. The street outside led down the hill and eventually the sea that Jonathan could just glimpse in the distance. The street, still cobbled, dated to the twelfth century; the buildings mixed from every century since. Now he was here instead of Spain he was going to make the most of it; this particular cafe did excellent coffee and pastries. This was not at all good for his waistline and he knew that he would have to take drastic action if he was to be fit enough for the next job; still he would have a couple of weeks at least, maybe longer. This latest series was paying rather well though; that was a little of a puzzle but he wouldn't be complaining. For now, he would sit here in the sunshine and watch the world go by.

Jonathan was probably past his prime but the experience he had gained over the last twenty years, particularly in the years since leaving the army would give him the edge over most adversaries he was likely to meet. He had gotten into this game in France; an old friend that had done some time in the Legion had been a little loose with his tongue after a booze fuelled night out. He had introduced Jonathan to a rather dodgy Romanian; the former Legionnaire had done a couple of jobs for the man and indicated it was money for old rope. He kept saying that Jonathan would be very good at it.

It was months later that the same Romanian was sat opposite him in a restaurant; this time very smartly dressed, and he had lost the accent.

"How did you know where I was?" Jonathan was a little concerned that this man who he had met in a bar in France had found him, months later, in the UK.

"We had the time, and you were not difficult to find as you are not hiding; something you could have done if you had wanted to I'm sure."

The Romanian had outlined the "job" that he wanted done; a simple assassination that was to look like a gang related murder. It had to appear that the killer was not an expert but rather someone who was just angry. Jonathan wasn't too perturbed about this; he had been doing similar jobs for years in his day job but this were to pay considerably better than the wage Her Majesty's Government paid him. Anyhow he was now a free agent on a poxy pension, so he had to find gainful employment somewhere; better stick to what you are good at.

The target on this occasion was a local petty crook that controlled a small drug supply empire in London; Jonathan was not sure why he warranted this kind of attack but he never was in the mind to ask; take the money and do the job.

This individual liked to carry a grenade around with him, often showing it to anyone he wanted to intimidate. The grenade of choice was one that had been made in Eastern Europe; a copy of a Russian design; slightly bigger yield than most grenades currently in use by the world's armed forces. Jonathan had no problem getting a hold of one on the many black-market outlets in continental Europe. Jonathan had then done some homework; taking note of the type and model of the target's car. He had gone to a car dealer out of town and sat in the driver's seat for a while, even dropping a tennis ball down between his legs to see if he could quickly retrieve it and to gauge his position if he tried to.

In the end, it was quite easy; Jonathan just stepped out of the shadows one day and dropped the grenade down between the target's legs. The open topped car continued on a pace as the target realised something had been thrown into the car but didn't know what. He may have realised what it was but too late; boom, the car slowed and crashed into a parked truck by the side of the road. The target lost both legs and received serious shrapnel and blast damage to his face and upper body; very dead. His minder was also sprayed with fragments and died at the scene. Eventually the police had concluded that perhaps he had been blown up by one of his own grenades; not quite what the brief had required, but the result was even better. The police would not waste too much time looking for anyone else.

After that, work had come Jonathan's way often; now he was much sought after. All these years later he could afford to pick and choose; he never went anywhere near anything that might get him caught or even killed; he left that to others. This one in Nottingham had worried him somewhat; much more money than was normal, and he had no real idea of who was paying; still it was straightforward, and it had gone without any problems except the man watching him in the car park and the team that had been trying to intercept him in Spain was a concern; he would have to be doubly careful from now on.

The phone in Jonathan's packet beeped once and gave about a second of vibration. It was a text reminder from a chemist in Brighton saying his prescription was ready. As far as he could remember he had never set foot in Brighton and he certainly wasn't waiting for a prescription. "Oh, the wonders of the internet." Jonathan said to himself as he erased the message. The chemist would have no idea that they had sent it to him; their machine had been hacked, and the number encrypted amongst a load of other stuff; this was then sent out amongst many reminders; there would be no trace of the communication to Jonathan. What it did say to Jonathan was that a new job was imminent and he should be ready to acquire the new tasking from the secure network that he used.

8.

Doctor Dudman and Professor Catchpole had completed the review of the paperwork; it was still not apparent why Professor Swift had made the notes or what they meant but David Catchpole was determined to find out; perhaps he would have another look when he was on his own. He thought at first glance that that Swift was using a fairly simple substitution code but he would need more time to experiment with the notes; it wouldn't explain why the Professor was making this type of note at all. He would make an assessment and report findings up the chain of command; perhaps then he could get on with his work. Hopefully the project would come to fruition in the next couple of weeks. His bosses, whoever they were, had told him about the closure of his old team only a couple of minutes ago, and that only two of his old workforce would be joining them. A great shame as he thought the team in the UK was better and more diligent than the one here despite the fact this lot were further ahead.

"OK Helen I think I have seen enough for now; I will use this office from now on so you can get back to work, we will have another meeting tomorrow with the rest of the team; the project is taking a different course so we all need to be pulling in the same direction; shall we meet in the conference room at ten hundred?"

"Right Professor I will stop by the main lab and let everybody know, I will see you at ten tomorrow." Helen turned and left the room, closing the door behind her. She now didn't like Professor Catchpole one bit and even considered leaving the project, but only for a couple of seconds; it paid way too much to leave just because she didn't like her boss;besides, she had other masters to serve.

David Catchpole sat at the desk and stared into space, deep in thought. It was twenty minutes before he stirred; he took a pencil and copied some notes that Swift had made; about ten notations in all. He then looked at page one of the document and noted down the first word in each paragraph and compared them to the notes written in pencil; nothing jumped out at him so he repeated the process using the second word, then the third word and so on until he has exhausted all the words in each paragraph; nothing, not a hint of what the pencil written notes were meant to say.

"Perhaps the key is not in the same document. If it was me, it would relate to the same document otherwise he would have to refer to more than one; clumsy.

"OK start again from the beginning." He said to himself.

Professor Catchpole started to read the document again, but this time looked at the grammar and not necessarily what was written.

After another hour, it suddenly leapt from the page; Swift has been using sections of the text that seemed to contain basic grammatical errors or simple typos to hide a second narrative. The notes were a quick guide to where they would be.

The pencilled notes using characters from the alphabet were easy to turn into a sequential set of numbers; the numbers then applied to the main text to identify certain words and, in some cases, phrases.

Catchpole took a fresh sheet of paper and began writing, moving backwards and forwards through the text until he had almost a full page. He sat back and read it several times. It still seemed to be in code.

"Dates and results!" He had it. "Not so sharp are we Professor Swift."

The coded notes referred to the main text and picked out the major steps and successes the team had had, against each item was the date. But was Professor Swift merely noting the progress for his own use or was he trying to hide something.

He read the document again and then compared the whole to the notes. It became obvious; the notes told the true story of progress and the main document detailed the whole project. The real progress was hidden in the main narrative and often talked around results that should have been in lights. It seemed that Professor Swift and his team were not just in front of his team in the UK but were very nearly at the end; success!

The team led by Swift had isolated and replicated certain parts of the genetic code of most of the sample subjects; they had traced and coded several traits that were passed on in the human population through genetic deformities. Of course, it had been known for some time that certain diseases and abnormalities ran in families so were passed on through DNA from the mother and father to any children; some of these even jumped a generation so the affected gene resurfaced in grandchildren or even great grandchildren. The big difference here, and it was a big difference, was this team had discovered a way to map most, if not all, variations to the gene sequence. They had discovered that they would be able to turn off certain variations that made a difference but not a critical one; such things as blue or grey eyes could be switched off in descendants simply by applying the switch to a mother or father before they had children. If all this information was correct, designer babies had become possible.

"But why were you hiding this, Swifty old mate?" The real or official narrative from the research said that they were close but much more work was required to reach any meaningful conclusions; there was even a note at the end of one of the chapters saying the team thought they may never get to a successful conclusion when in fact they were already there. Were the whole team in on this deception?

And then Professor Swift had been killed in Nottingham! Perhaps he had been in the wrong place at the wrong time but why was he even there. Was he trying to hide the results from the project management? Was he looking to sell the research to someone else? Wasn't he a little dim writing all this code down in the main document? Catchpole was very bright, but the code had not been that difficult to break; the experts would have had it hours ago, so what was Swift up to?

"Should I worry about this?" Catchpole stood up and put the files back into the cabinets. He knew that he had to fire this up the project chain; after all that was what they were paying him for; no point in carrying the research forward when they were already at the end. Professor Catchpole was getting more and more concerned over the things he had discovered; the whole project was now looking a little odd. What was going on? The briefing he had received from the project management had not hinted at anything untoward; the project was going well, and he was to replace Professor Swift in France. Swift had been murdered, and that was now part of the Police investigation; nothing, at the moment, indicated why he was in Nottingham or why he had been killed.

9.

Jonathan Brown was sitting at a small table, upstairs in a medium sized coffee shop in the centre of Bourges, a very nice city about 250 kilometres South of Paris and about ten from the facility where the research was going on. Apparently, it was where the man in Nottingham was working. Jonathan had received the tasking the same day as the warning text; quite unusual and he was in two minds whether to go or not. Anyway, he was here now so he would sit and wait for the target to show. He knew the target always used this place on Saturday and that they always come upstairs to read the papers and drink their hot chocolate. They were invariably on their own. The shop was on two floors; downstairs by the entrance was the counter and a small display that offered cakes and biscuits; further in was a small seating area. A single flight of stairs led to a much larger area that held seating for many more customers. The walls upstairs and downstairs were filled with large format photographs of places and architecture from various towns in Italy.

Jonathan sipped his espresso and looked over the top of a magazine he had taken from the rack. He had chosen this seat carefully on a previous recce; he could see the whole room but more importantly he could see down the stairs through the waist high glass partition; the only way into the room, except through the fire escape that was down at the other end, past the toilets on the left. This would be the way out after the target was dead. The fire escape opened onto some iron stairs that led down into the courtyard at the back of the building; from there it would be easy to slip into the main road and disappear.

Jonathan counted the people in the room and made a mental note of anybody who looked like they could intervene. There were eight; all except two were sat on the right side of the room, and he estimated that all would be of no assistance to the target. He would make sure they didn't get the chance. The target's preferred seating, down towards the fire exit, was empty so they would be in the ideal position when they sat down. It would appear that Jonathan was walking down the room towards the toilets. He adjusted the position of the blade on his forearm under his jacket and waited.

Right on time the target was at the bottom of the stairs; drink in one hand and a cake or pastry of some sort in the other. The target looked up the stairs locking eyes with Jonathan for half a second before taking a step up. There was suddenly a loud bang over by the main door from the street.

Just a loud bang to most people who heard it but to Jonathan it was the unmistakable sound of a high velocity bullet being fired. The first shot was followed by many more, all fired in short bursts; AK; fuck! Jonathan couldn't see who was firing or where they were but he decided that he wasn't going to hang around to find out. In one swift movement, he was out of his seat and down the length of the room, through the door to the fire escape and was down in the courtyard at the back of the building; the job can wait.

As he got to the bottom of the stairs he was confronted by another gunman; this time the weapon was already on display and was coming up into the aim; to be pointed right at Jonathan. The gunman was too slow; the blade went into the man's neck and was withdrawn in less than a second; the Internal Carotid Artery sliced open. There was much more blood than Jonathan would have liked but he didn't have the time to be picky. The man with the gun went down like a sack of potatoes; not fully knowing what had happened; he was dead, a few seconds later.

This was all going badly wrong for Jonathan; he must now get as far away from here as possible. No doubt the whole episode had been caught on CCTV and the country's security forces would descend mob handed onto this one. The borders would be closed or at the very least closely watched. He joined a group of people who were fleeing the area, away from the coffee shop and away from the serious danger that was still there. The sound of gunfire abruptly stopped and followed by a loud explosion then all was silent except the sound of multiple sirens coming down the main roads that led to the open area where the coffee shop was.

Jonathan paused at the junction of two major roads that ran through the city; the sounds of the police and ambulances still filled the air; everyone was gossiping and watching the episode unfold; many concerned faces.

There was the sound of more shooting; two single shots from the direction of the coffee shop, then silence. Jonathan was in escape mode; he didn't care what had just happened he had to think of self-preservation; nothing else mattered at this point.

He need not have worried in the short term. There had been two gunmen; the one inside, who had killed three people on the ground floor and the one outside that he had dealt with. The gunman inside had moved to the upper floor to continue the mayhem but had found that the fire exit was open and everybody had followed Jonathan out and down the stairs, stepping over the prostrate gunman in the courtyard. The second gunman had stepped onto the metal stairs and exploded in a fireball that sent hundreds of small metal objects flying in all directions. Whether he intended to destroy himself or the bomb detonated by accident was never ascertained but because the wound that the blade had inflicted had pierced the man's neck, through the artery and out of the back it looked at first sight that it had been a bomb fragment that had done the damage. The shooting after both men were dead came from a policeman shooting at shadows as he entered the building.

It would be a couple of days before Jonathan left the country; couldn't risk the journey just yet; he would let things settle for now then make a move later on in the week. For now, he would disappear. He would be on holiday, relaxing in central France then East into Italy. He had no idea what had happened to the target; perhaps they had been killed in the coffee shop; at this point he didn't care one way or the other; self-preservation for now.

It was to be two weeks before he could exit France; he could have done it sooner, but he was now super attentive to any threat or possible threat to himself. The two gunmen had not been positively identified and the motive for the attack was not at all clear. The authorities had said that it was thought it might have been a gangland hit on persons unknown but the purpose of the explosive vest remained a mystery. Jonathan had watched an interview with a French security expert talking about the usual operating methods of criminals and terrorist; the presenter had concluded that the attack did not fit into any of the profiles that had been seen in recent years. There had been no mention, or even the suggestion, that the man outside had been stabbed. This concerned Jonathan as he knew that the autopsy would have identified the cause of death quite readily. The list of the casualties did not include the target so Jonathan had failed; he was sure he had a good excuse.

Jonathan stepped onto the dock side from the ferry that had just carried him across Lake Como; he had left his car in the car park of the Britannia Hotel on the western side of the lake. The Britannia was a large hotel that catered for many nationalities so he was able to merge into the crowds quite easily. This was one of his favourite places in the world; Bellagio in Lombardy; excellent food and not that touristy, not the usual type of tourists, anyway. The weather was pleasant and the sun would be going down in an hour or so; very beautiful and very upmarket; several millionaire film stars from Hollywood lived around the lake. He was here to pick up his next instruction, and he hoped that he may get some explanation of what had happened in France; he also considered that he might not and would have to turn jobs down for the foreseeable future.

The walk from the ferry to the main part of town was not far; across the flat area beside the lakeside then up quite a steep hill to a traditional restaurant, off down a side street. He would sit here, have something to eat and wait.

His phone beeped once; this time it was from a dentist in South Shields reminding him of an appointment, that didn't exist, for his annual check-up. He hoped that he would be given some information regarding the episode in Bourges. He set his phone to download and waited; the phone beeped again and a number one appeared on the face of the phone. Jonathan entered an eighteen-digit code and waited; the normal screen image reappeared. Putting the phone to his ear Jonathan listened.

"The episode in the coffee shop was intended to kill you; you were the only target; it was supposed to appear as if terrorists had carried out the attack. It seems that they have seriously underestimated you. The police will not be trying to find you; all of that has been taken care of and the official line is what you have seen in the newspapers. We still do not understand why the gunman had an explosive vest or why it was detonated. However, we think that you are still a target so be aware that something similar or even very dissimilar could happen. Your target did escape unhurt; more to follow." The recording ended, and the phone beeped once. The message had been streamed to the phone from somewhere close by; no trace of it would be found on the phone if anyone ever had the opportunity to look for it.

He sat back in his chair and closed his eyes, thinking hard. Why was he a target? None of this made much sense but his instincts were shouting in unison. "Leave this and get the hell away from all of this; it isn't going to end well Jonathan."

10.

Helen Dudman was in her office; the events over the last couple of days had been very traumatic. What had unfolded when she was in her favourite coffee shop had put her into overdrive; she now slept very lightly and would be alert at the slightest sound that was out of place. She analysed the event; she had run up the stairs, discarding her coffee and cake, as the shooting started. By the time, she had made the top of the stairs the man who had been looking at her had gone. She ran straight across the top floor and out through an open fire door, having to jump over a body that lay at the bottom of the stairs; from there she had run down the street to collapse into a shop doorway. She was rounded up with a few dozen others and taken to the municipal hospital for assessment and treatment; the police had carried out long and exhausting interviews over the rest of the day. Professor Catchpole had suggested that she go home for a month or so but her tasking would not allow that; besides, she was now interested in what had happened; was she involved or was she an innocent bystander who just happened to be there? She would stay at work in the secure area until things became clearer. She had spent the first few days reading all there was in the newspapers regarding the attack; lots of supposition and things that were simply not true, but that is the norm when there is little real evidence for the feature writers; they simply make it up. The article in today's paper was different though; it concluded that the man at the bottom of the stairs had been killed by a bomb fragment when the man at the fire door had blown himself up. "That is not possible!" she had said out loud, reading the article several times. "He was lying there when I left as I had to jump over him; the bomb went off as I went down the street." She would seek clarification on this and request advice.

Helen had told the police all of this, several times but it seems that they either didn't believe her or they knew something different; was the body there or not? Did the bomb go off earlier than she recalled? Had she known that she was to be the only dead person at the coffee shop she may have been even more stressed. The two gunmen had saved her life.

"How are you keeping Helen?" Professor Catchpole had his head around the door.

"Not bad but I keep waking with the same bad dreams; I expect they will fade over time and I can go to bed and actually sleep through. The work is keeping me busy so I will be alright." Helen was lying about the dreams; she was sleeping more lightly, but that was due to the circumstances and the training she had undergone on previous jobs; *stay focused and stay alert*

"If I can do anything, please let me know; I still think that you should go back to the UK and have some time away from the job."

"Thanks, I will keep that offer in mind; we will see how this week's goes; we are nearly ready for the testing."

The door closed and Catchpole was gone; Helen considered the option of requesting a replacement but knew that a replacement was not going to happen. Over the last week she and Catchpole had finalised most of the results and presented them; they were only waiting for the go ahead from the project management and they would be done. The test, whatever that was, would progress but there would be little need to keep her on here in France. At this point she wasn't all that sure what the test would be or how it would pan out. They did get some vague instructions last week and had prepared a sample to introduce to a test subject, who would be a middle-aged man, but no real detail on what was expected. She had put the secrecy down to money; after all this project was rumoured to be worth an absolute fortune; billions of Euros.

She locked her filing cabinet and put the key into the key press on the wall by the door; closed the door and waited for the tumbler to rotate; locking the box.

Time to go and eat and perhaps have an early night; she was still working over the coffee shop episode in her mind.

She locked the door to her office, put the key into her pocket and walked down the corridor; five minutes later she was in her room watching TV. Dinner was in the restaurant at eight.

Down the corridor in his room Professor Catchpole was speaking over the secure line to the project manager; he had never met him but he had spoken to him many times over the last year. It was the project manager who had called him in the UK to reassign him here in France.

"The report regarding Professor Swift and his notes was very interesting but we feel that perhaps you have misinterpreted the notes and come to some wrong conclusions." Professor Catchpole was already annoyed; he had gone over the information a dozen times and each time he arrived at the same answer; Swift was hiding the true nature and progress of the project. Or was he recording this information so that someone could discover what was really going on should things go bad? *Well it certainly went bad for Professor Swift.*

"I do feel that it is perhaps your team that has not fully grasped what Swift was recording; as to why I have no idea, but the notes are clear enough; the project is coming to a conclusion and the use to which the research will be put is not what we all think it is." The man on the other end didn't say anything for a good two minutes; Catchpole was starting to think the contact had fallen out.

"No matter; the project is taking a new direction and your team will be reassigned; we will dispatch a drawdown team in the next couple of weeks; full briefing notes will be in your Inbox tonight; we would like you to brief everyone once you have read them and got back to us with any questions. Your current work is to end tomorrow midday. Is everything clear so far Professor?"

“Well not really; are we all to return from France? It is all a bit short notice; the team here has been working very hard over the last couple of years and they might be a little more unforgiving when the news is broken that they are no longer needed.”

“May I remind you Professor that at the start you all signed up to a contract of employment and by doing so you all agreed to carry out the work that was required, working to the end point. That end point had now been reached therefore the contract has come to an end. We have been paying you and the team a considerable salary; certainly, way above what you might all expect outside of this project.”

“Yes of course; forgive me; as you may realise we have all become quite close to the work here and in the UK.”

“How is Doctor Dudman getting along after her experience?” The man at the other end had changed the subject.

“She is moving along but still has broken sleep; the nightmares are getting less.” Catchpole was a little surprised at the question because he had briefed this same man only the day before yesterday. *Perhaps he doesn’t read all his emails.*

“Very good; we will let you know when the drawdown team is on its way. Goodbye Professor Catchpole.” The connection ended.

Catchpole was very surprised; he had gone from running part of a multimillion dollar project that looked like it would make shed loads of money to unemployed in less time than it took to make a cup of coffee.

11.

The man Catchpole had been speaking to turned his seat around so he could look out of the window; Central Park was nice this time of the year; the temperature outside was very pleasant; he remembered the times he used to take a walk over lunch down there; times long gone, he didn't suppose that he would ever be able to do it again; certainly, not in the short term; much too much to do and absolutely no time to waste. He had another call in two minutes; this would get heated he was sure; he took a deep breath and calmed himself as best he could.

The desk phone rang; the man picked it up and waited for the tone to indicate the connection was secure.

"Yes?" He was getting wound up already.

"You wished to speak to me regarding the episode in France Principal."

"Indeed, I do; what was that all about? Why did you send those two buffoons after Brown? He was not a problem, and he was in our employ."

"We thought that he may have been gaining more knowledge than could be permitted but we were wrong; the shooting was supposed to appear like a terrorist attack or a gangland turf war incident.

"Instead, you fool, your two men got themselves killed and attracted all manner of scrutiny; what was the bomb for? That was completely mad." He was getting heated and was starting to shout.

There was a brief silence from the other end; thinking before saying anything that would make matters worse.

"Principal, the plan was a sound one, but we underestimated him; it seems he dealt with our man without the slightest effort; our team stood no chance."

"But why the suicide vest? Fifty per cent of your team killed themselves and the other half of your team was dealt with very easily, despite being armed. He still couldn't believe how dim this lot had been even though it was now a couple of weeks since the incident.

"The explosives were meant to be abandoned when the team made their escape but for reasons we do not understand they were detonated whilst still attached to our man." The man on the other end of the phone was hoping the call would end very soon; experience told him that the longer it went on the worse it would be for him.

"From now on you are to pass all, and I mean all, plans through this office so perhaps we can stop you lot embarking on any more hare-brained schemes in the future. This has not been good. Your target in France is no longer a target so make sure your people are in control.

The Principal put the phone down and made a mental note; get rid of that idiot sooner rather than later.

The situation had very nearly got out of hand with one side of the organisation attacking the other. It had taken some considerable work to close the whole thing down; luckily the people in France were on it very quickly. The attempted hit was now recorded as another gangland attack by persons or group unknown. It had ended with five dead people, two of whom only wanted to serve coffee to a third who only wanted to drink it.

The death of the two clowns with guns was of little concern to him now. It would require a case review by the top three to determine how a tasking for a hitman had turned into the hitman becoming the target; perhaps the team was getting too big and fragmented. Doctor Dudman would have to wait, it wouldn't help if anyone connected her death to the episode in France, *better leave it for now.*

"Perhaps there are elements that are still against me and the project." He was talking to himself as he often did when searching for clarity.

The intercom beeped once. "They are here Principal."

"He thought for a couple of seconds. "Show them into the conference room I will be there directly." The intercom clicked off without further comment.

The conference room was the smaller of two that were in the building; the larger one was the venue of choice for most of the meetings that were held. Both rooms had similar panelling on the walls on which were hung pictures of previous, but not all, principles dating back a few hundred years. The main difference other than the size was the lack of any windows. This small room was equipped, as was the larger one, to maintain the confidentiality of any meetings that went on. It was swept on a daily basis to ensure no eves-dropping could go on; state-of-the art counter surveillance equipment was employed from when the delegates entered the building to the moment they left.

A tall athletic looking man stood by the conference room door as the Principal approached. “What news David?”

David was head of security in this building and had, in the past, shown himself to be very good at his job.

“We have excluded one individual and confiscated a device from another; the other two are clean.” It was normal practice to exclude attendees if there was the slightest doubt about anything they brought with them to meetings; no chances were ever taken. “What was confiscated David?”

“Smart phone; didn’t pass the test so we have it. The details of the exclusion are on your device, ready for you when you enter”

“Thank you, David.” The Principal opened the door to the room and walked in, closing the door behind him; David stood at the closed door and waited, watching down the corridor. He, of course, knew the full details behind the exclusion of the delegate; it had been coming for some time; he expected a big work load once the Principal had read the brief.

The other three were already seated at the small conference table waiting for the much younger man to sit down.

Before acknowledging the three, the Principal read through the report that was on the small device in front of him; a small black, rectangular tablet that looked nothing out of the ordinary. It was very unusual in that only the person that it was coded for was able to get anything from it. The Principal placed both hands onto the edges of the screen and waited; the screen blinked on and displayed a series of pages of text. The Principal read quickly and then put the tablet down; as soon as he let go of the device, it switched itself off; the information that had been streamed to it from the secure network within the room now gone.

“Brothers we have a problem that must be resolved today. As you are no doubt aware Brother Trevor has been excluded from this meeting; he is still in the building and will have to undergo some further investigation regarding some indiscretions on his part. Another of you has had a problem with a mobile device I am told. The guilty party looked a little sheepish and started to speak in his own defence; the Principal quickly held up his hand to indicate that this was not going to be a debate about the rights and wrongs in acquiring a new mobile phone.

“I’m very confident that the rules governing the use of portable communication devices have now been reinforced so I see this matter as closed.”

"Bother Trevor, however, is another matter."

"As you all know the project is nearing completion; we are very close to the goal that was set by my predecessors over the last ten years. We will soon be in a position to manipulate the population of this country, and others, in a manner that was quite impossible previously."

The three other men sat at the table looked on without comment; they all knew full well that the time had come for action and from this day on nothing in the great world outside would be the same.

"Brother Trevor will be detained and debriefed. For the moment, he is no longer the holder of the authority; perhaps he will re-join us in the future." The Principal looked around the table to gauge opinion; he was met with blank faces; all in the room knew very well what the "Debrief" meant and none of them would wish to go down that route themselves.

The Principal was silent for more than five minutes; gathering his thoughts for the briefing that he was about to undertake.

"Brothers; we are now ready to undertake the first field trial of Project ninety-one." Each man turned over a single sheet of paper that had been placed in front of them. It listed ten bullet points detailing times and locations but not any specific detail on what was to happen.

“Gentlemen, as you can see the subject is in North America so we will be able to monitor his movements quite closely; we should not have to intervene once the start point has passed.” All of them were looking at the sheet of paper and all had been surprised that the Principal had used the term *Gentlemen.* At meetings at this level the form of address was always *Brothers*. It wasn’t the first time this principal had changed procedure in an arbitrary manner and it would not be the last. More than one of them at the meeting hoped that the next incumbent would be more of a traditionalist but that would be two years from now.

“We have had a man in place for a number of years now; he is very well trusted and will have little difficulty in deploying the element to the target. He will stay in place to report back as and when required.” The principal looked around the table, inviting comment.

“Will he be discovered once the element is deployed? It could indicate to them that we are involved.” One of the three said.

“No there will be little or no evidence present that we have intervened and anyway our man could not be connected to the project in any way. He has no knowledge of what or why things are progressing the way they are. They could interrogate him until the end of time but they will learn nothing because he knows nothing.”

"As you can see the insert has been scheduled so we have to make sure we are ready at our end. The project will start closing from today."

"Are there any questions or observations at this stage? No? Then the meeting is closed."

The three men got up and pushed their chairs back under the table; the Principal remained seated and watched the men leave. The meeting had been a bit of an indulgence as the three already knew the project plan but were only waiting for the start to be announced. They could have been informed by any number of other means but this principal liked to be personal. *You can't beat a face-to-face meeting*. As he often said.

David entered the room and gathered up the pieces of paper the three men had left.

"David, have we learned anything from Brother Trevor?"

"Not yet principal, we are still in the early stages but we think that he might be involved in some sort of financial operation not connected to the project. We have segregated him and all his contacts as a precaution for the time being."

"Thank you, David, keep me informed." David would of course keep the principal informed; after all he was the boss running the whole show.

The principal left the room, leaving the tablet on the desk. David picked it up and had a look around the room to ensure nothing from the meeting had been left. *All good; now for Brother Trevor.*

12.

Professor Catchpole was at his desk not quite believing what he had just read. It had arrived as an email but then had to be decrypted using the small key book he always carried.

You are to cease operations immediately; the project has reached the completion point. Your team will be largely reassigned but in some cases, will be let go. The close down team will be on site when you are ready to declare closure. More to follow. It was the same as he had been told over the phone but it still riled him.

“All a bit sudden don’t you think.” Catchpole said aloud still puzzled that the project was to end so suddenly. They were near the end but he didn’t think that it all would suddenly stop in this way. He wondered when the *More to follow* would arrive. *Hopefully soon.*

He got up and left the office; he would go and find doctor Dudman and give her the good news. He wondered if she was to be reassigned or let go, he had enjoyed working with her over the last couple of weeks and had gained a real respect for her abilities and professionalism. Even the episode in town had not affected her work to any great degree.

Doctor Helen Dudman was in one of the small labs that processed the work done on the main floor of the facility. She was checking through a small pile of progress reports that had been marked for archive. This was a standard routine job that stopped information disappearing because it had been marked as complete and then incorrectly filed.

“Helen.” Helen was surprised Catchpole had used her given name, it was usually Doctor or Doctor Dudman but now it was Helen.

“We are to start closing down the project from today, the work has been completed, or at least our part has been completed.”

Helen was puzzled; it wasn’t at all apparent that they had reached any final conclusions from the project and this seemed to be a very strange time to call a halt.

“Have we run out of money?” Helen asked.

“Don’t think so, in fact I’m sure we haven’t, the original budget was way over the top for what we needed. Some projects I have been on in the past would have loved half the funding we have here. No I think that the plug has been pulled because the project has delivered the answers they were after; whatever that was.”

“I will receive further instruction in due course, in the mean time we will brief the team and set about collating all the information and closing the project down, we are to get a close down team later to clear the site. It has been a privilege working with you over these past weeks Doctor Dudman.”

Back to Doctor Dudman now is it. Helen smiled and tilted her head.

“Let’s say we let the team now and then have a coffee; there is no rush for anything now.

The two of them walked down the corridor to the main lab where most of the technicians worked. Helen went next door to round up the remainder and bring them all into the meeting.

It didn’t take long; Professor Catchpole announced the end of the project and answered questions regarding future work and any reasons he might know about the conclusion of the project. He had to admit that he actually didn’t know much more than they did but he would let them know when it all was a little clearer.

“At this stage I think we should all go and get a coffee.”

It was three days before Professor Catchpole received further instructions by which time the team had closed down the research and had almost completed filing and cataloguing the results from the years they had been working. Gossip was rife but rumour central indicated that the project had lost its funding.

Catchpole had been sat at his desk for long periods looking at the notes that Swift had made against the project file. He began to think that the *easy* code was nothing of the sort and that the decoded information was another code in itself; he was intrigued. *What was Swift doing with this information and why was he making notes?*

"Helen, can we meet later on in my office? We need to discuss something." He put the phone down and wondered if Helen Dudman was part of this or completely oblivious as to what Swift was up to. He would have to take a risk and assume that she was in the dark.

It was the next day before Doctor Dudman and Catchpole were sat at the same desk looking at the notes that Professor Swift had made in the project files.

"You see here" he indicated a long string of two or three letter sequences in the margin halfway through one of the files. The records detailed the progress and purpose of a series of experiments that had been done the year before when the team was trying to identify gene patterns that determined the colour of people eyes. Several samples taken from volunteers within the team had been used. Both read and re read the records and tried to make sense of Swift's notes.

"Would you mind putting some time onto this Helen, I think we need to know what Swift was doing before the project closes down completely and all this information is out of reach. You and I have to compile a report for the control team before we leave this place, I don't want something jumping out of the woodwork later on that we should have known about. I have a bad feeling about these notes."

"Of course, we are nearly done in the labs anyway and only waiting for the close down team to show up. Do we need any help from some of the team? There are one or two who might be useful" Helen was thinking of two in her section that were very good at seeing patterns in seemingly random results but it was only part of the duplicitous act she was performing; the professor would not discover anymore from the project if she could help it.

"Not at this point, if we are still getting nowhere in a day or so we will think again but for now let's keep this to ourselves.

13.

Hector was reading a message he had just received. “It seems we are about to experience another leak from the site in France.”

“I thought the project had terminated and the French thing was to close.” Remarked the small man.

“Indeed, it has but we someone looking into information that was left by our Professor Swift. They don’t yet know any of the story but they may in a couple of days. They may not, of course, but we will have to ensure they do not get near the truth or you and I will be having some very big problems.” Hector was less concerned than he indicated to his friend but something would have to be done, and soon.

“Is our man in Spain still available after we very nearly killed him?” The small man came over to the desk and sat down next to Hector. Hector offered him the tablet with the message still displayed.

Hector waited for him to finish reading then spoke. “He is still available and fortunately still in our employ, we were very lucky to keep him after the cock up in Bourges. We do not want to go through that again, the principal was most displeased and some of the dirt undoubtedly has stuck to us. However, we cannot get him to strike there as the whole place is now on lockdown ready for removal; perhaps when the team leaves and is reassigned, we will have a good chance.

The small man took a sip from the coffee he had just made. "Is the trial run on schedule?"

Hector thought that it was a rhetorical question because the small man knew as much as he did about the planned trial.

"The Principal has decreed that the trial will go ahead, and it seems that all is in place to make it happen tomorrow. I am sure we do not know the full picture as we have been side-lined on several matters over the past year. I think that our role in this operation is drawing to a close. In the meantime, we must ensure that we are dealing with the number one priority and that dear friend is the potential for a leak from France."

Hector paused not sure he could be bothered to continue, not only on this project but the job in general. He had been doing this for some years now and he was a little tired. He wondered if it would be possible to retire at all with the current Principal; perhaps not but he wouldn't be around forever.

"We can only wait for the trial to produce results, good or bad, before we have to move on any outstanding issues with the people from the two research teams. I think that most will fade into the woodwork and not cause us problems but one, or maybe two, is already showing up on the radar. What about a coffee?"

The small man took this as a request to go and get a drink for Hector.

“Fortunately, we have not lost our man in Spain; if he had been compromised, we would not find another of his calibre very easily.” The small man handed Hector his coffee and sat down. What the two men didn’t know was that the trial had in fact started months before, even before Professor Swift had been murdered in Nottingham.

The real control over what was happening was in the hands of the Principal. Even before he had been raised to the position of Principal, he had made sure that all authority and the power to initiate things would be placed in his hands once he was in the chair. He would be in control, under current rules, for just over three years; the three-year ruling would be circumvented if the next phase of this project was a success. If it was not a success, he anticipated that he would be gone in less than one, but for now he was gathering all the power and control that he could; most, if not all his enemies would fall by the wayside as the project gathered pace. He had taken a gamble with the project when he had ordered the trial to be brought forward; only a few people close to him knew of the change in plan but it allowed him to manipulate the other members and drive them around in circles vying for position; *they were all wasting their time.*

Two thousand mile away the Director was waiting in the small reception room that his medical team used to brief him, and others, on the current situation regarding the many varied but closely related ailments that they treated. Today the Director was to be the centre of attention. He sat with his back firmly into the seat looking across the room at a poster that advertised the services of the centre. He wasn't reading it but was deep in thought; his wife was gone now, but she was in his mind every day; hardly an hour would pass without him thinking of what she had said or what she would have said if she was still here. *I wonder what she would have thought about me living for so long.*

The door to the room opened and the Director's doctor entered with two other people; Doctors he guessed, one a man and the other a rather striking woman, probably in her fifties.

"Good morning Simon." The Doctor used the Director's first name; he hadn't done that since he gave him the bad news that he was unlikely to survive until Christmas; that was nearly five years ago, but here he was.

"I would like to introduce Doctor Powell and Doctor Rutherford." He indicated first the woman then the man. "They are both part of the team that have been looking after you but you will not have seen them before; they are the backroom boys so to speak.

The Director was taken aback that all three sat down in the small room; usually he would be invited into the main consulting room down the corridor. *Bad news to follow I think.*

"Simon, we are a little surprised at the latest tests that we carried out on you some two weeks ago; you remember we took blood and some bone marrow from you to enable us to determine the progression of your illness." The lady Doctor was now speaking.

It is the end! Thought Simon, suddenly wanting to flee this room and keep on running. He didn't feel any different but now it seems he had reached the end.

"Simon, are you OK?" Doctor Rutherford was looking at him with a concerned frown.

"OK tell me how it is and please get on with it; it's not as if we haven't been waiting for this to arrive have we." Simon reverted to the Director persona; always in charge and always in control.

"We can tell you today that your condition has not got any worse from the last time we assessed you; in fact, the condition has changed somewhat; if it is for the better we do not yet know, but it has changed.

The three doctors went over his treatment from the beginning to the present; most of what they were saying Simon knew of course. The slow decline in his health due to the genetic problem he had inherited from his father and his father before him. There was no cure, only a chance that the disease might be slowed, but it would kill him. The progression of the disease had been modified somehow.

"We are not at all certain what has happened but several things have shown up from the latest batch of tests and no we don't think there has been a problem with the tests and we have false indications. Doctor Rutherford pre-empted the question from Simon."

“As previously the physical tests were carried out before the bloods were taken; the same every time. The tests have also been run using the control samples that we take at every occasion; as you know we take two sets of samples every time we monitor you. One sample is tested, and the other is held in isolation just in case we have a significant change in what we expected. We have only used the second sample once before and that was two years ago when an analyser malfunctioned. Since that occasion the test results have been as predicted and without anything unusual. This time it is somewhat different.

“OK so far but what is going on. Am I to die sooner rather than later or what?” The Director was not at all happy with the way he this was going.

“How do you feel Simon?” Doctor Claire Powell was now speaking, looking the Director squarely in the eye, unblinking.

“I feel pretty much like I always do except that, if I think about it, I am not as breathless as I have been in the past. I could put that down to me consciously slowing down. Don’t run if you don’t want to be out of breath sort of thing.”

“Well let me go through the results from the last set of tests we did with you.” As you know we carry out exactly the same tests every time, the only variation was last time when a new lung function device was used to assess the progression of your complaint.”

A complaint, now is it? Simon was still irritated that they were not getting to the point but kept quiet.

When we first compared the figures, we thought that the equipment was probably at fault and that your lung function was not changed." Doctor Claire Powell was staring at him again.

"However, we then looked at your bloods to see what had changed in the indicators that are produced with your condition; low and behold the markers connected with the disease are almost non-existent. They do show that you still have the problem but you are not very far away from when you were first diagnosed.

"What does this mean? Have I somehow been cured?" Simon's mood was on the up.

"It appears that your health is improving and that that the condition is fading into the background. However up until this point we would all agree that this is not possible, and this has never been encountered before; believe us when we say that the medical records and articles relating to this have been exhaustively researched. Your test results have been checked and counter checked by a whole new team completely unconnected to you. You are the first to show any sign of improvement. I'm sure that no one here believes in miracles but we at a loss to explain what has happened" Claire sat back into the seat, still staring at Simon.

"So, you are saying that my health is now improving and that the prognosis is now better than it should be?" Simon had long ago resigned himself to an early death and had become quite used to the idea. "Will it return or is it going only one way?"

"We don't know because this is outside our experience, we will have to monitor you very closely from now on to determine what direction this is heading. Your case is now at the top of the tree so to speak but be assured your identity is not known outside the small medical team that has been looking after you for these years." The Director's own physician, Doctor Jones, was now speaking.

"We would like to carry out further tests over the next two week to determine the speed of the change; would that be alright with you Simon?"

"Yes of course I can be available whenever you need me." Simon was in fact very busy and could hardly spare the time to be here today but this was important and he would make time; getting little sleep had been one of the consequences of his job so he could go there again for a short time. A number of the projects he was overseeing were winding down, anyway.

"Can you come to the clinic next Monday at 15:00 to some more testing?" Doctor Rutherford scribbled into a small black note book.

"Yes, I will make time and be here whenever you need me. One question though; do I need to keep taking the medication at the same times as I do at present?"

"Yes, we don't yet know the cause and effect of what has been happening to you so, for the time being, we will keep everything the same if that is alright with you Simon." Doctor Jones got up and offered his hand to Simon. "We are very pleased but quite amazed at the turnaround of your condition and believe me we will leave nothing to chance in your care."

All four were now on their feet, they all shook hands before Simon was left alone with Doctor Jones. "This is really quite amazing you know Simon; this thing that is happening to you is quite impossible."

Simon smiled. "Yet it is happening; thank you very much Doctor, see you next week."

Simon was sitting in the back of the agency car that had brought him to the meeting. "Back to work Jimmy, take your time." Simon closed the window that separated the driver from the rear of the car. *Well maybe a lot more years than he thought. Who knows?*

The car was just making the turn onto main from Woodstock when the secure phone in the car beeped once.

"Director." Simon said wondering who this might be. The one beep indicated that it had come from within the organisation and at a fairly low level.

"Simon, how are you feeling today? I expect you have had the good news from your medical team and are pretty pleased with the outcome."

"Who is this?" The caller had not introduced themselves but speaking with a slight accent – perhaps

German. He was using the Director's first name, something no one at work ever did.

"It does not matter who I am but I'm very pleased that we could help you with your small medical problem. We have succeeded in turning it off Simon but we can just as easily turn it back on, Bye for now." The line was disconnected.

"Get a record and trace on the last call to the vehicle phone, I want to know who and from where. Get back to me as soon as possible." Simon had used the emergency contact phone that was in the car. It didn't matter that the call was no longer in progress; all calls to the Director were monitored, traced and recorded as a matter of course. The system should throw up the caller ID and location without too much effort.

The car drove down the ramp to the underground parking area as it came to a stop the phone rang.

"Director we have a problem, the call was registered by the system as in progress but nothing else, no content and no indication from where it came; I have never come across anything like it before. We think it carried a sub command with the connection that wiped the content from the recording but I have no idea at this point why we cannot determine where it came from."

"Thank you, keep on it will you please, I need to know who it was."

The Director made a mental note to investigate the medical team but as far as he was aware only the three doctors at the interview knew who he was and what he did. Even he hadn't known the other two doctor's names before today; the whole idea was to keep it blind. That had obviously not worked in this case. He pondered what the future would now hold. His problem did seem to have gone away, his was sorry was that his wife was not here to see it. He felt more lonely than usual.

The Principal sat back in his chair and pondered what he had said on the phone. Most of what he said was true, but he knew full well that once the change had been made in the director's condition there was no going back. *We can turn it back on* was an empty threat, but that didn't matter as long as the Director believed the lie. What the Director and his doctors didn't know, of course, was that the change in his condition had been initiated some time ago, the change had only been apparent over the last month or so. The medical team had picked it up in the routine checks of course but had delayed informing the director this long because the results of the tests had been so unlikely.

Why had this particular target been chosen? The Principal still thought that they had the right person; he had a disease that was related to an inherited genetic anomaly. The problem had come from his father and through the male line before him. It was very rare but was well understood although until now nothing much could be done about it. The Director's lung function would slowly get worse until his heart failed and he died; he was already living on borrowed time when he was chosen; the fact that he was now in little danger because of the intervention was fortunate for the director and good news for the group who would be the subject of the next test. The Principal sipped his coffee and smiled; it would be a long day getting the next phase launched and all the players in place.

14.

Helen Dudman and David Catchpole were sitting at a long table that was laid out with piles of documents with several that were open. The table was covered in post it notes with scribbles and notations on them. Professor Catchpole was also keeping a log in an alphabet indexed note book.

"See this Helen." He indicated a column that he had compiled on page one of the notebook.

"This is Swift's notation laid out sequentially with the page numbers referenced against each entry." Catchpole indicated a long list of letters in three or four-digit groups.

"If we reference this back to the pages, they came from it seems to indicate a simple short hand notation so that Swift could quickly gauge where they were in the project. At first I thought it was a quick way for him to reference material when he was compiling a report of some kind."

Helen was looking at the figures and cross referencing them with page numbers that related to several reports piled in front of her.

"You're right, they appear to be just a quick reference that Professor Swift was using to enable a quick search for the main points on each of these reports; are you saying that this is not the case?" Helen thought that the notations were exactly that and Professor Catchpole was chasing shadows.

“Yes, they certainly do but look here......” Catchpole was indicating a string of letters that all began with the letter F.

They do relate to the page numbers in the same way but they also indicate something else; it took me all night to see it. Remember both teams did the Blue Eyes test to see what remained of the gene as it progressed through the generations and why it could be found in family lines that had no blue eyes at all. Well this set of notes refers to something else in that line of thought; you see it is relating to somewhat unconnected pages and comparing the fairly straight forward Blue Eyes line to something else.”

The Professor went on to explain what he had found the night before; the notes left by Professor Swift kept indicating a hidden factor in all that the team had been doing; a hidden genetic marker that was indicated to be present in a very large number of samples.

“Look at this; the marker looks like it is in 98% of the test population, which it is, but the test population here in the test are all from a certain genetic background. In this case, they are all European of Scandinavian decent. This other group are from a small enclave in Argentina that originally came from Scotland, so essentially the same group. This information is only apparent if you read the reports in conjunction with Swift’s notes and use a bit of lateral thinking.”

“But why was he proceeding in this direction? The research was only designed to map genetic traits across ethnic groups; this seems to be way more than that. Has the research wandered or are we looking at a parallel line of results, and if we are why was Professor Swift doing this?" Helen was getting irritated; she had put some considerable work into all this research and she was completely unaware of any deviation to the research line. *It appears that I have been taking my eye off the ball on more than one occasion;* she would have to report this as soon as she got the chance.

"I don't think Swift was directing this or at least not in the way he thought the project was going. I think he stumbled onto a duel research route that he was not formally aware of. That is why he kept all these notes. I think he stumbled on a covert line in the research and was concerned about it." The two scientists fell silent and gazed at the scribbles that were Professor Swift's message to them.

"Professor Swift was murdered." Helen stated what everybody knew, of course, but this may have something to do with it.

"Are you suggesting that he was murdered because of something he had discovered within the project?" Helen was trying hard to think that it wasn't.

Professor Catchpole let out a long breath and sat back in his chair.

"I have no idea Helen and I'm unsure as to what I, or we, should do about it. Swift obviously found a secret line within the research but why did he keep it to himself and make these coded entries. Even that is a mystery as we were able to crack it in a fairly short time; I'm sure an expert would have little trouble getting into it.

"Who is controlling the project? I thought it was one of the big pharmaceutical companies who would naturally be keeping things close to their chest but come to think of it we have never had any visitors from the people who are paying us. Professor Swift was always the point of contact and he always had meetings off site; we never saw anybody; it is paying more than the usual though." Helen was wondering what she should do about this.

"Yes, it was similar with the UK site until I came here. As the project manager, I would attend weekly meetings that were always held away from the facility but I can assure you nothing regarding what we have found here was discussed; only the progress to the plan was ever talked about. Your thoughts on who is providing the cash are almost there but I cannot discuss that with you or anybody else."

"Well this project is now ended and the closedown team will be here over the next couple of days to remove all this to heaven knows where, if we had not been curious about Professor Swift's scribbling we would be none the wiser. We could always forget about this and take the money; a considerable amount of money as things go." Helen was now all for this plan and hoped that Catchpole would fold and they could all go home without a worry, she could then leave it to others to dig into the reasons for the research.

Catchpole was thinking. The team will be leaving tomorrow; transport will leave here at ten in the morning that will leave you and I to make sure all the research and equipment is removed before the buildings are handed over. Why do you think we have been selected to do this last, rather mundane, job? Catchpole held Helen's stare.

"Helen, I thought that I was in charge but as the time passes, I have realised that I don't have the faintest notion of what is going on.

"Perhaps we are staying because we are the lead on the project." Helen was now wondering why the two grownups were left to last. She had been on previous projects not too dissimilar to this one and the upper echelons were always the first to leave once the job folded.

"All very well but what are we going to do about this info from Swift's notes. It may be that we are putting two and two together and getting five of course but I feel that we should flag this to someone, but whom?" Catchpole was trying to convince himself; if Professor Swift had indeed found a hidden line of research that both teams were unknowingly carrying out, what should they do about it? At least the final meeting would give him a chance to bring it up. A wild thought crossed his mind, what if he told the press that secret research into genetic manipulation was going on but was disguised as something else? He thought that this would be a bad idea because if it was all completely harmless he would not only lose his job but may well end up in court somewhere.

"I will bring it up at the closure meeting next week in the US. I won't mention our conversations so your name will not come up; don't need to blot your copybook, unnecessarily do we?"

Helen thought it would be likely that the Professor would mention her involvement if only to reinforce his argument and concerns. She would still flag it herself.

15.

"Gentlemen; I would like to say that I have been very happy with the way the project has progressed and the job satisfaction experienced by the teams in the UK and in France." Professor Catchpole was speaking at the end of the close meeting for the project and so far, he thought that he had been made welcome with no sign of any hidden agendas.

"I do have some questions on the direction and purpose of some of the research that we have been carrying out."

The four men in the meeting with him stared blankly at him as if waiting for him to say something more.

"Why did we pursue the genetic variations of the groups that had become isolated from their parent group? In particular, the large amount of work on the group that had originated in Scotland but had moved, centuries ago, to the Northern part of South America. They had largely, but not exclusively, remained as originally settled in their genetic makeup, most still spoke a form of Gaelic."

Again, the four men stared at him, giving no indication that they were even listening to what he was saying.

"Professor Catchpole, we would like to remind you of your contractual obligations and responsibilities that were outlined when you first agreed to the rather substantial salary that we have been paying you and indeed the agreement that we would continue to pay you for the following two years. Do you not remember the second to last paragraph in the contract?"

A man younger than the other three was speaking; he had a very expensive looking, well-tailored dark suit; he didn't look at all friendly. There was something about his stare that Catchpole found very unnerving.

Catchpole squirmed; he knew this had been a bad idea to question anything; *just take the money.* He did remember the paragraph of course; it outlined the confidential nature and the penalties for disclosure of sensitive information that could come from the research. The penalty was the forfeit of the two years' salary that was promised at the close of the contract. He hoped he wasn't staring this in the face.

"Yes of course; please forgive me but I am still geared to the busy regime of the research; sometimes I don't know when to stop."

"Well Professor I suggest that you do stop and just concentrate on the completion of the project and confirm that all is now tidied up. Remember what was agreed – the research was for reasons that were not fully disclosed at the time of the contract start; you seem to be the only one from the team that has difficulties with this.

"I'm sorry it is just professional interest gentlemen." Catchpole was getting nervous, the reaction from the men in front of him was way beyond a contractual argument, he could feel the animosity coming from all four of the men opposite, they were not happy; *better to quite while you still can Catchpole old mate.* He stopped and waited.

"Does anyone else on the team share your curiosity Professor?" The younger man was staring, unblinking.

Catchpole hesitated, unsure as to what to say. "No, not at all I haven't discussed my questions with anybody except you good gentlemen."

The younger man carried on as if there had been no awkward moment. "I think we are almost there Professor, you will need to return to France and carryout a last check of the facility and give the good lady Doctor the good news that she will receive her two-year bonus directly. We wish you luck in your future endeavours Professor Catchpole."

The Professor took this as an indication that he was to leave, *don't think about any of this, have a nice life,* if only he could.

"Thank you, gentlemen, perhaps our paths will cross again in the future, I have enjoyed the work that you set me. Goodbye." He shook hands with all in turn, the younger man last, none of them showed any enthusiasm. The Professor turned, picked up his briefcase and left; it would take about an hour to get to the airport then he would be in an aircraft for six or seven hours; altogether he had been in the US for less than twenty-four hours.

The four men had got up and were now drinking coffee that had been placed on a small table in the corner.

"Well do we need to do anymore with the professor and the good doctor" The small man was speaking.

"He wasn't telling the whole truth Principal, we know that much from the surveillance that has been in place over the last couple of months. He and Doctor Dudman have discussed the South American group at length; I feel that we should plan for the worst with these two." A large and very overweight man was speaking.

"Indeed, but we will have to move quickly before they share their thoughts with anyone else, the next stage is ready to begin but I think we will delay until we have contained our two ex-employees." The younger man was about to say more but thought better of it. "OK get our man from Spain to sort it at his earliest convenience will you."

"Of course, Principal I will contact him today and pass the details; have you any preference on the order of things?"

"Not really but let us stick to seniority; the professor being the senior can lead the way. Thank you, gentlemen, a pleasure as always." The Principal left the room, following the overweight man. The remaining two continued drinking coffee, they would all soon be very busy.

16.

Jonathan Brown was unsure what to do; he had been tasked again by the same people who had nearly got him killed in France. He had been assured that it was all a bad mistake on their part but how could he be sure? The past couple of weeks he had been on high alert; was he being watched or followed? He didn't think so unless the people after him were far better than him; an unlikely scenario. He sat in the sunshine; drinking his coffee and watching a group of tourists go by. His target this time was in London so if he was to proceed he would need to be a little closer to plan the job and make sure he would be able to extract himself without anything getting in the way.

Professor Catchpole was a deeply troubled man; he had left France and returned home to South London; his mortgage was now history, and he had enough spare cash to enable him to do exactly what he wanted for the rest of his life. The project had paid him off with a more than generous settlement and a monthly payment that would stretch into the foreseeable future. The agreement was way above what the contract had said at the start; and that had been very generous. No; something wasn't right; he had been censured at the meeting in the States and the people employing him had not been at all friendly when he had asked questions about the project. It wasn't until the last day in France when he and Helen were about to leave that the full severance package was announced. Payoffs like the one they had been given didn't happen in the real world; was this an attempt to shut him up? He wasn't at all sure. It was true that he could now do whatever he wanted or indeed do nothing at all except enjoy life. Truth was Professor Catchpole was not the sort of person that could do nothing for any length of time; he had always been busy and had enjoyed the work that had come his way.

Since returning to the UK he had put some feelers out to get another research job but the questioning had taken a similar route on all his applications; "What have you been doing these past years Professor Catchpole? When are the results of the research to be published?" and many other similar lines of questioning. The fact that he couldn't tell them what he had been doing was partly because he wasn't sure; anything he could have a stab at he was not permitted to divulge. He had become almost unemployable at the level he wanted. He was on the way to another interview at the British Library; they were looking for a person just like him; a little over-qualified but he had the experience, and they had agreed to interview him for the post. Catchpole wasn't all that sure if he would like the job but he would attempt to get it non-the-less. He would get onto the Northern line and go three stops to Kings Cross; then a short walk in the morning air and he would be there. This was a journey he had made many times in the past, carrying out research and other jobs for several companies in the UK and abroad.

Catchpole put his Oyster card on the reader and went through as the barrier opened. The station was very busy, so he had to queue to use the escalator. No matter how many people used the tube it always seemed to function well, moving millions of passengers around

London every day. This day Catchpole would be one of them getting on at Camden.

Jonathan Brown watched Catchpole step off the bottom of the escalator and walk towards the platform where many more commuters were waiting. The crowd grew by the second with more and more arriving on the platform. Catchpole made his way to the front of the people waiting, careful not to get too close to the edge; he had heard many lurid stories about people who had fallen onto the track and been either electrocuted or run over. The scientist in him thought that there must be a way to prevent both, but he wasn't quite certain. Some station platforms had been segregated from the edge by sliding doors that only opened when the train was in the station and stopped. Camden station had yet to be upgraded.

Jonathan Brown was waiting for the opportunity; it might not happen on this journey but the tube was a good place to do it. The area was teeming with people who had no interest in their fellow passengers and only wanted the journey to end. There would be hardly any eye contact and Jonathan would bet that no one would attempt to intervene if there were to be trouble.

Catchpole pushed into the carriage and moved to the far side holding onto the rail that was just above his head. As he turned around to face the way he had come Jonathan was facing him and almost touching. The young girl behind Catchpole, who had been fiddling with her phone, suddenly looked up at the station sign and leapt forward trying to exit the train. "My stop I think."

Jonathan couldn't believe his luck; the blade was deployed and entered Catchpole on his left side, into his heart and then moved sideways destroying the function of the organ in an instant. Catchpole gave a sigh; unable to stand. Jonathan held the front of Catchpoles jacket and eased him backwards into the seat just vacated by the girl. The surrounding passengers gave no sign that they had seen any of it.

Jonathan rode another six stops placing himself in front of Catchpole but facing away from him. He left the train as the numbers started to thin out and was away into the crowds leaving the station. Catchpole looked like he was having a nap and would probably ride backwards and forwards on the line for a couple of hours at least. The police would spend a lot of time searching through surveillance records but it was unlikely Jonathan could be identified from one camera to the next; it was amazing what a different coat and a pair of glasses could do. They might find the weapon sometime in the future; Jonathan had put the blade down a drain several blocks away. Even if found it wouldn't be recognised as a weapon by the ordinary man in the street; more like a piece that has been taken from a metal container of some sort. Jonathan was very proud of the design; *pity he couldn't register a patent.*

Within an hour, Jonathan was getting onto a coach at Victoria; he had already signalled the successful completion of this part of the job, he hoped that the payment would arrive in his bank directly; he would be in Leeds by the late afternoon; *time for a sleep and ponder the next phase of this tasking.*

17.

The small man brought Hector's coffee over to the desk and sat down. "What is going on Hector?"

"I really don't know but I aim to find out." The two men had just received the latest tasking from the Principal. It ran to almost three full pages of instructions and timetables.

"At the start of this trip we are asked to ensure that the two are removed without delay, which we were already doing, but at the end we are told to hold on the female until given further guidance. What does that even mean; further guidance!" The small man was seeing Hector winding himself up into one of his moods again. Hector was not happy.

"Most of this stuff is already known to us; we could have written these ourselves.

"Hector tossed the paperwork onto the table and sat back with his eyes closed. The small man kept silent waiting for Hector to speak.

"What did this say about our man in Spain and payment options?" Hector still had his eyes closed as the small man picked up the top page and read the third paragraph.

"Here it is; '....is not to be paid until the final job is completed successfully." The small man didn't look up but read the line again to make sure he wasn't hallucinating. The agreement with this chap had always been on a stage payment basis; some money at start and payments when the job was proceeding to plan. He had never been paid all the money at the end of a job.

“That will not work!” Hector was now very irritated. “If you remember back to the beginning, we agreed with him that the payments would not be altered unless all parties agreed; at the time, he said that if we tried to modify ‘payments’ he would walk and we would not hear from him again.”

“He also said that you will get what you have paid for.” The smaller man was as concerned about as much as Hector.” If we don’t get this rectified, the whole thing could unravel. He is halfway through the tasking and we haven’t been paying him. He won’t be very happy and he will stop. If and when we proceed with the woman, our man will not be available. Outstanding!”

The phone on the desk rang once and was silent. “It seems the Principal wants to speak to us.” Hector picked up the phone and entered a five-digit code into the keypad. “Principal, how nice of you to call.” Hector made a face and listened. “But principal......”

Hector took the phone away from his ear and looked at it. “Our world is starting to change for the worse my friend; how we got this far with him in control is a mystery to me.” Hector tossed the handset onto the table, something the small man had never seen him do before; Hector always put the phone down with the cable facing the same way; he had even seen him rearrange the phone on someone’s desk if it had been put down ‘incorrectly’. Hector was not a man to simply toss the phone away.

“OK this what our illustrious leader wants us to do; we are not to proceed with the removal of the good lady doctor at this time; we already have two leaders of the team that have been murdered, and it is thought that it now has the potential to attract too much attention. He says that the two separate police forces have not yet made a connection; it is thought that it is only a matter of time before they do. At present, Doctor Dudman is unaware of Catchpole’s departure and is not trying to pry into the project; it seems that she has taken the money and is just relaxing with her new financial security; she has even bought a house. She will be monitored until the organisation is satisfied that she won’t try to dig further or contact anyone with information regarding the project in France.”

“But what do we do if she does become a nuisance?” The small man thought that they should just remove her and be done with it.

Hector smiled. “Yes, dear friend, we should really get rid of her before she does anything we cannot contain but our leader, our principal, thinks otherwise. We are to only act against her on the orders from him and not before. I will have to send him a note regarding the non-payment of our man; the principal wasn’t in much of a listening mood on the phone.

18.

Doctor Helen Dudman was sitting on a bench eating her lunch and watching the world go by. She had been hard at work these past weeks in one of the labs at the university working as a research assistant on an extremely boring project that was looking at the way certain organic molecule behaved, or didn't behave, when subjected to different levels of heat. She wasn't doing it for the money and it was not rocket science but it kept her busy; something she needed to be or the whole project in France kept coming back. *Be professional and just wait for the next job, stay sleeping.* A large National Express coach come around the corner from the main road and pulled up at the stop that was the usual jumping off and on point for many students every day at this time; a queue with those who were leaving had formed; mostly students carrying rucksacks of one design or another; it was the same most days; a bus load getting off and a bus load getting on.

She watched the passengers leave the bus and wait at the side so the driver could retrieve their bags from the storage under the passenger part of the vehicle. One passenger, about the tenth to get off, didn't wait for any baggage but went off down the path that ran straight towards the seat that Helen was sitting on. As he went past the man briefly made eye contact with Helen. *Something familiar about him.* Helen thought to herself, not quite sure where she could have seen him before. Perhaps it was in the University; after all there were a few thousand people in there every day and he was walking that way. No, it was him. "Now what on Earth are you doing here?" Alarm bells started to ring.

Helen turned and watched him walk off down the road that led away from the University. Had he seen her? Was he here because she was? And if so why? She would need to get guidance before she continued.

Jonathan Brown was not happy; *what is it with this woman? Every time I get near her something goes wrong.* He was pretty sure she had not made the connection but he couldn't be sure so would have to modify his plans to keep well away from her until the time came to remove her; whenever that might be. The planning and reconnaissance would have to be at arm's length from now on. He wasn't at all sure how he would take the target down when he was told to but it would probably follow the sequence that he favoured; quick and out of the blue for the target and an easy getaway for him.

Jonathan picked up the pace and went down the street, past one of the entrances to the university; he would be at the cheap and cheerful hotel in five or some minutes. At least the chance meeting hadn't been all bad; he had at least noted that she was alone on the bench and eating lunch; perhaps she did that every day or at least most days when the weather was good.

He counted the steps it took to arrive at the hotel; estimating the distance he looked at his watch and made a mental note to allow five more minutes to ensure he could arrive at the target, if she was to be there, on time with a little fudge factor.

Jonathan checked in and went to the room that he had asked for; it was on the top floor at the end of the corridor adjacent to the fire escape. Jonathan looked at the door mechanism and noticed a small sign on the wall indicating that the door was alarmed and that the customers were not to use it for normal access but to use the main entrance. The alarm would be a simple circuit that would flash a warning down in reception when the door was opened. *Easily bypassed.*

Jonathan went into the room; put his small bag on the table by the TV and lay on the bed.

Helen Dudman was back at work; the image of the man walking towards her and the way he looked at her had stuck in her mind. There was something odd going on that she couldn't let go unchallenged. The eye contact had probably lasted less than a second but it had stuck.

Jonathan took a shower; it would be around three hours before he would need to leave and go looking for Helen Dudman; he assumed that she would leave at the normal finish time for that department; half past five except Wednesdays when it would be five. Once showered and changed Jonathan felt much better; he lay on the bed for a while watching the news channel on the TV. There was a big presentation on some global warming event; it seems that the whole world is doomed unless mankind does something about it. "Fat chance of that." Jonathan said to the television; Jonathan closed his eyes and considered what the next few days might bring. He had been instructed not to act against Doctor Dudman but to prepare a plan to remove her nonetheless. He was unsure of how the target would be attacked but he always considered several options; the blade was his preferred method but that wouldn't always be practical. She wasn't a big woman and as far as he knew at this time, she was not any sort of Martial Arts expert; *just because you have seen no evidence of capability do not assume that there is none.*

Jonathan made the journey to the main entrance in good time; he hoped that she would use this side of the building but she may leave by a side entrance that he was unaware of but judging by the research he had done online the checking in and out of the facility was via the main entrance. He also knew that not everyone in an organisation like this would obey all the rules all the time.

At twenty past he was standing under a tree that was part of a large wooded area just off to one side of the main road that led to the parking area; it looked like it had originally been put there as a small park so people could get away from the concrete; all a little overgrown now. If anyone noticed him, they would assume that he was waiting to collect someone who would come out of the university.

Right on time a number of people exited the main entrance; *they must have been on the starting blocks to leave* Jonathan said to himself.

Doctor Helen Dudman was one of the last to emerge at around five to six; Jonathan was beginning to think she was either working late or had indeed gone out another exit. He wasn't sure how she would get home but he knew from the initial research that she had bought a nice house about twenty minutes away. She may have a car in the car park but he would wait and see.

Helen Dudman set off walking at a fairly brisk pace. *A little fitness training on the way home.* Jonathan followed at about a two-minute interval, being careful not to close the gap but keep her in sight. He knew where she was going so it wouldn't be that bad if he was momentarily out of sight. She turned the corner from the main road that led to the street where he knew the house was.

"Hello, who is this then?" Jonathan said under his breath.

As the doctor was about a hundred metres from her front door a figure, probably a man emerged from a small side entranceway and began to follow her. He was about six feet tall and wearing sports trousers and a hooded top, both hands firmly pushed into pockets. Jonathan stopped and watched. As the Doctor turned into the small driveway to her house, the figure closed the gap between them; it looked to Jonathan that he was going to intercept the Doctor as she was going in towards her house. Just then a car stopped; the window wound down, and the man was distracted. The car driver was asking directions to somewhere or other. By the time the car driver was satisfied Helen Dudman was inside her house. The hooded figure looked at the closed door and then carried on down the road.

Jonathan was puzzled; *what was that all about?* Was there someone else tasked to remove the doctor or was it some random low life that was taking the opportunity to have a go at a lone female?

Jonathan had to make a decision; the Doctor was now at home and probably not going anywhere in the immediate future whilst the person with the hood was getting away.

It wasn't hard for Jonathan to keep pace; he paused outside the house to get a good look at the front door; *no problem with that; easily breached if he had to.* Jonathan followed the man down the hill and into a children's play area; he watched from across the street as the man sat on a bench; *not an expert, he is totally unaware of his surroundings.* Jonathan was now thinking that the man was an opportunist and was out to rob or assault the doctor; perhaps he intended to follow her into the house when she opened the door.

It was ten minutes before the man got up and walked out of the play area and down a small lane that went towards the railway line. The path was boarded by dense undergrowth on one side; the other side a low wall with a fence that prevented walkers straying down a steep bank onto the railway line. The fence was broken down in places as if someone had used it for a shortcut to cross the railway. The bank was covered in gorse bushes and years of rubbish that had been thrown over the fence.

Jonathan was now close to the man. “Hey.” Jonathan said when he was close enough to touch; the man turned to see who was behind him; Jonathan’s fist went into the man’s stomach just below the ribcage; all the air was driven out of him and he went straight down gasping for breath.

The man was way out of condition and was having serious problems with his breathing. Jonathan searched him and found a small kitchen knife and a roll of duct tape. “What were you going to do with this old friend?”

“Piss off.” The man was still struggling to speak and was trying to get up. Jonathan fell onto the man’s leg, bringing all his weight into the side of the knee; a loud popping sound indicating that the knee was now not going to support him anytime soon. The man started to moan, the pain in his leg almost overwhelming.

“What were you going to do with this old friend?” Jonathan repeated the question.

“I was just going to have a bit of fun with the bird, that’s all.” The man was now starting to cry. “Don’t hurt me anymore......” His pleas were cut off as Jonathan jabbed him in his throat, crushing the Larynx; the man stared to gurgle and then lay still. Jonathan checked the man was dead, feeling carefully for a pulse in the carotid artery.

“No more having fun old mate. Jonathan picked the man from the floor, hoisted onto his shoulders and threw him down the embankment towards the railway line. The body disappeared into the thick gorse and was invisible from the path.

Jonathan walked up the path to the end and checked if he may have been overlooked; there was no housing in the immediate area and no noise came from the small road that ran about fifty metres away towards the town. Satisfied he was unseen Jonathan made his way back through the playground and retraced his steps past Helen Dudman’s house and walked back towards the hotel. He would have to reconsider what the future would hold for Doctor Dudman; he had stepped completely away from his usual practices. Why had he intervened and removed the threat to the Doctor? He wouldn’t have previously. Jonathan had only been instructed to watch Helen Dudman but not to keep her alive or unharmed; this time he had put his own safety at great risk; what if someone had seen him and called the police or tried to intervene? “Perhaps I am going soft in my old age.” *He would seek clarification on this job* when he next had contact.

19.

Hector was in a meeting with the Principal, the smaller man was also in attendance; both had been summoned the day before to discuss the next phase of the trial period. Spaces at the large conference table were filled with the usual people; there was one empty chair that Hector was surprised at; Brother Trevor was always there; he considered asking where he was but immediately thought better of it.

"Gentlemen, let me outline what has already been done on this latest test sequence." The Principal looked directly at Hector for a couple of seconds. *What is he looking at me for? I don't have any direct responsibility with this testing, anyway.* Hector became nervous.

"As you all know the work done in our research programme has enabled us to manipulate some genetic traits that have been known about for some time; blue eyes, red hair, some cardio pulmonary defects etc. that exist in the wider population. Some weeks ago, we targeted a small group of individuals that have a particularly rare form of Psoriasis; in this case, it only affects the finger nails on some people; they all can trace their ancestry to two individuals that arrived in the area more than a hundred years ago. Locally they are referred to as the Brookes; Mr and Mrs Brookes were the first to be recorded as having this problem once they arrived in the new world. The community of which we speak has not moved location and has not had too much contamination with other Europeans and has only mixed with Asian or Native American groups. The Psoriasis only emerges in individuals that have a direct line to the Brookes; in number about two dozen."

"Principal, what are we doing with this?" Hector was puzzled by what had been said. *Are we after a treatment for bad nails?*

"We have already done something dear Hector; nothing too complicated at this stage. We have determined that we can switch off some genetic anomalies and this test is going a little further in our testing; if it works, we will be well on the way to overall success. Previously we would have to wait for the next generation to appear but thanks to the recent research, that has cost a fortune, we can alter some things now so that the affected individual and any future offspring will be problem free. Item three on your tablet will give you the general details and results of this trial."

The brief was just a more detailed explanation that the Principal had just given; the small group had been chosen because the defect was genetic and had been passed down through a small but a specific line from an original pair that could be identified. The report concluded that it had indeed worked and ninety per cent of the targets had seen a reduction in the psoriasis of the type they all had. Some fifty percent now showed no signs at all. The report went on to detail the mechanism of the treatment process; it had been administered by including the new treatment in the existing medication that all the targets were being given.

"I bet the fifty percent are happy with this." Hector threw away the line and didn't expect anyone to say anything; no one did.

"Moving on gentlemen; where are we with the team leaders that were in France; we must ensure that nothing regarding this matter escapes into the public domain." The Principal was looking directly at Hector.

"We have removed Professor Catchpole and are monitoring Doctor Dudman; so far she has shown no inclination to dig into the reasons for the project; we think that she has taken the money and moved on. We will of course continue to watch her and report back. If she does stray, we have a mechanism to remove her." Hector was surprised that the Doctor had done just that, he had expected that she would have to be removed once the news of Catchpole had emerged.

"What about the remainder of the teams that were involved in the two sites."

"Principal, we have kept a close eye on all of them and to a man, or woman, they have not shown the slightest problem; the majority of them didn't know much anyway as they were only sequencing unidentified threads that we passed to them. I believe they all considered that they had a very well-paid job and were thankful for it. The surveillance teams consider them to be low risk." Hector finished, hoping that the Principal would order that the large-scale monitoring of the bulk of the teams would be discontinued; it was tying up a large element of the workforce available to him.

"In that case Hector I want you to withdraw the monitoring on the group except Doctor Dudman; she is the one who has the potential to make waves if she so wishes. We will keep her in sight for another couple of months; after that it won't matter anyway as the project will have passed the point of no return."

20.

The Director was back in Canada; he knew, of course, that his team didn't like the operations being run from here but it allowed him to relax and think clearly. He was much more settled here and had no wish to return to the bad old days when he spent sixteen hours each day in a windowless office. The new tech world had allowed him to escape all that, but it did mean that he was never *out of the office*.

"How are we going on the search for the man who called me in the car?" The director was speaking over a live link to the team that monitors all the communications to and from the office.

"We are not any closer than we were at the start Director; we think that perhaps the caller was one of ours but we cannot say for certain; we will keep on it."

"OK thank you." The director closed the link and opened another one. "James, good to speak with you, I am just catching up on some of the smaller ops we are involved in; what had become of the two we watched in New York and the man in Spain?"

James was a thousand mile away but was well used to communicating with his boss in this way; on most occasions, it was better as he could get on with work even as he spoke to the director. "We have kept a quiet eye on the two and think that they are near to starting whatever they are up to. The projects in the UK and France have ceased and all the staff paid off. At the moment, we think that they are involved in some sort of commercial enterprise that is worth several billion dollars if successful. We are still concerned at the effort they put into keeping it all secret. They have removed the second head of the team that was in France. It is thought that the same asset from Spain was used as the damage to the subject was near identical."

"Are we doing anything about him" The Director already knew the answer.

"No director he is operating outside of our interest and authority so we will let him go on his way for now. If he becomes a problem, we may have to remove him."

"Thank you, James, we will talk again later in the week; you know where I am if you need to talk." The link was disconnected, and the director sat back in his chair and looked up the coast to the storm that was coming towards the land, about ten miles away; with any luck, it won't bother us down here in Prospect. The Director closed his eyes and thought of his wife; a great pity she was not here now to see he was on the mend from a seemingly incurable disease; *he hadn't felt this well in years*.

"Come along dear it's time to go." It was Margaret's voice; his heart slowed and stopped; the director was dead.

It wasn't until the next morning that the Director's aide found him; in the past, he would have visited his boss several times during the evening to administer the treatment or simply see if everything was fine. Since the Director's miracle cure the reliance on the aide had fallen away to a point where he hardly saw the Director on some days.

The security went into overdrive and closed off the whole area; it was very soon determined that there was no obvious foul play at work and the original statement from the medical team indicated that the Director had suffered either a stroke or a heart attack. Only the post mortem would prove conclusively either way. The director's body was recovered from the house and returned to the US late in the afternoon. Two days later his replacement was already in charge and being briefed on the current operations that the agency was overseeing. Mrs Amelia Cordner was a career spook; someone who had spent her whole working life digging into other peoples' business Amelia was no longer married; that had gone down the drain some years before she reached senior management; no children but a determination that, at times, would border on the manic obsessive.

"We talked about the pharmaceutical research that was going on in France and the UK; allied to that we had been watching a hit man that we thought was under orders from the people supplying the money for the research. That was the last time I spoke to him."

James fidgeted with a pile of paperwork that he had on the desk in front of him. The briefing was coming to a close with the new Director seemingly happy with the way the agency was working. The former director's body had not given them any clue as to the death; it was as if the heart had just stopped for no reason. There was no indication of heart problems or a stroke; the director was healthy and the underlying condition that had threatened his life was gone.

"James, I would like a review into the hitman; just to make sure we are not missing anything here; get a handle on where he has been and what he has been up to since the guy on the train. Get it to me as soon as you can; hopefully we can put all this to bed in quick time. It looks, at the minute, like my predecessor has simply died; let us hope so."

21.

Helen Dudman was still alert; she had been followed on several occasions and she had got to the point that she was continually looking for the man who she had seen in various places on the way home after finishing work. Several days before, she had become aware of a man stepping out of a side entranceway that led to the rear of the houses where she lived; he was hooded and was following her; she was convinced of that. Once inside her house with the door securely locked she had stood at the back of the front room so she could see the gate and the street beyond. The hoody had stopped and looked at the front door for a while but had then moved off down the road. She was nearly going to go into the kitchen to sort out her evening meal when a second man stopped and looked at the front door; it was the man from France she had seen when she was on the bench outside the university and the same man who had been following her home these last weeks. *She was supposed to be sleeping and not involved in any operation; what was this person doing following her; was she in danger?*

Helen considered phoning the police but thought better of it; what could she say? Excuse me but I have seen two men in the street outside of my house; one I may have seen before but the other I haven't. No, they didn't speak to me and didn't loiter for more than a couple of seconds. Besides, that would bring her into direct contact with the authorities and her control would like to avoid that.

The first man in the street she had never seen again, but she was sure, well almost sure, that the second one had been in the area when she walked home in the evening on more than a couple of occasions. She even kept a watch at work, always looking for the man to appear in the workplace; he never did, she only ever saw him outside when she was walking home. *Perhaps I should confront him; maybe not, but why had there been no comments or reports about him?*

Doctor Dudman had decided that the job at the university was way too dull to keep at it for more than a couple of months and that time was fast approaching; she would have a big long holiday somewhere hot. She had been very well rewarded by the company for all the hard work she and her team had done in France even though it wasn't her full-time day job. It was a pity that she could no longer speak to any of the people she had worked with for several years; but that was the nature of her kind of work. Professor Catchpole was unlucky and had found himself in the wrong place at the wrong time; murdered on the tube. The police had concluded that he had been the victim of an attempted robbery by a lone assailant who had not been identified. The people who controlled her had not said anything different.

She had only recently bought the house, but it had gained in value already; not a vast amount but she wouldn't lose any money on it if she put it back on the market. It had seemed like the best thing to do when she had been paid well above what she had expected. There had been a rather rigorous disclosure agreement that, at the time, had amused her. Outside of her work for the agency it did not worry her unduly; she never did talk out of work anyway; a habit that she had got into years ago. The work at the university would come to an end pretty soon; maybe only two or three weeks to go before the funding ran out and everybody went looking for other jobs; it was time to assess her future and decide what she was going to do. The money that she had earned in the last two years would enable her to have a pretty easy life if she was careful. Perhaps putting the house up for rental would be the better option; she would make that decision when she finished at the university and they had decided where she was to go. He full time employment was looking like it would not re-start anytime soon so she would remain sleeping and do what other "Jobbing Scientists" did and move about from one job to another as they were presented.

Jonathan Brown had not been close for a couple of days as he had completed the survey of the Doctor; he would be able to act at short-notice should he be tasked. The surveillance had gone well except the interception of the stalker, but that was now past without any complications; the body had not been found and would likely remain undiscovered until the railway authority decided to do something with the embankment and that wouldn't be anytime soon. In the meantime, he was out on the coast enjoying the fresh air, a little sunshine even for this time of year.

Doctor Dudman's routine had been carefully recorded; Jonathan Brown had even been into her house when she was out; fairly straightforward entry without leaving any trace. He now knew all he needed if it went any further; she would be hit in her home on a Friday evening; that way she wouldn't be missed until Monday morning when she didn't show up for work; add to that the slow response from her employer who would be unlikely to raise concerns until Wednesday at the earliest. Because of the casual nature of her contract they may never investigate why she hadn't shown. Doctor Dudman appeared to have no friends who she met on a regular basis so she would not be missed in the short term.

Jonathan Brown had other, more pressing, concerns; he had not been paid! He and his employer were out of contract.

22.

Jonathan had decided that he would do nothing more regarding the Doctor until he had been paid; he had contacted the people who had tasked him but had yet to receive any sort of answer that explained the change in the arrangements. Helen Dudman could go her own way and do whatever she liked; he was not going to expend any more time on the matter.

His phone beeped once. *Perhaps we have an answer.* Jonathan inputted the code and waited for the system to connect; a long stream of text appeared on the screen.

You are requested to continue to monitor the target but not intervene again if she is compromised by any outside agency. Payment has been arranged under the normal method. END.

"What am I supposed to be doing then? Making sure she stays alive unless someone else thinks that she should be dead? Sounds like bollocks to me." Jonathan was speaking to the phone that was now showing nothing at all. The connection had terminated in the usual way.

The episode with the random man by the railway had been reported when he checked in after the event but no comment had been made until now; *I suppose it sort of makes sense; I was putting myself into a situation where I could have easily have been compromised; that would not be good.*

Jonathan did think it was a little strange that he was being paid an awful lot of money just to follow and report on someone; any number of local agencies would have done the job at a tenth of the price.

"Well tomorrow back to the daily routine of Doctor Helen Dudman for the rest of time." Jonathan used his phone to enter the code that communicated with his bank in the Caribbean; he had never watched or been in contact with a target for this long and it was getting a little boring, but since his money was now in place, he would do as they had requested.

It was two days before he was sitting outside the university waiting for the end of work that would push a few hundred people out onto the street; Doctor Dudman was right on time; she was very rarely early or late; a woman of routine and habit. Jonathan didn't bother to follow her but made a mental note of who came out and went the same way; there never did appear to be anyone that was with the Doctor, sometimes she went some way with others but it was never the same people and the group always split up as it progressed into the area where they all lived.

Now he was outside her house, waiting to see if anyone came or went; so far, she had made the journey in the same time and taken the same route without fail; she never had any visitors.

He had intended to watch Helen come home and then hang around for an hour or so to make sure her routine was the same as other nights. She seemed to shut the door and double lock it, have her evening meal quite early then watch TV before going upstairs to bed between half nine and ten o'clock; the process never varied much.

This time it was different; the light in the kitchen didn't come on and only ten minutes after entering her house the door opened and the doctor reappeared with a small suitcase. At the same time a taxi came around the corner and stopped outside the house. The driver got out and helped the doctor with the case, putting it into the boot of the car. They both stood chatting for a good five minutes before they both got into the taxi and it drove off.

Jonathan needed to act fast. He telephoned the taxi firm on the number that had been on the doors.

"Hello, excuse me but my wife ordered a Taxi for about now to take her to the railway station; any idea when it will be here?" Jonathan gave them the address.

The woman at the other end was very apologetic and assured Jonathan that the car would be there any time now and not to worry but the cab had been ordered to take the doctor to the Leeds Bradford airport.

"Yes, of course, did I say the railway station? Silly me it's the airport of course. Thank you very much; I can see the taxi now, goodbye."

Where are you going Doctor Dudman? Jonathan started walking back to the hotel; it would take him twenty minutes at this pace; time to plan and contact his paymaster.

Jonathan messaged his contact with the situation but didn't get an answer until he was walking into his room at the hotel.

She is getting a late flight down to London Heathrow and is booked onto the New York flight at 10:30, gets into JFK 13:20. She hasn't booked a return. You are on the same flight; get yourself to London Heathrow as soon as possible, more to follow whilst en route.

Jonathan thought for a moment; no sense in trying to get to Leeds Bradford and get the connection because she may see him; way to suspicious if that happened. No, he would make the flight from Heathrow if he took the train down tonight. He wasn't expecting to get much sleep, anyway. *The train it is then.*

Jonathan left the hotel and walked to the railway station; the next train would get him into London about eleven o'clock; he would then get the tube up to Heathrow and wait for Doctor Dudman to appear in the morning; he expected that she would be staying in one of the many small hotels on Bath road or thereabouts, getting to the terminal a couple of hours before her flight. He had plenty of time to get in front of her.

23.

Exactly two hours before departure Helen Dudman walked into the terminal building; she had a small bag over her shoulder and a suitcase that she was pushing along on its four wheels.

Jonathan was sitting across the concourse with a good view of the entrance. *Not going for too long Doctor Dudman.* Jonathan knew she had a one-way ticket but judging by the size of her luggage she did have a return date in mind.

Doctor Dudman went straight to the bag drop off and then made her way to departures and waited in the queue for the security check; the terminal was very busy as was usual at this time of day. It was twenty minutes before she was through and into the departure lounge. Jonathan was close behind but not so close that she might catch sight of him. He took a seat next to a stand that was trying to sell draw tickets for a ridiculously expensive Porsche car that sat gleaming in the middle of the shopping area. Muscle cars never held a fascination for Jonathan; a car was just a means of transport; as long as it was reliable that was good enough. There didn't seem to be a shortage of hopefuls, mainly men, buying the tickets.

Helen was sat about ten yards away with her back to him, reading a magazine that she had bought from the newsstand. Jonathan could see the large format high definition that the magazine held; some sort of wildlife publication he thought.

The board above the walkway indicated that the gate was now open; Helen put the magazine into the shoulder bag and started walking towards the gate; it would be about a ten-minute walk Jonathan estimated; plenty of time. Jonathan walked at the same pace as Helen but far enough back not to be noticed. Helen went through the entrance door of the aircraft and was directed down the right-hand side to her seat. He knew his seat had been chosen to put him on the opposite side of the aircraft and ten rows behind Doctor Dudman. The toilets were close to the Doctor, so it was unlikely that she would wander past the area he was sitting and he had no reason to get any closer to her during the flight.

Jonathan settled down for a long sleep; he was against the window so would not be disturbed by his fellow passengers who were in the same row. Doctor Dudman was not going anywhere so he could catch up on his rest; no telling where this was going to go when they reach New York.

The flight was uneventful; Jonathan was left alone by the cabin crew who were quite happy to let him sleep against the window; one less passenger to work on. He could just see the top of Doctor Dudman's head, and it seemed like she hadn't moved from her seat except once to let the inside passenger past her. Just over eight hours after leaving the UK Jonathan was standing in the aisle waiting for the passengers in front of him to exit the aircraft. Helen Dudman was still ahead of him and would probably get to the exit with about twenty people between him and her.

Jonathan had no hold baggage so he could follow the Doctor at a safe distance and make sure he wasn't seen. He and the doctor passed through immigration without any problems and were soon in the baggage reclaim area. Jonathan made sure the doctor was waiting for her case and then went through the customs area into the arrivals to wait for her to come out.

He stood at the far end in the crowd and waited; twenty minutes later the Doctor appeared and walked straight towards the exit. *She seems to know exactly where she is going.* Jonathan was a little surprised at this as he didn't think the doctor had been to New York that often. Most people visiting this great city at least take in the surroundings when they arrive.

Where was, she going? He thought that he may lose her in the crowds outside the entrance but Helen Dudman made a bee line straight to a waiting people carrier that was in the short stop parking areas just in front of the taxi rank that served the terminal. Emblazoned down the side of the white and gold vehicle were "Mannington Hotel, Times Square" and an enhanced colour picture of the hotel set at an angle across the vehicle.

"Excellent!" Jonathan said to himself; he knew of the hotel so he could now take his time and make his way there and see what she gets up to later.

Jonathan had little difficulty in finding the hotel and checking in under the name that was on his passport; this time James Smyth. With a smile and little charm, he had discovered the room number that the Doctor was in; it was very straightforward to link his Smartphone to the wireless security camera that was in the corridor just down from her room; clever little app that alerted him anytime there was a movement. But despite the phone beeping away, no one other than the hotel housekeeping and other guests used the corridor outside of the Doctor's room. It seemed that the good doctor had gone to the hotel, checked in and not moved. She even had room service for her meals. Jonathan was beginning to wonder why on earth she had come all this way to sit in a hotel room?

Helen Dudman was sitting at a desk in the main part of her room. Opposite her was another woman who was slightly older and much more expensively dressed. About six feet tall and auburn hair tied up into a knot she looked like many of the high flyer business women that could be seen moving around the power centres of New York City. Amelia Cordner was not a business woman at all of course; her interests were far more serious than mere business. As the new director of the agency she has been getting up to speed with all manner of critical projects. This one had been low on the briefing notes she had been given but, for now at least, it had been elevated; there was something not quite right about it.

"Claire" The Director was using the Doctor's real name and not the one she had been used to over these last years. Claire had actually liked Helen as a first name. Her name was Claire Steele, an apt name for a spook if only part time, she thought.

"What should we make of this going on with the assassin? He has been following you for some time now and it is not at all clear what he is after. He does not appear to be sending back any sort of detailed reports but he is there none the less. In fact, at the moment he is one floor below and a little further down the corridor. You already know that he was in the cafe when the two gunmen met their demise but I can now tell you that the gunmen were a distraction of sorts and that you were the target; the assassin was to kill you while you had a coffee. The two gunmen, believe it or not, were actually after him. Why all this was going on and why he was being targeted, we cannot yet understand. We believe that someone suspected you, along with Swift and Catchpole, of leaking information to the press or some other organisation. Not completely wrong as you were indeed passing information to us."

The Director paused as if waiting for a response.

"We are pretty confident that they do not know you are one of ours and that is partly why you are still with us. We think that there is no doubt that you would have been removed if they suspected our involvement. Why they are simply following you and have not made any attempt since France to remove you is unknown."

Claire sat without saying anything; this debrief had been going on for some days now but this was the first time the Director had been present. Claire was uneasy to know that the man who had been following her in the UK was now here, in the same hotel. He was obviously very good because she was sure that he had not been close when she left the UK. More worryingly was the fact that the agency had not done anything about him and had not informed her.

"So, Claire we are about to embark on a new direction for this project. Our man on the floor below us is very competent but not remarkably so; he has been watching the comings and goings in the corridor on the other side of your door, by connecting a wireless device to the camera outside. We knew straight away what he was up to and he should have anticipated discovery but he didn't. We have been feeding him images so he will have been completely unaware that you have left and returned to the room or that you have had several visitors over the time you have been here. I would bet considerable money that he doesn't know I am here. All that is good and the way we wanted it to be. It won't be long before we can meet him face to face and recruit him to assist us on the next phase. We will leave the detailed briefing for you both when we have enlisted his help. If he rejects our offer we will have to think again."

24.

One floor below, the team that was to take down Jonathan was waiting for the order to launch.

They had been monitoring Jonathan for some time; feeding his device not only the fake images from the corridor above but also the traffic information that he was watching in the corridor outside his room. Mr Brown had only left his room once during the time he had been there and that was to place counter-surveillance items in the corridor and the emergency escape stairwell; pity none of it would be of much use. His meals and a daily paper were all delivered by room service. They had substituted the hotel employee who delivered to the room with one of their own after day two; they did think that perhaps Jonathan would become suspicious, but he hadn't; he never let anyone into the room but took the items from them at the door; he never gave a tip and didn't say anything other than hello and goodbye.

Today would be different; a slim, tall hotel worker was pushing a small trolley down the corridor towards the door to his room. The team knew he was watching her from the moment she stepped from the elevator. It was all going to the same routine at the same time; sandwiches for lunch with an oversized pot of coffee. As she stopped outside the door Jonathan was looking through the spy hole; he had modified it so that he could see left and right from the door all the way down to the exit stairs at one end and the elevators at the other. He could only see the single female with the same bored look on her face that was always there.

The waitress knocked once on the door; well used to Jonathan opening the door almost immediately. Jonathan would open the door, say hello, pick up the plated sandwiches, and the coffee, then goodbye as he closed the door with his foot; always the same. A low whine came from the device in her right hand.

The door opened and Jonathan reached for the plated food and the coffee pot. The waitress brought the Taser up into the aim and fired immediately. The Taser generated 50,000 volts as the trigger was pressed and the weapon deployed. The barbs contacted Jonathan's chest just right of centre; the voltage passing into Jonathan was now just over a thousand volts but the amps being delivered stopped him in his tracks. He was unable to stand and fell to the floor; the coffee and sandwiches clattering into the door. Two men came out of the door opposite, brushed past the female and turned Jonathan Brown over, putting restraints onto his ankles and wrists. They then picked him up and carried him into the room placing him onto a chair that was near the bed. Once seated another restraint was passes around his right leg and attached to the chair. A hood was then placed over his head and secured at the neck. The female replaced the power cartridge in the Taser and waited out of reach of Jonathan. The two men cleared the mess from the doorway and entered the room, closing the door behind them. The two men stood back on opposite sides of their captive; both keeping well away from any attack that might come from Jonathan.

Jonathan Brown was more than angry; mainly with himself. How could he have been so amateurish as to get taken down so easily? He had never been this compromised in entire his life. Perhaps he had been distracted by the good-looking maid or he had just missed some vital part of the picture. One thing was on his side; the maid could have easily shot him with something deadlier than a Taser; so, they did not want him dead because if they did he would be on the floor with a couple of holes in him. They were not amateurs; two men who had trussed him up very quickly and expertly and a woman who was very practised; the weapon was discharged immediately she had it in the aim; very good snap shooting. He was still attached to the Taser; good thinking by the woman; keeping away from him but still having the opportunity to zap him again if he became a threat. The two men were in the room but he didn't know where. What did they want? Was it anything to do with the job he was on or had he stumbled onto something else and upset someone? He decided to play compliant and say nothing; not much more he could do at this stage. One thing troubled him; the team that had taken him down were very competent; not a group of thugs at all. He was not subjected to any undue violence; indicating the two men and the woman were calm and professional. Apart from the pain and injury to his chest from the Taser device he was not injured. He estimated that he had been secured to the chair for at least an hour.

He heard the door open and heard two female voices. He wasn't sure if it was two new people or one and the woman who had shot him.

"Jonathan Brown or whatever your name is today, we meet at last."

Jonathan didn't recognise the voice, but it was female and there was a slight smell of a perfume that was familiar. He estimated she was keeping her distance from him. Got it; the last time he had smelled this particular brand was inside Doctor Dudman's house in Leeds; surely not!

Someone stepped close to Jonathan and released the ties that held the hood in place; the hood was pulled off by one of the men who had dealt with him so successfully; the man moved out of reach and stood in the corner tossing the hood onto the bed. In the room Jonathan could now see that the female maid/waitress was still holding the Taser. Five people were watching him; the two men who had handcuffed him, the female maid and two other women. One he didn't recognise; about six feet and slim, a woman in her fifties perhaps and long auburn hair tied up. *Very neat and business-like* Jonathan thought to himself. Then there was the other woman; unmistakably Helen Dudman but with shorter and now black hair. *It didn't suit her.* Jonathan smiled.

"It's been a while since I was in a hotel bedroom with three ladies but I must admit I have never been in one with this many players before or for that matter tired up, but don't knock it until you have tried it." Jonathan was making light of a very serious situation but he was already making assessments of his ability to get out of here. Leave Helen Dudman to whatever she was up to and flee as far away as he could manage. But first he had to escape, and that looked particularly unlikely at the moment.

The older woman moved a little closer to him but still stayed well out of range if Jonathan had free hands; *still not taking any chances at all are we?*

"We know all about you Jonathan; everything from your history in the military to your mast recent jobs when you took care of Swift and Catchpole. The Catchpole job did elude us for a time but with a little digging it certainly pointed to you. We even tagged you with the somewhat random killing in Leeds; we didn't quite understand that one but never mind. You have been getting rather slack as of late. You may have deduced that Doctor Dudman was a somewhat different fish from the usual people you get to deal with and we are also puzzled as to why you were told to remove her and then told to follow and report back; you are probably way too expensive simply to be employed to follow someone halfway across Europe and then into the United States, any number of cheaper more available people could have done that. You are too well connected for this opportunity to be wasted"

The woman paused as if thinking where she wanted the story to go. Jonathan held her gaze wondering why they had taken him and why they were still talking; he fully expected that this might be his last conversation in this world; the cards were well stacked against him.

"Mr Brown, we would like you to work for us for a short time."

"Just suppose I don't want to." Jonathan was now very confused; *what were they after?*

The older woman smiled. "If you decide that you do not want to work for us then your life ends here today; this will be the last day of your life."

Jonathan was silent; t*his is serious then.* He was still a little unsure that they would kill him without more justification; at worst he thought they may hand him over to answer for the people he had killed but the way she was speaking it seemed like she didn't care one way or the other about his victims. If he did agree to work for them what was it that they wanted him to do; he was sure they could manage anything he could do on their own. Of course, they could have simply asked him like most other people had done in the past.

"OK what is in it for me; other than staying alive?"

"Mr Brown, if you decide to work for us you will not only stay alive, as you say, but you will be able to retire safely to wherever you wish. Even if you escape us, which you won't, you will never be able to relax because we will find you. We want you because of your unique knowledge base of the people we are targeting and they trust you."

Working for a government agency again; that will be nice. Jonathan wasn't convinced it would be good at all but it seemed that he might not have much choice in the matter.

“OK whatever it is that you want me to do; why don’t you simply do it yourself? You obviously have the resources and the expertise.”

“Well, we believe that you will be excellent value for money and that you will carry out our bidding in a most professional manner. You are, after all a one man show. The most important thing about you is that we have deniability; if you are noticed it will have nothing to do with us after all you are a man for hire and you have been involved in some serious criminal activity over these last years. Think on it for a few minutes Mr Brown, there is no hurry.”

One of the men who had been standing away from the discussion picked up the hood from the bed and replaced it over Jonathan’s head, tightening the neck strap; Jonathan heard the door open and close; the room was silent.

Jonathan sat and listened; he was sure they had not all left but he couldn’t hear anything in the room; the team was impressing him even more, no conversation between them and absolutely no unnecessary noise coming from them; *perhaps they have left*. He closed his eyes and began to doze.

25.

Jonathan heard the door open and close again; still no sound from the people who had stayed in the room or anyone who had just entered. All part of the detention/interrogation techniques that he was familiar with. *Don't get close to your prisoner, either physically or mentally. Say nothing to the prisoner unless it is a direct question.* All the clever mind games should be left to the experts at a later date. For Jonathan, this was something he had experienced many times in training for his former life. At least they weren't beating him.

The hood was removed; the same people were in front of him except the girl with the Taser was not in view; Jonathan suspected that she was now behind him.

"Mr Brown, I hope you have had enough time to give our very generous offer some consideration." It was the older woman speaking again.

"I think that I might be interested since the alternative doesn't sound all that attractive."

Jonathan thought that at the moment he didn't have any other choice but to go along with them; he may be able to get away if they thought he was cooperating but what should he do if the opportunity came where he could escape. He would be on the run from this lot for the rest of his life whereas the job they wanted him to do might be fairly simple and offer a way out. To stay out of their way he would have to be lucky for the rest of his life but they would only have to get lucky once.

"I would be only too willing to assist you in whatever you are up to. That's if I actually can be of assistance, you may be overestimating my abilities somewhat."

"Fine, then we would like you and Doctor Dudman here to work as a team but not appear as a team; if you get the drift. You should have killed her in France we know; you were a little ahead of us then but eventually we got the kill instruction changed to just follow and report. You see, we have contacts and others in the organisation that we are interested in but we still do not know exactly what they are up to. That is where you and your new partner come in."

The woman nodded to someone behind Jonathan; one of the men who he thought might not be there was undoing the cuffs on his wrists and legs; the tether from his leg to the chair was left attached.

"That might make you feel a little more comfortable; let us get to business. In the next two days you will be briefed on the outcomes that we expect; obviously not all plans run true but this one should get us what we want, at worst it will close down the operation that we are interested in."

Jonathan still didn't know what he was supposed to do, but he was a little more comfortable the restraints had gone.

“Any chance of using the loo? Bathroom if you like, it has been a while.”

Another nod to the same man and the leg tether was removed. Jonathan was puzzled; why didn’t they remove that the same time as the others? *Just a simple request to have a piss and it was gone; should have thought of that sooner.*

Jonathan got to his feet and pulled the barbs from his chest; he noticed they were all staying out of reach but the girl with the Taser was ready with another one. The bathroom was just inside to the door of his room, he could have been in any of the middle market hotels around the world; all pretty much the same layout. He went through and closed the door.

There was no escape from here and he soon found that the weapon he had hidden down the side of the bath was gone; also the blade of his design was not there. He had hidden it behind a pipe that ran along one of the corners behind the fixing for the shower. This again demonstrated that he was not dealing with amateurs; it would have been almost invisible to most people.

“Oh well, onwards and upwards.” Jonathan wondered how this would all play out as he dried his hands and opened the door. The same people were still in the room. “Feeling refreshed are we Mr Brown?” The older female was speaking again. “Please sit down and we can get this out of the way.” She motioned to a seat that was at a large desk that had three other seats placed under it on the opposite side.

I wonder how they got that in here so fast. Jonathan rubbed his hand over the leather table top as he sat down.

The older woman, Helen Dudman and one of the men sat down opposite. The female with the Taser was in view again but didn't seem to have the weapon. The other man stood by the door looking bored but not taking his eyes from Jonathan.

"Are you not going to tie me up again?" Jonathan hoped not.

"No Mr Brown, we have moved on from that sort of thing; as I said before, you either work for us or you die; not much of a choice is it."

Jonathan didn't answer.

"There are a group of people that we would like you to deal with; you won't be acting alone. Doctor Dudman here will be with you for the rest of the operation. Your former employers obviously know both yourself and the Doctor, so it will not raise any flags for them when you two are moving around the country together with you just following her and reporting back."

The woman nodded to Helen who pushed a very thick file of paperwork towards Jonathan. "We would like you to take some time and read through this; you never know once you see what we up against you might not need any coercion at all." All three sitting across from him got up and left the room as did the Taser lady.

"Just me and happy then." Jonathan smiled at the man stood by the door; he didn't smile back.

26.

The information in the file was extensive; it started out with information on him; not all of it correct, but the details, in some areas, made him feel uncomfortable. The most comprehensive information was from his time in the armed forces but he supposed they could get a hold of that once they knew his name and nationality. There wasn't much about his life after he left the Army until he got involved with this current episode; from there the information was extensive; even images from a long lens camera of him outside Doctor Dudman's house and following the guy down the road. There was a black-and-white photograph of the body in amongst the gorse. *How the hell had they got that? Jonathan would have bet serious money that this photograph was impossible; the angle that it was taken would have meant the removal of a large amount of gorse. If they had done this why wasn't the death reported anywhere?* He had been severely compromised on this job; they even had pictures of his house in Spain; *so, it was them in the Mercedes.*

An hour and a half later Jonathan had seen all he wanted to; the stuff about him was a surprise, but it was there so he wasn't in any position to change that. The information about the project the doctor was involved in was sketchy and the purpose of the research that was taking up lots of time and money was very vague so whoever was controlling it were a few steps ahead of the people who had him.

The door opened and Helen Dudman walked in with another file under her arm.

"Starting to get the picture Jonathan? You don't mind me calling you Jonathan, do you?"

"Not really and no to your questions Doctor."

She sat down opposite and smiled. He was taken by how athletic she suddenly appeared; not at all like the woman that he had followed these past weeks. She moved with an ease that indicated that she was very sure of herself and was ready to react to anything very quickly. *That explains why she was able to get out of the coffee shop in France so quickly.* He thought. *Would I have had any problems if I did attempt the hit? I think I would have.*

"Why the change to your hair?" Jonathan held her gaze.

"Just part of the job; I usually have it like this."

"Doesn't suit you." The Doctor didn't smile or make any indication that she had heard him.

"Jonathan, you and I are to embark on a somewhat risky adventure together; I am going to play the retired scientist part and move around the US; you are to follow me and report back to your old masters; as you have been doing over the past weeks. We expect that things will go as planned for the short term but things may kick off if they suspect that I am up to no good, so they may instruct you to end it by killing me. If they do instruct you to end it, we will know in advance so that you will not be compromised by any failed attempt.

“You think I would fail?” Jonathan was smiling again.

“Undoubtedly; I am more expert than you could imagine and I have almost unlimited backup; you are on your own. The best you could hope for would be a painless death.” She smiled back at him.

“How long have you been collecting this stuff about me” Jonathan tapped the file that he had just read.

“Believe it or not I have no idea; I only became aware of you when you showed up at Leeds but even then, I didn’t know your involvement with Swift and Catchpole; they didn’t tell me.”

Jonathan could understand that; most organisations like the ones at play here operated on a need to know basis; the more competent terrorist groups did the same; no information to individuals that could be a problem later on.

“OK Jonathan from here over the next couple of days you and I will get to know each other and prepare a plan for the next phase; food and a man to dress your wounds will be here in a moment. I think that it is time to check in with your old masters to let them know what I am up to.”

Jonathan retrieved his phone and entered a code and waited for the device to synchronise. He then tapped in a long sequence of short groups of numbers and letters then switched off the phone and put it on the table.

"Aren't you worried about what I have just sent?"

"No Jonathan, we have been monitoring everything that had come or gone from that phone for some time. A lot of the traffic, at first, was undecipherable but we can get the gist of the message very easily. Besides, at the moment it hasn't gone anywhere as we are looking at it; if it is OK, we will let it go; if not we can discuss it further; not rocket science."

Jonathan resigned himself to be their employee, at least for the time being. It was looking extremely unlikely he would be able to get away from this.

27.

The Principal was sitting at his desk looking out of the window; he had just read the latest briefing notes from the project and in particular the deployment to the people with the bad fingernails. It seems the monitoring has had to be curtailed because the CDC had closed the area to determine the cause of the recent problems the people of the small town were having. The whole local area was involved with some sort of flu type bug. It was thought that it may be a strain of the Asian flu that had caused problems but it had become quite serious, and some people had died. The team monitoring the project had been caught up in the quarantine and were still reporting back but they could not monitor the individuals that were related to the project. This was a pity because it will slow down the fielding of the next phase.

Let us hope the CDC does not find anything that we are doing. He picked up the phone and dialled 1.

"Yes Principal."

"Janet can you get a hold of Hector and ask him to call me as soon as possible." He put the phone down and continued looking at the world outside.

The phone on his desk beeped once; he let it go through the sequence of lights that indicated the route was being switched through the secure system; the phone rang twice.

"Hector, good of you to get back to me so soon. How is our surveillance of the Doctor going?"

Hector was a little irritated about this question; he had only just forwarded the routine report to the principal the day before; does this boy not read his correspondence?

"Principal we still have our man looking after her; she has not done anything out of the ordinary since she came to New York except that she seems to like her hotel room more than the great outdoors; she hasn't moved from the hotel.

"Things have changed slightly with our little project; some other disease has got in the way so we can't tie up all the loose ends at the moment so I think that our man should stay on the job and make sure the Doctor doesn't do anything else."

Hector didn't agree; they were paying well over the odds for the service that the man from Spain was providing; in Hector's view they should either abandon the surveillance or deal with the Doctor and have done with it.

"Yes Principal, we will continue to get reports from him but I must admit the reports of late are a little boring as she isn't doing anything. Perhaps we should deal with her and be done with it." Hector thought that he had been disconnected as the Principal didn't say anything for a few minutes.

"No Hector let her go on her way and we will re-evaluate if things change; I'm sure your department can absorb the cost in the short term; Goodbye Hector, nice speaking to you."

“The principal picked up the phone.” Is David in the building Janet?”

“Yes, principal he is next door.”

“Can you get him to come and see me when it is convenient?” He put the phone down without waiting for an acknowledgement.

A short time later there was a knock on the door; the head of security entered without waiting. “Principal you wanted to speak to me.”

“Yes David, please take a seat I won’t keep you long; I just need a face to face update on our brother Trevor; what did you find out?”

“The report is on its way to you so you should have it by Friday. In essence Brother Trevor has not done well, either for us or the people he has been talking to. He has been passing information to the government agency for some time and I must offer my sincere apologies for the time it has taken us to discover him. I will of course resign my post if you require it Principal.”

“No need for that David we are very confident in your handling of this and our security in general; please carry on.”

“Well, Principal he has been passing information over the life of the current project, he was also the instigator of the little episode in France; we believe that intervention was directed by the opposition; Trevor used our resources to get it underway. He played us against ourselves for a while. The conclusion we have reached is that Doctor Dudman is a very valuable asset to them. At the moment we do not understand why but she is still under the tightest scrutiny and if it is determined we can have her removed immediately if you decide to do so. Currently she appears to be sitting in New York doing nothing at all."

"Do we think that the enemy know the detail of our endeavours?"

"No Principal, we are sure they do not know enough to put the project on hold; as far as we can determine they suspect that a multimillion dollar intervention in the pharmaceutical industry is underway, they have not linked us with the director's death or the project in the small community."

"So, David what are we going to do with Brother Trevor?"

"We have completed our work with him so we await your decision on the way forward; he has a small business with eight employees and a wife who he is separated from; they have no children and both sets of parents are dead. Trevor has no close relatives who might miss him."

"Leave it with me David, when I read the full report I will let you know our decision but prepare for the usual disposal so that Brother Trevor can depart with the minimum of fuss.

"Thank you, David, that is all for now."

28.

The group under test was not faring well; the true results of the application had been masked by the flu that had laid low most of the community. The death toll had been unusually high for a flu outbreak in a well-nourished and basically healthy group.

The two-man team that had been reporting back about the progress of the intervention in the Brookes group had been extremely satisfied on the progress of the agent. The trial was progressing as anticipated until the flu arrived in the town and then spread to most of the test subjects. Some had been hospitalised and others seemed to be completely unaffected by it. Some had died, but the fatalities were not in the likely groups who were old or had an underlying condition that would normally put them at greater risk. At the moment the authorities had not made a connection with the Psoriasis and the flu. *They would need to check in with their concerns.*

It was some days after the two men had asked for guidance that they were found dead in their hotel room. The hotel manager had found them when he had gone to see them about a non-payment of a bar bill. The door had been locked, and he had suspected that the two men had left, intending not to pay the bill at the end of each week, as was agreed with guests before they were allowed to check in.

Both men were in their beds seemingly asleep; there was no sign of anything amiss in the room; the door was locked and the men's clothing still hanging in the wardrobe. When the police had been informed they came and searched the room; nothing out of the ordinary was found; it appeared that the two men had simply died. Perhaps the flu, but that couldn't be determined until the autopsy was carried out.

The identity of the two men was not immediately apparent to the police but checks on some of the paperwork left in the room identified them as US citizens on a short holiday in the area. No relatives of the two could be identified and none came forward to claim the bodies; the short and very cursory autopsy found nothing wrong with either man and they had shown no symptoms of the flu. The medical review of the autopsy finding concluded that they had died of natural causes but the exact mechanism had not been identified. They were both interred in a corner plot of the local cemetery reserved for unidentified individuals.

The office of the principal, however did know of the fate the two men had met. The operation was closed down in a very short order and no connection to New York was made. David had done a very thorough and clean job in masking the true reason the two men were in the area.

"Do we know any more than the police about the cause of death David?" The Principal was leafing through a file that the head of security had brought into the room.

“No Principal, we do not but we think that the death may have been related to the very serious flu that is the area; unconnected to our project.”

“Leave this with me for now David I will make time to go through it; we have to make sure that this is now buried and these two do not cause us any problems even in death.”

“As you wish Principal, I will call and collect the file when you have finished with it.” David turned on his heel and left the room; closing the door behind him.

The Principal was not convinced that the death of the two men had gone completely unnoticed but he was confident in the efforts that the security team had made in the cover up. The project would be in serious jeopardy if the two were connected to the delivery of the agent. As far as they knew the project wasn’t even on the opposition’s radar. At least the agent that had been delivered was performing as predicted and the incidences of the psoriasis had been reducing. *Perhaps I am being too cautious at this stage.*

29.

Over a month had passed since the episode in the New York hotel; both Jonathan and the Doctor had been moving around the United States in what would appear to a casual observer to be a random holiday wander by Helen Dudman. Jonathan had learned that she was in fact a fully qualified research scientist and that the job she was doing now for the agency had started off as a side line to earn extra cash. The involvement with the agency over the years had grown and now Claire Steele had become Doctor Helen Dudman almost full time. Her conscience did not seem to be compromised at all by the fact she was a spy passing information to a third party.

The briefing to the pair had been extensive and Jonathan was concerned at the amount of detail that was being passed about what the agency was up to. *Why were they telling me all this?* It didn't make sense at first but it soon became apparent that the agency did appear to trust him. Later into the process it was obvious that they were trying to recruit Jonathan as a main player and not just a temp for a single job. He was being trapped, of that he had little doubt; but what to do about it?

Jonathan had just collected his bag from the reclaim at the airport that served the town of Marion, Illinois. He was always impressed how the Americans acknowledged their military veterans when most of their allies did not. This airport was renamed the Veterans Airport from the Williamson County Airport in honour of the veterans only recently. He toyed with the idea of getting a free coffee from the stand but that would identify him; only a passing thought.

The closest big city to this place was Chicago, a place he and Helen had spent several days; she wandered about and he had followed and reported back about what she was, or what he thought she was, doing. He had received little guidance from his masters as to what they expected him to do; when asked the answer was always the same; keep close and report back; be ready to target the women at a moment's notice if instructed to do so.

How long he would be able to maintain the illusion of hunter and prey was beginning to feature more and more in Jonathan's thoughts. It was bound to be uncovered eventually as by now he seemed to have miraculous powers of observation regarding the travels and whereabouts of the Doctor. If this was real, he would have lost contact with her a long time ago. To the outside observer she was taking a leisurely wander around the United States and only making travel plans at the last minute.

His phone beeped once; a code appeared on the face instructing Jonathan to make contact as soon as possible. "This might be interesting." Jonathan thought to himself; what if this was the time for action to be taken?

Jonathan sat in the arrivals area and keyed in the code sequence to unlock the message.

You are to prepare to remove the target.

"Well that is a bit obvious; haven't I been there all this time."

He closed the message and dialled in his bank information. He noted that they were still paying him a huge amount of money for what he was actually doing.

"OK let's see what my masters really have to say about this." Jonathan walked to a payphone that was near the entrance; putting his bag down he lifted the handset and dialled a five-digit number; there was a short pause, the voice said "Second." Jonathan dialled in a further five-digit sequence and waited.

"Mr Brown, how are we today? In fine health we hope." This was odd, he was actually talking to a real person; not normal.

"I am well Mr...?"

Jonathan thought he heard a suppressed chuckle but the voice on the other end didn't give his name.

"We would like you to pay particular attention to where the doctor will be this afternoon; we think she is to try to gain access to a facility that we own in the centre of town. If she looks like she is about to enter the building she is to be removed immediately; if she remains on the outside, you are to carry on as before and report back."

Both sides of the conversation were silent.

"Is that understood?" The voice didn't sound impatient.

"Yes, of course, but the timing of the hit might be a problem as it might have to be done in an instant regardless of the surroundings; I may be compromised, depending upon what is going on around her."

"I'm sure you will manage; the details will be sent in the usual manner; goodbye."

The line went dead and was followed by the dial tone; Jonathan put the handset back on the hook.

"Well here it is."

Jonathan was now thinking about how he could avoid this tasking, if it came up, and what he should be telling his real masters at this present time. Could he kill Helen? More importantly could he escape if he did? He thought No to both these questions.

He picked up his bag and made for the entrance; he would get a cab into town and the hotel he had already booked; it was across the street from where Helen was staying, she had arrived in town earlier in the day. Jonathan was two flights behind her; he would look at his phone and get the detail when he was in his room. For the first time in many years he was unsure as to what to do.

The instructions that were streamed to his phone seemed simple enough; Helen was intending to visit a large distribution centre near the railway station on the edge of town. He already knew this as Helen had told him the day before; she had been probing several places across the States to try to get a response; this was the first time the other side had reacted.

Jonathan was in his hotel room within the hour; the journey from the airport into town was, almost, a one road trip. He could see from his room window across and down the street to the boarding house that Helen was in.

From the cupboard, under the sink in the bathroom, Jonathan retrieved a small smart phone; this had been left by the team that was supporting him and Helen. It was the only way that he and Helen could communicate directly.

He keyed in the number to connect with Helen's phone and waited; after a series of tones and silence the other end rang.

"Jonathan; how are you today? I assume you are in your little room across the street by now."

"Yes, I'm here and I have been tasked to remove you if the situation requires it."

Helen was silent and Jonathan thought he heard her, or someone else, talking in the background. "Don't worry Jonathan I will not present a need for you to act at this facility; I do not intend to try to enter the buildings or indeed get any closer than the perimeter road. You can carry on with the reporting back as usual. Have a pleasant stay in Marion." The connection ended with another series of tones as the network closed.

Helen turned and faced a screen that was set up on the table in her room. Well here we are Director, it looks like we have gained a response from the other side; Jonathan has been instructed to remove me if I attempt to enter the facility for any reason; there must be something in there that they are very sensitive about. They haven't responded to all the other probes that we have been doing.

The Director was speaking to someone out of shot as Helen finished; she didn't answer Helen immediately.

"Helen, we agree with your assessment and the plan you have for this location; do not attempt any incursion even if the opportunity presents itself. I think we now all agree that the town of Marion is of great interest but we will have to do some digging on the side-lines to find out what is in there. Do take care; we have our friend under surveillance 24/7 but we all know that he can be very quick and efficient should the need arise. We will do our best to ensure that he stays on our side. Hopefully there will not be any relapses to his old masters. Thank you, Helen, more to follow."

30.

"Gentlemen; our person of interest is now at the site five; hopefully she will do her reconnaissance and leave like she has at the other two locations. We believe she and her organisation are still in the dark as to what we are doing and actually do not know what they are looking for except in the broadest terms." Our man from Spain is still providing day-to-day information and has not missed anything that the Doctor has been doing. We have given him the standard instructions that we agreed upon at the last meeting; if she tries to gain access, she will be removed."

The Principal was speaking over a live conference call to the three most senior members of the group; all remained silent waiting for the Principal to finish and invite questions.

"We are close to the end of the trials; only one more, then we will be ready to assess the results and proceed to the first major deployment; more about that when the time comes. From now on we must double our efforts in this matter and ensure that it continues on plan. Are there any questions?"

"Would it not be prudent to remove her now so she is no longer a distraction Principal?"

The question came from the next most senior and was expected by the Principal. *I will keep my eye on that one.*

“No, not at this time; we have been monitoring her and we believe she is not acting alone. We think that she is part of that other organisation that has the capacity to close us down completely if they so choose. We are on top of what they know and believe me they don’t know much. If we suddenly take action against one of theirs at this stage, we will arouse much unwanted interest that may put the project in jeopardy. We are so close to the conclusion that we are at a stage where we could never recover if it was ended now. No, gentlemen we will let the Doctor go her own way unless she gets too close. However, as we know, that might happen today but we think it won’t, this is the last site that we have concerns about and she is almost at the point where she will report that nothing is to be found; when that happens, we will launch.”

“Can we be sure that our man can remove her before the site is compromised; does he have the capability, and the time required to stop her?”

The same man was asking the question. The Director made a note on a pencil pad.

“Yes, we are certain our man can stop her if ordered and I can tell you that you would not want this man after you; he is very capable and I can assure you he does have enough time to act. Are there any more questions regarding this matter? No? Good then we are nearly there gentlemen; we are on the brink of something momentous, let’s stay focused on this and not get distracted at this late hour.

The principal closed the link and sat back in his chair, closing his eyes. The time has come to rid the team of the clutter that is trying to unseat him. *Was he being paranoid? Perhaps, but he would act anyway. Of more concern was their ex-employee from the project running around the United States looking for heaven knows what; how she was getting the information to target their primary sites had been a mystery, but it seems that she has now exhausted her list of things to investigate; as far as the organisation could determine she had found absolutely nothing of interest.*

The director picked up the secure phone and waited for the connection; "We are ready to proceed to the next phase but I recommend that we wait until the person of interest has concluded her investigation and left." He listened to the response knowing full well that the person on the other end would agree and let him run the show his way. Yes, we have an asset in place to deal with her should the need arise." The connection ended, and the director replaced the handset.

31.

Helen was sat in the hire car that she that had been delivered; a car a little bigger than she had ordered but it would serve the purpose. In any case, by this time tomorrow she hoped to be away from all this and let the agency get on with the rest of it.

She saw Jonathan sat in a parked car across the street and about two hundred metres down the hill; how he had managed to acquire the beat up of Ford he was driving in such a short notice was a mystery; he had continued to impress Helen with his resourcefulness and even at a moment's notice he could be relied upon to deliver the goods.

From where she was she could see the main entrance to a large building that came almost to the sidewalk; there didn't appear to be any land that separated the structure from the public pathway that ran along the side of the road; the building seemed to have been constructed to utilise all the available land. Helen couldn't see the rear but from the height of the building behind she guessed there was no "out back" to the property. The building was square in structure and if it was another story high would have presented itself as a cube. She mused what it would look like if painted to resemble a very large Rubik puzzle. *It would be a great advertising exercise.*

Just then a medium sized white van stopped outside, one of two large roller doors opened in an otherwise featureless wall of the structure. From where she was she could just see inside; nothing much; bright lighting near the door but got very dark and gloomy as her view got further into the building. There didn't appear to be another floor, but it was rather a large storage type facility with no upstairs. The van drove in and the door closed behind it; she didn't see anyone in the building while the door was open.

Perhaps if I move further up the street and past the door, I will be able to see into the building from another angle and some more of the inside. She engaged drive and moved off down the street and parked on the same side but almost adjacent to the door that had been opened.

It was just over an hour before another van identical to the first made the turn into the street from the main road behind her; as it approached, the door opened, and the van turned into the building; the door closed. Helen did have a better view into the building but the amount of detail was the same; no people, bright lighting near the entrance and darkness into the rear; the first van she had seen was not visible; the second van continued moving forward when the door closed. *Two in and nothing out so far.*

The building was registered as a storage facility for surplus clothing from several large retail outlets waiting for disposal; not a charity but working on behalf of several agencies that recycled textiles. Helen thought that they could get a bit of extra advertising if they had marked the vans with something that would identify the work they were up to. A plain white van was pretty nondescript and would hardly add to any company profile; perhaps they didn't want to be noticed or at least to not stand out.

Helen gave up waiting just after four in the afternoon; the door in the building had not opened again; perhaps it was just a place to store surplus clothing waiting recycling. *Then why were they getting twitchy about her being there?*

She decided that she would suggest that an attempt at entry to the building should be attempted over the next few days; the director would have the final say.

32.

"Hector, we have a plan; she was outside the building for most of the day yesterday but didn't try to get any closer than the street. Is our man still on task?"

The Principal has called Hector at three in the morning wanting to talk about Doctor Dudman's exploits. Hector knew all about them as the man from Spain had kept all concerned up to date with what was happening or, in this case, what wasn't. *Does he intent to deprive me of sleep? Or does he not understand time zones?*

"Yes, principal he is still there; he has been keeping us up to date on a regular basis; as he always does when the target is out and about. Does anything concern you Principal?"

“No, we are not concerned but we need to make the agency feel there is nothing to see in this place; it is time to let them have a look inside the building; when they find nothing of interest, they will leave us alone. All the other sites have been investigated by them and they have moved on. We think that they will do the same here.”

“How are we going to invite them in principal? If we are too obvious, they will become suspicious; after all they think we do not know they are here.”

“Hector, the plan is a simple one; we will leave the main door open for as long as they are interested; if they then try to get inside, we will let them. We are almost ready for this incursion so when she comes back tomorrow there will be nothing to find.

Helen was sitting in her car the next day; to her surprise the large roller door was fully open; she had not seen a van or anything else come or go from the building as she drove up and parked across the street. She could see inside quite easily from her new position; a large open space with two white vans parked in the rear corner and piles of what looked like bales of material staged in a row two or three high. She couldn’t see any people and all the lights appeared to be on. After waiting an hour with nothing happening, she took a series of photographs and drove away. To Helen it looked like the building was what it said it was; a storage facility for surplus clothing and material. The fact that the two vans were still parked up from the previous day indicated they were not doing a lot of business. Why were our friends into this side of charity work? The agency knew full well that the main income and almost all the legitimate outgoings from the organisation revolved around charity work; perhaps this building and the others were simply what they purported to be.

On the way back to her hotel Helen considered that they had been misled and had been chasing shadows; still the director would make a decision and perhaps she could go back to sleep.

33.

The next day Helen flew to Chicago and checked into the Airport Hotel; it would be a couple of hours until the debriefing meeting; she wasn't sure who and how many would attend but she continued to hope that this was the end. She took a shower, sorted out her clothes and waited; the television was playing the usual daytime stuff; lots of old movies and endless weather predictions.

There was a knock at the door; looking through the spy hole Helen saw a well-built man in a suit; he seemed to be looking directly at her.

"Deputy Director, nice to meet you again." She had not worked with this man for some time. She hoped that his involvement indicated a slowdown in the operation and that they could indeed all go home.

"Good to be working with you again agent Steele" Deputy Director Tim Logan said as he came into the room. A couple of inches over six feet tall and with a wide athletic build he looked the picture book image of a spy from the movies. Helen couldn't tell if he was armed but made a mental bet that he was.

Deputy Director Logan put his briefcase down on the table and poured himself a coffee from the flask that had been delivered ten minutes before; he sat in the chair next to the desk and looked at Helen.

"It's a pity we can't convince you to work with us full time Agent Steele."

Helen was a little confused that he was using her real name and not the cover; they were, after all, still on the operation. *Perhaps it is ending here.*

Helen didn't answer but smiled briefly as there was a tap on the door.

"The rest of the team I think." Tim Logan said as he got up to open the door. Outside in the corridor were two people, a man and a woman; both had paperwork under their arms. Only one more then we can wrap this up." No sooner had closed the door there was a single tap again. This time he looked through the spy hole, something he had not done before which had puzzled Helen.

"Come and join us Mr Brown, we are ready to start and I expect this not to take too long, we can then all be on our way."

"That suits me fine." Jonathan said, and he walked across the room and sat down at the small table that was just big enough for the five of them.

The Deputy Director, Helen, Jonathan and the other man sat at the table; the woman stood back near the door and waited.

Deputy Logan passed around several sheets of paper so all the group that was sitting had the same three pieces. Two large format photographs and a page of notes relating to the images.

"Image number one was taken about two months ago by one of our assets; it is an aerial view of the whole block; as you can see the building, we are interested in sits in the plot with little room around the perimeter; there is only one pedestrian access point, and that is round the right-hand side as viewed from the road. The other entrance is the one used for vehicle access; the door being controlled, as far as we can determine, either from inside or from a remote device inside the vehicles. Other than the drivers we have not detected anyone else inside the building."

The Deputy Director paused to enable the other three sitting to examine the image.

"Next we have the best image that was taken by Agent Steele; as you can see we are able to see to the back of the building interior right up to the rear wall. The only area we cannot see is just inside the roller door to the left and right."

The picture showed almost the whole inside; the two vans were parked at the rear. The lighting inside was all on so the whole area was lit extremely well. The bundles laid out in a row didn't have any identification on them but appeared to be bales of clothing of one sort or another.

"Has anyone got any comments on what we can see?" The Deputy Director intended to get this over as soon as he could; he had far more pressing work to be getting on with.

Helen was the first to speak. "No, it looks as though this is the same as the other sites; nothing there to interest us. Why are they being so secretive when we nose around them? We know the research they, and I, have been doing is of great importance to them but this....?" I don't get it; have we been misdirected to chase bundles of old clothing rather than the real thing?"

"You are right of course; we do now think that these sites around the country are a distraction and not to do with anything that would be of interest to us. Has anyone else got any points that they wished raised." Jonathan and the other man remained silent.

"Excellent, then we are done here; Mr Brown you can go but be aware that we still have an interest in you; please do not attempt to kill any of our people."

Jonathan got up and moved to the door; the woman who had arrived with the Deputy Director opened it for him.

Once Jonathan had gone the Deputy Director outlined what was to happen from then on; Doctor Dudman was to remain with that name and go to sleep back in the UK; she may be called upon regarding these last weeks, but he thought that would be unlikely.

"You can go back to the UK now Agent Steele, have a safe trip and enjoy the rest that you deserve.

In less than five minutes Helen was alone in her room.

Well that was interesting; all this chasing around and now it is over. I have still got the shadow that may or may not try to kill me." Helen spoke aloud but was very concerned that she had been directed back to the UK. *A little out on a limb.*

Jonathan was across the street from the hotel watching the Deputy Director and the two others get into a large car that had been parked outside. After a few minutes the vehicle pulled out into the traffic and was gone.

None of this made sense to Jonathan; the two photographs they had been shown were contradictory; obvious to even an amateur. Why had the Deputy Director and the other guy not said anything; Jonathan was very surprised that even Doctor Dudman had not indicated that she had seen the anomaly. No, something was not right here but Jonathon was unsure. Should he have said something at the meeting? But what if the Deputy Director already knew about the contradiction in the images? Better to step back and say nothing; pretend he hadn't seen it.

34.

"They have given up Principal." Hector was on the phone to his boss, having just got the information from their man inside. "It now looks like we will have a free hand from now on. Do we need to let our man from Spain go at this point? He is costing us a considerable amount with little return."

"Yes, Hector he can go; make sure that we have paid what we owe him. The next phase is already in play, from today things will progress very quickly."

The connection ended.

Hector was still annoyed that he and the small man did not know fully what was going on; the "next phase", whatever that was, had not been mentioned before today. Why had they been chasing this female doctor around the country? They should have dealt with her when they first suspected her, not let it get out of hand. At least it now appeared that she had taken her fill and come to the conclusion that there was nothing to be found.

"Signal our man that he can go back home but warn him off for another job in the near future; best to keep our options open for now don't you think?"

"I couldn't agree more Hector." The small man said as he reached for the code index that he used to communicate with the assassin. "It is always good to have this asset in our control and not shared with the organisation."

He began keying in the code sequence to the smart phone he had taken from the drawer. Once finished he waited for the series of sounds from the phone that indicated the message had gone and the record on the phone was deleted. The phone was returned to the drawer.

Hector had been thinking for some time that the project, as it was progressing, was not to the organisation's benefit; too many things had been changed or had been taken into sole charge by the Principal; this is not how it should work. There was a mechanism whereby any principal could be challenged, and indeed removed, but that would place a huge amount of risk on the accuser. At this point Hector didn't feel confident that he would be supported should it ever come to a vote. He was beginning to think that he might be the sole dissenting voice if ever a challenge was made against the principal. He watched as the smaller man-made notes in the small note book that he always carried. What is he writing in that book? Is he on my side or has he got a hidden agenda? *Stop it Hector you are getting paranoid.*

35.

Jonathan was on the same flight from Chicago as Helen Dudman; he would transit through Heathrow and onto Portugal and his second house; it had been a long time since the start of this tasking and he was looking forward to a rest; he might even pack it in altogether but he had thought that before on many occasions.

He was sitting two rows behind her on the aircraft; one of the new Boeing things that seemed to carry more and more passengers with less and less room in economy and reduced area for club or first class, all profit driven of course. Helen knew he was there; there was hardly any point in hiding now. He had considered getting a seat near or even next to her but thought better of it; it was not a good idea, after all she had been the target once.

The aircraft was on time; Jonathan was walking down towards the point where the traffic was diverted to either transit or baggage reclaim.

"Goodbye Jonathan, I think it is likely that we will never meet again."

Helen stood with her hand out towards him on the corner as Jonathan made the turn away from baggage reclaim. He must be getting slow in his old age; he had not seen her come past him and he was sure that he had exited the plane before her. He didn't know what to say.

He took her hand; a very strong handshake that he didn't expect. She held his gaze with a half-smile playing on her face; *was she mocking him?*

"Cat got your tongue Jonathan?"

"No, I didn't expect to be meeting you like this. Goodbye Doctor; it seems that things have worked out for the better, at least for the two of us.

She held his gaze; Jonathan stared back. *What is it about you Helen Dudman?*

She let go the handshake, turned and walked down the ramp to the baggage hall; Jonathan stared after her a little unsure what had just transpired. Helen didn't look back. Jonathan decided that, even if he was tasked to remove her, he would decline the job; the first time he would have done that; perhaps it really was time to call it a day and retire.

Three hours later Jonathan was getting off the plane in Portugal, another half hour and he would be home; at least his home for now. He was still thinking about the meeting in Chicago and the two photographs; perhaps he was imagining things, perhaps not.

Jonathan left the airport and took a taxi to his house; the car he had left in the airport car park would still be there but he had decided to let that one go; it was registered in the normal way and would not be connected to him; some cars had been in the car park for years, now covered in dust; some with wheels missing. The Portuguese authorities didn't seem too interested in abandoned cars. Occasionally they would tow one away but there didn't seem to be much of a plan.

Jonathan sat at the table that was next to the large picture window in his house; the view of the sea directly ahead and the mountains to the left was quite spectacular; he liked this house but didn't have an idea of how long he would be able to stay. His escape plan had already been made and practised before he left for the states; he was quite sure that it would work.

On the table in front of him were two pieces of A4 paper laid side by side; Jonathan's eyes were closed; he was visualising the two images the Deputy Director had shown him. It was a skill that he had first recognised when he was at school; he only needed to see something once and he could remember it in minute detail. All he had to do was clear his mind and map it out in his head. The skill had been very useful on many occasions when he was serving.

He began to draw on the paper; first the aerial photograph that showed the roof and some of the surrounding area. Once complete he stared at it for a few minutes to make sure he hadn't missed anything. The road, the side walk and all the detail of the structure that had been on the image were on the paper. Satisfied he drew the detail that had been on the photo that Helen had taken.

"There it is, or in fact there it isn't." The inside of the building didn't match the aerial picture. There was a skylight of some kind at the rear of the structure and in

Helen's photo it was missing. Not conclusive as the skylight could have been removed after the aerial photograph was recorded. There was more though; looking at the whole image of the inside Jonathan had noticed a mark that seemed to run across the right-hand side of one of the vehicles; there was also another mark of similar shape and size on the wall at the other side.

He had seen these types of marks on images before.

Years before when he was working for Her Majesty's government he had been involved in some prototype camouflage stuff. At the time it was secret but since then it had progressed and was widely used around the world. At the time it was a tracked troop carrier that Jonathan had worked on; one side of the medium sized armoured vehicle had a large array of LEDs on it; on the other side a series of cameras that fed the LEDs. The time Jonathan had first seen it, the tracked vehicle had driven up and parked against the wood line. The operator had then switched on the device. The vehicle had disappeared and only the wood line, trees and all were visible.

At that time the device was not practicable as it didn't work too well if the vehicle was moving and in some lighting conditions the ambient light reflected of the LEDs. Later on in the experiment it was discovered that the frequency of some electric lighting might render some parts of the display inoperative. Jonathan guessed that this one in the building was being affected by the fluorescent lighting.

The only other device Jonathan had experience of that could hide a room behind an projected or displayed image was the charged water vapour device they had experimented with in the early nineties. A long strip was set into the floor directly underneath a similar strip set into the ceiling of a room. Charged water vapour was released from the ceiling device and was attracted to the one in the floor; onto this water curtain could be projected anything you liked. It worked very well and people or, if it was big enough, vehicles could pass through it; it would only take a couple of seconds before the curtain flattened out and the fake image returned. The major problem this device would have here would be the air currents that would be encountered in a large open space; it would be fine in a closed room but not this warehouse with the door open; no this was the first one using a fixed display screen that would not be affected by wind or anything moving close to it. It could also be something else but the purpose was the same; to hide what was in the building.

Bad luck fella's, you didn't convince me.

Jonathan circled on the paper where he remembered the anomalies on the image. No doubt about it, the inside of the building was a projection, or rather an image that was displayed so it looked like the building was almost empty. Jonathan was still puzzled that no one else had noticed it. More importantly what was being hidden within this building in the middle of a small American town? This sort of effort and the resources required did not come cheap.

36.

"Good morning Principal, how good of you to return my call so soon." The Principal was sitting in his office looking out the window at the grey skies and pouring rain.

"I must admit that I was surprised you needed to speak to me so soon after our last briefing session, but I am here now. How can I help you?" The Principal looked at the speaker phone on his desk.

"Principal the next stage is now in motion; there is nothing now that anyone can do to stop it; soon the device will have completed delivering the material into the Chicago area water supply. We hope to see results within a month."

The pause indicated that a response was required from the Principal but he wasn't sure what he could say; he did know that this phase was going to happen any day, but it now transpires that the sequence has started without his involvement.

"Thank you for informing me; is there anything that you require of me in the meantime?"

"No Principal, you and your organisation have performed as expected; the rewards coming to you will be far more than you can imagine. You can now decommission and remove any evidence from the sites; I would suggest that the one in the town of Marion that had been under investigation be cleared first. Goodbye Principal."

The line went dead. What on Earth is he talking about? He remembered back to the early days when this project was in the planning stage; he hadn't even been in charge back then but the promise of massive gains for them had always been there. *Why else does he think we are at this?*

The Principal pressed a button on the internal intercom. "Yes, principal how can I help?"

"Get the seniors together tomorrow evening here in the conference room; Hector's people as well; push the time back if any of them cannot make it by then and let me know when the meeting is finalised; I want everyone to attend. If there any that suggestion they cannot come you persuade them otherwise; they must be here."

The principal closed the connection without waiting for a reply he was beginning to think that they had been too trusting. He thought back to those days when this project first saw the light of day; he, nor anybody in the organisation had ever had a face to face meeting the people that had provided the direction and funding for it all. Most of the communication had been by email and telephone; no, this was the time to get a grip of this and make sure it was under control; his control.

The delivery sites had been chosen carefully; this one in Marion was on the fresh water network that eventually fed into Chicago; all the sites chosen for the deployment had enabled the targeting of groups with positive ethnic traits. There were two main groups that interested them in Chicago; the Irish community and the

Italians; both long established and both still retaining many direct blood lines to their home origins. Unlike the first and second large experiments, they had not targeted any particular genetic ailment or trait that could be traced from the two groups origins in Europe. The more the principal thought about it the more uneasy he became; where were the plans for vast profits from the pharmaceutical empire they now controlled going to come from; the experiments were beginning to make less and less sense. It seems that the promise of their empire being able to offer a “fix all” solution to millions of people were not yet within grasp, but they should be.

37.

Jonathan was standing outside the house in Leeds where he had spent many an hour previously. He didn't know if Doctor Dudman was in or if she would be at all happy to know he was there. He suspected that if she had seen him arrive, she would have immediately called for support. He had been there more than an hour and nothing had happened yet so maybe she hadn't, or more simply she wasn't at home today.

It was soon after he had got to his house in Portugal that contact had been made from his employers; he was to stand down and not pursue the Doctor from then on; the operation was completed. Jonathan was now unemployed and a free agent that could pursue further work if he chose to. The two photographs still interested him but if asked he would find it hard to explain why, it was not his concern and he should walk away. *Perhaps he was more interested in Helen Dudman than he was in the images.* As far as he was aware he was not under surveillance from either side but he had made sure that his departure from Portugal went unnoticed. But now he was here outside the former targets house in plain view; he was asking himself why.

"Jonathan, what brings you here?" Jonathan was taken by surprise; Helen Dudman was standing not three feet from him and had approached him from the rear; he had not noticed her; very, very sloppy on his part. *Things were getting worse by the day.*

Helen, you continue to impress me. I would have bet money that you could not get this close without me noticing, but here you are."

"Since you are not here to kill me I suggest we go inside and have a coffee; or tea perhaps."

"Coffee will be fine thanks."

The doctor turned on her heel and walked up the short path to the front door, she already had the key in her hand. Jonathan followed with saying anything.

The hallway had three doors, one left and right and the third at the end; all were closed.

"Go and sit in the lounge and I will put the coffee on." Helen Dudman walked towards the door at the end of the hallway and went into the kitchen."

Jonathan stood for a few seconds and looked at the departing Doctor. *I must be mad.*

Jonathan was sitting on an oversized soft chair when the doctor returned with two mugs of steaming coffee.

"You knew where the lounge was then Jonathan." She said smiling and holding his gaze.

"Err lucky guess, I suppose."

"You were being watched for some time Jonathan. They saw you enter this house the time you were investigating me. You didn't find the surveillance though did you Jonathan?"

Jonathan looked around the room, still unsure where this was going.

"Don't worry, the equipment is gone; we are getting ready to release this house, we were only waiting for you to show up. I must admit you surprised us by being here so soon after you were let go. I take it you have come to talk about the images that you were shown in Chicago."

The doctor was sitting opposite Jonathan sipping her coffee; Jonathan still held his in his right hand and appeared to have forgotten about it. "Drink your coffee Jonathan; we have some things to go through before you can definitely retire."

To Jonathan this was getting more and more unreal; the Doctor was not who he originally thought and now she was turning into someone else. He thought again if he would have succeeded in France when she was the target.

"Why was the investigation wound up?" Jonathan drank from his coffee.

"We were closing down leaks Jonathan; Deputy Director Logan is batting for the other side; what other side we still can't determine. He was put in charge to see what he would do and lo-and-behold he ceased operations in double quick time. It was just what we were after of course. The project is now closed and the investigation can continue without the leaks. Logan had been reassigned to a project where he will be happy but not able to rub against this operation."

Jonathan looked around the room thinking that this was far from over for him; was he to be a full time employer with this lot? He hoped not.

“What do you want from me Doctor Dudman?”

“Call me Helen; please let us be on friendly terms from now on, we might be travelling together for a little while yet.”

Helen got up and retrieved a file from a cupboard that was at the side of the room. She laid two sheets of paper onto the table in front of Jonathan.

“Here we have the image taken previously and the image that I took from outside when the door was conveniently left open. The skylight in this one seems to have disappeared in this one.” Helen tapped the photograph with her pen. “This one here is a projected image; it could have been done in several ways but how it was done is not important. I’m sure you and everybody in the hotel room when we looked at these saw it.”

She was looking at him waiting for a response.

“OK, yes I did see it at the time but since no one else said anything at all, I decided to keep quiet; after all what is to do with me.”

“You are right Jonathan, at the time, it was nothing to do with you; we did intend to let you go and have a nice retirement in Portugal but things have changed somewhat.”

She was staring at him again; Jonathan was making plans to flee this thing as soon as he had the opportunity.

"I take it this man Logan also saw it but closed the operation, anyway."

"That is correct, he was trying to shut us down and since no one said anything at the table, he had the opportunity. He has always been an arrogant sod and actually does believe he is better at this job than anyone else. The only problem we could have had was you; we were not at all sure that you would keep quiet, but the gamble paid off. Logan was persuaded that no one had seen it because he thought that you had not; an independent pair of eyes so to speak. That gave Logan the chance to close the project; something he, and others, wanted.

Helen gathered up the papers into the file and put if back in the cupboard.

"What I would like us to do for the rest of the day, Jonathan, is go over what we would like you to do from now on. We are somewhat on our own from this point; you are retired from both your jobs and I am sleeping so we should have a free hand for the next stage. The only downside from this is that our support is severely curtailed; we cannot continue if the forces ranged against us are aware of what we are doing."

38.

The meeting in the Principals office was not going well; a group of ten people, all men had been summoned, all arrived on time; this was unusual in itself but the Principal was in no mood to compromise on his instructions given a few days before. Something was going on within this group that he felt he was not in control of. This would stop here, today.

"We have ceased operations against the two teams that had been doing the primary research as instructed."

Hector was the last of the group to speak and he was underlining that fact that he and his colleague had only done what had been asked of them. Hector knew full well that the Principal was feeling the strain of this undertaking and was now demonstrating he was severely out of his depth. *Do not get a boy to do a man's job gentlemen.* He had never endorsed this boy to be in a position so high in the organisation; funnily enough this principal actually thought he was in charge and didn't answer to a higher body; laughable!

"Thank you, Hector, now we have heard all your reports we must now decide what, if anything, we should do."

All the men around the table wished this would end and they could leave this dark, claustrophobic room.

"The deployment has gone to plan but we are now in a position where we do not control what is happening. The Director of the agency, as you may remember, died of unknown causes some time after we intervened; the cause of death was not established but at the time it was believed that it was of natural causes. The targets in South America went the same way; a partial cure then death. At this time, we thought that the intervention of some sort of flu pandemic was the agent but now, we are not so sure. You do remember, brothers, that the death of our two men was not fully explained."

The Principal paused and moved some papers around on the table, not looking at anyone of the men who were all staring at him. None of this information was new to the group; all had been briefed and consulted by one another on several occasions. The group also knew that a major deployment of the agent had been underway in a large conurbation in the United States. Many of the men had become uncomfortable with the direction this conversation was going.

"Gentlemen; we are at a crossroads, or at least I hope we are at a crossroads." The principal was now looking around the table, pausing to gather his thoughts.

"So far the large deployment has not indicated anything untoward; the agent is now firmly in the water supply and all indications show that there is nothing unexpected happening. The targeted individuals are still going about their daily business and show no signs of illness. It is believed by the control group that the agent has been absorbed by the targets and is sitting in the background waiting for the trigger; exactly as we had planned."

There was more shuffling of papers. Hector found this interesting. *He is not at all sure of what he is in control of.*

“One problem we may have to deal with has presented itself in the small South American town that was the site of the first multiple deployments. As you remember there were some deaths which included the two who introduced the agent. Initial investigation had concluded that the rather severe strain of flu that was in the area was responsible. The CDC now thinks that there are other factors involved and have reopened the investigation. This is not good news for us but it is also not all bad news. The CDC will now be fully employed on a major tasking that is well out of our way. We are confident that they will not be able to determine our involvement with the genetic manipulation project at this stage. Should they eventually discover the genetic link it will be too late?”

“Brothers; we are now to implement the secure protocol that had been used only once in the last one hundred years.”

What? Hector was now getting a little worried; the secure protocol the Principal had mentioned was indeed a rare occurrence and was last used just before Hector joined the organisation. It was a last stand device that was put into place should there be a serious, a very serious, chance that the organisation was infiltrated.

The Principal now had the undivided attention of all in the room; things were going to change that was for sure.

"Brothers, it has come to my attention that we may be being manipulated by a third party; all the work we have been undertaking during these past years have been at the behest of someone outside of our group. We have been duped into providing the expertise and logistics for someone so someone else can progress this genetic project. I'm sure you will agree that if this is the case, we must put a stop to it as soon as possible. We are not a group that has ever carried out the bidding of others nor will we ever do that."

"Principal, how has this been found out? The project is well into the final stage, surely there should have been indications before now. Are we under investigation by the government? Are they deep into the control cell? Was Brother Trevor involved?"

The Principal let the questions come until finally he held up his hand to request silence.

"Let us not get carried away with what might happen and concentrate on what has happened. Brother Trevor was not involved in this; he was taking funds from the support side of the organisation; obviously we could not allow that to continue; Brother Trevor is no longer a member; rather sad after fifty years with us. No, the organisation has not been infiltrated, but we have been duped on more than one occasion; we now appear to be working for someone else."

“How is that possible Principal? We have strict protocols in place to prevent that; we generate the requirement on each occasion and we do nothing that is not for the good of the organisation. We are always in control of the planning and execution.”

The Principal was looking less and less confident. “We were in control of the planning; it was our project from the start and only members were involved in that; however, we have received some substantial funding from a source outside of the organisation.”

He paused to allow comment; something he rarely did at these meetings.

Hector was annoyed now. I knew this boy would overstretch himself; give him sufficient rope and he was sure to hang himself.

“Is the project in danger of failing principal?” Hector would not let this go; it was time for this particular principal to depart the position.

“Yes and no Hector; the project is on track and it appears we have been more successful than we anticipated but we find ourselves not fully in control of the direction it is going. In other words, we are no longer deciding on the scope of the project at the fielding level.”

The principal could see where this was going; somewhere in the room would try to remove him; at a guess it would be Hector; after all he had been the

Principal in the past and his history in the organisation was impressive.

Hector stood up; something no one did unless they were to challenge the principal.

"Principal, I forward that you are in breach of rule nineteen of the office of Principal and thereby unfit to carry on in the position of Principal."

Hector sat down; the formalities now started to remove the incumbent from the chair. Hector was a little pleased at the way things had very suddenly taken a change for the better. This young upstart had been a mistake from the start but he still had many friends that might interfere and keep him in place. If he was to survive, then it would be Hector and a few others that would feel it.

"Thank you, Hector." The principal was gathering up his paperwork, making ready to leave; there would be no argument at this stage; protocol required him to withdraw without comment once the rule nineteen had been invoked. The one problem they now had was that the organisation would be leaderless, or at least not have a leader who knew all the detail of the project that had been compromised; there would have to be an investigation by the committee to determine the best course of action. Until then the project would be on hold.

Once the principal had left Hector resumed the formalities and spoke in a manner that he had not used for years; he was already enjoying this.

"Under the remit of rule nineteen I assume the office of Principal for the duration of the investigation that will take place starting tomorrow. I may remind you all that this is a serious matter and personalities are to play no part. Any blame, no matter where directed, will be investigated and action taken. Of course, it may transpire that there is nothing to redirect in this project and we can resume as we were. At this time, I would like it recorded that a vote of thanks be given to bother Ridgley for bringing this matter to the attention of the committee and standing down from the office of Principal without argument." Hector was making sure that all the formalities were carried out to the book; at this stage he did not want to make a mistake that would invalidate any action that he had taken. He knew as well as the rest of them that the outgoing principal was in no position to argue; under rule nineteen it was cut and dried; the matter had to be investigated and action taken if required. Since the outgoing principal had raised the problem at a convened meeting, he had no argument to make.

38.

Helen was reading a message that she had received earlier; it ran to more than a dozen pages and it seemed to Jonathan that it contained much interesting information; Helen had not looked up even for an instant since she had started reading.

"What is it then?" Jonathan asked trying to sound uninterested.

"The opposition have stopped their project; it seems there has been somewhat of a struggle at the top of the organisation. This is excellent news as we can now make a move which should go unnoticed in the short term. The project they are conducting, whatever it is, has stopped. Our people on the inside seem to think that the head of the shed has upset someone, and they have made a move to remove him. The problem is that this has not happened before and I doubt that we will see a big change of the direction that this particular bunch of criminals is going."

"Well where do we fit into this? What are we going to do other than monitor what they are not doing?" Jonathan hoped this would allow him to get out and stay out; he was definitely going to retire after this."

But before we do anything else we have a building to look at in Marion."

The flight to Chicago and onto Marion was uneventful, it was the first flight in a long time on which

Jonathan could relax, he even watched some of the movies that were on offer.

The storage facility in Marion wasn't expected to give any clues but since the building was now unoccupied, it was worth the effort. The users had handed back the structure shortly after the project ended. The deputy director took a particular interest; coincidence or not the building was now up for rent to whoever wanted it.

They met the agent from the letting company, a small man, outside on the street; Helen had booked the meeting the day before; she and her business partner required a medium storage building for around six months. The story given was that they were willing to pay the premium for such a short let.

Once inside Helen listened to the sales pitch from the agent while Jonathan walked around the floor. At first sight it seemed the building was just a large open plan structure that was ideal for the intended purpose of storage. Jonathan found no evidence of anything that would allow an image to be projected to hide the rear parts when viewed through the large roller door that opened onto the street. One thing on the back wall did look out of place, however; there were several electrical boxes attached to concrete posts about half a metre from the wall. Jonathan checked the date on the safety label; only installed six weeks previously. There was also another small card tag that was attached to each control panel; on it was a series of characters that appeared to be Chinese or perhaps Korean; Jonathan pulled one off and put it into his pocket. Walking back to the agent who was still talking to Helen a piece of metal caught his eye; it was another tag; a small steel disk about an inch across with a hole at the edge as it if was intended to be attached to something; it had similar characters on to the tag on the equipment

"Excuse me, can I ask a question?" The agent didn't answer but looked at Jonathan.

"Why did they install those three phase electrical points; it seems a bit over the top for a place that is just a store. It looks like the previous users of this place had some sort of high usage machinery in here."

"I am afraid I don't know the whole story behind that Mr Brown; we were asked if they could install all of that about six months ago; they wanted to use some fixed handling equipment to move stock around on the floor. All of it was built to current regulations, and they agreed to leave the "plumbing" so to speak, when they left. It has added value to the building we were quite happy with it." The agent looked at his watch to indicate this visit was taking a little longer than was required.

"Thank you, Mr Jones we will be in touch. There is another building that might suite our needs across town but this looks like it will meet our requirements. It has been nice talking to you."

Helen held out her hand for the weak and the limp handshake from Mr Jones.

Helen and Jonathan were back in the car before the agent had locked the door.

"What do you think?" Helen looked at Jonathan not really expecting an answer.

"They had some heavy load machinery in there; maybe it was to move stuff around but it would have been easier and cheaper to rent a fork lift truck; there is plenty of room and the image you acquired didn't show the place loaded up with lots of stacks that would have been a problem to move."

"I agree Jonathan, whatever machinery or equipment was in there was doing something else other than moving boxes about but at least we know that they are definitely gone from here."

Helen's phone beeped once. "There other sites are empty too; it looks like they have gone or have finished what they were doing. We will get those tags translated to see if they can tell us anything; well spotted Jonathan; I noticed you had them but our friend didn't; he wasn't paying too much attention to anything except me."

Helen had taken photographs of the two tags and forwarded them to the department that translated this sort of thing; it was always done this way so as not to miss any nuance in any text that might be found. Helen already had an idea about the steel disk Jonathan had found on the floor; it appeared to be a sequence of steps in a process; she had seen such items before when working with some people in Hong Kong. The card tags she had no idea; it looked like a random set of characters but her Chinese wasn't anywhere good enough to get the true meaning from the two tags.

They made the airport in under half an hour and after handing the car back to the rental company they made their way through check-in and sat in the corner waiting for the flight to Chicago and a couple of days rest until the flight out of the US.

Helens phoned beeped. "This is very interesting Jonathan, it seems that the tag attached to the equipment only refers to a shutdown sequence and relates to the equipment that was attached. On the back is a company that works out of Hong Kong but only by registered number; their licence to work in the United States. The steel disk is much more interesting; it has on it a small sequence that refers to DNA if you can believe that.

"Are you sure? Why would that disk have that sort of info on it?"

"Believe me Jonathan I have spent the last two years looking at DNA strings and parts of strings; this is definitely related to DNA but why it's on this disk, I have no idea." Helen's phone was communicating again.

"In Chicago we will have the tickets and the direction for the next phase Jonathan; we are off to China, to be precise Hong Kong; ther latest intelligence is telling us the project is directed and funded from there; a little unlikely but there it is. We will leave next Tuesday, bouncing through Amsterdam; if anyone is watching us, it will keep then guessing."

"What are we looking for in Hong Kong then Helen?" Jonathan was not really expecting a blow by blow account of what they would be expected to do but it was worth a try.

"We are going to see the company that produced and installed the equipment in Marion; at first sight they appear to be just an engineering company but they have shown up on the radar previously. The agency has been aware of their operation for some time. There have been three big investigations into large scale criminal activity in the states that have had links to this company in Hong Kong. The head office is in a large building in the New Territories but the main manufacturing effort is done in a dozen different places. The plan is to visit head office and see what we can find."

Jonathan was no longer listening; he had noticed a man come into the departure lounge at the far end. He would have gone unnoticed by most people but to Jonathan he was displaying all the signs of someone who was not just the usual traveller. He paused at the entrance and checked to whole are; he was very quick, but the scan was unmistakable to Jonathan. It was only had only taken seconds but the way he logged Helen and Jonathon sitting in the corner was very clear.

"We have company Helen; a man about five ten in a dark jacket, now sitting at the far end by the entrance; he clocked us the minute he entered the room. On the face of it he is a professional. Not sure if he is armed but I would guess that he isn't as he has just come through the security. He might be armed if the system here is supporting him. I would think that he is alone."

"Who is he then; my lot aren't here and your old lot should not be here; perhaps it is something we have stirred up by the second visit and the translation request that I instigated. Our empire is not without its leaks and divided loyalties as you know; look at the deputy director. I doubt it is him and the department as I would have been informed by now. For now, we will keep out of this man's way, it might be necessary to do something about him as time goes on."

"Hopefully we are only under surveillance from this guy; if he is planning some sort of hit we may have a big problem." Jonathan thought that the second option was the one in play here; he had seen this sort many times; after all he himself was one of them. The question here was what was he after? Both of them or only one of them? If only one, which one?

39.

The flight to Chicago was uneventful; the man that had been noted in the departure lounge stayed well away from the two of them and didn't seem to be paying too much interest. Perhaps he wasn't what Jonathan had originally thought. It didn't matter at this point but if things changed Jonathan was ready.

They both made the gate for the connecting flight to Hong Kong in plenty of time; it would be a couple of hours and they would be on their way.

"Is he still with us?" Helen was reading a magazine she had picked up on the way in.

"Not sure, he was close when we came across the airport to this side but I don't see him now; maybe he isn't interested in us at all. We had better be alert for this one though, he was displaying all the signs; perhaps he is after someone else, who knows?"

The man was watching the two across the central divide; his target today was the female, he had been well briefed about these two and had been warned that the male was more than capable if he was to be given the chance to intervene. He planned that she would be taken down when they were separated and didn't intend to let the male have an opportunity to upset things. The male would be left alone after the hit; he was not a concern to the people paying for this. It might be easier to deal with both at the same time but orders were orders. He watched Helen to see what she was doing; was she aware of what was going on around her? It didn't look like she was; just looking at a magazine. The male however was very alert, maintaining a look around all the time. *You might be good but you haven't clocked me since disembarkation, have you?*

"Time for the washroom I think, I will use the one over by the duty free." She indicated the female washrooms with a wave of her arm. Jonathan watched her go, paying attention to those that were around the area; all seemed to be normal with just the normal coming and going that is normal in a busy airport.

The washroom entrance was down a short corridor; female at the end and the males about halfway down on the right. A sign had been placed against the male toilets to say that they were out of order and that other facilities were available a short walk down the concourse in either direction. The airport authority was very sorry for the inconvenience. *Someone is being funny.* The assassin thought as he picked up the sign and followed the doctor towards the end of the corridor.

Jonathan hadn't seen the man make a move but Helen had. She was aware that the man would come into the washroom behind her; she closed and locked the end cubicle with a coin she had removed from her purse on the way in. She then moved back to the door and stood against the wall and waited for the man to come in. It was likely he would not notice her behind the door until it was too late; distracted by the closed cubicle he would, hopefully, assume she was in it. It was fortunate that there were no other travellers in the washroom.

The man came into the room, holding the door open for a couple of seconds. Letting the door go me moved towards the closed cubicle and was started to bend down to look under the door. He saw Helen coming, but it was too late, her kick connected on the side of his neck just under the jaw line; he continued to go down and lay quiet on the floor. Helen checked his pockets and felt for any hidden weapon. There was only a small metal disk in his pocket and a UK passport in the inside of the jacket. She checked his pulse, strong and regular; he would survive but he would not stay unconscious for very much longer; it was time to get away from this. Helen replaced the passport and left the man where he was; sprawled out in the centre of the room; anyone coming in would trip over him and raise the alarm for sure.

"What took you so long?" Jonathan had been about to go looking for her but as he was about to get up she had sat down beside him. She explained what had just happened, and that she had left the washroom closed sign against the door so the first person through the door to the corridor would likely be the assailant. They both sat and watched the end of the small corridor that the man had to emerge from, nothing happened. *Perhaps there was another way out that wasn't obvious.*

He had not appeared when their flight was called twenty minutes later. Now on high alert they both made their way down to the gate and joined to queue; it was another ten minutes before they settled into their seats at the rear part of tourist class; from there they could see most of the passenger that were on the flight. Unless he was in first class, he was not on this aircraft.

The two didn't know but the threat from the assassin had disappeared; he wouldn't be found for another two hours when the maintenance man appeared to fix the leaking pipe in the gent's; finding the sign on the wrong door he checked to see if there had been an unreported fault or someone had simply moved the sign. Random movements of warning signs were not unusual in this airport, like most others. He had seen it many time in this job; put a sign up telling people they cannot go that way and they simply ignore it or move the sign. Once he had found the man lying on the floor, it took only minutes for the police and the paramedic to turn up; he was dead but why he was dead and why he was on the floor on the ladies' washroom was a mystery. Heart attack, drugs perhaps, it wasn't the first time the police had found such a person; there was no sign of injury, it lust looked like the poor man had simply fallen over and died. The airport didn't know at the time but this incident would not be the last by a long way. Soon the whole area would be in dire need of an explanation as to what was happening, but that was later.

40.

Neither Jonathan, nor Helen could detect anyone that might be following them; the flight went without incident but they had taken turns sleeping just to make sure that they would not be surprised.

The aircraft landed on time in Hong Kong and the journey through immigration and baggage collection was quick. In an hour they were inside the Harbour Heights hotel that overlooked a large part of Hong Kong Island. Jonathan had been in the area more than twenty years before when the Island belonged to the Crown; the place had changed a lot since then; more buildings and a lot more people. Mainland China now held sway here and apart from a few protesters routinely complaining about it, the place appeared to function as it did when the British were in control.

The two were sitting at a low table on very comfortable chairs in the bar area; the view from the window was quite spectacular as the sun was starting to disappear over the horizon.

"Fancy a Car Bomb Helen?"

"What?"

Jonathan was reading the cocktail menu.

"A Car Bomb; a medium glass of Guinness with a shot glass of Whiskey dropped into it; sounds nice."

“No Jonathan, I do not want a “Car Bomb” thank you. A glass of white wine will do.

Jonathan ordered the drinks from the waiter who had been hovering around. Minutes later the two drinks were on the table; three glasses, one with the wine and two for Jonathan.

“Guinness and whiskey can’t beat it but I’m not sure what they will be like together.

Jonathan picked up the shot glass and dropped it into the Guinness; the top turned to a foamy grey/ brown colour and didn’t look at all appetising.

“Oh well don’t knock it until you have tried it.”

Helen retrieved the token that she had removed from the man in the washroom and handed it to Jonathon.

“Looks the same or very similar to the one I found at the warehouse. Are they both same?”

Helen explained that they did, at first, appear to be the same but there were two small differences. The lettering around the edge seemed to be transposed when the second disk was compared to the first. The second disk did not have a hole where it could be attached to anything. It looked like the sort of token that some old-time casinos used in the slots before the advent of pay by card. The general lettering on the face was identical to the first, and the disks were the same size.

“What does the different letting say that is not the same as the first disk?”

Helen took out her notebook and flipped to the middle.

“The gist of the lettering again refers to DNA strings or at least, a small part of a small part so to speak. It is referring to a slightly different sequence to the first one. Is it two small parts of the same string? We don’t think so but we cannot be sure. We don’t even know why they would be putting this stuff onto a small metal disk that are in random places. Why would that man be carrying one?”

The two discussed the significance of the disks, and what they would do the next day, well into the late evening.

41.

Just a short walk from the hotel to the city transit system; it was possible to get to most parts of Hong Kong and never come up for fresh air. The transit system was a long way from the London underground with the old, narrow tunnels and walkways. This one was relatively new and very clean by comparison; even the ticket machines were simple and the both of them got the ticket they actually required rather than some odd combination of travel. Two people even stopped and offered help.

It was several stops and a number of changes before the two got off and ascended to the surface. They were not far from the race course in the New Territories; an area covered in high rise apartments that some of the wealthiest in Hong Kong lived or did business. The net wealth of the people living here was eye wateringly huge. The business that was controlled from these few square miles reached to the furthest corners of the planet; fingers in every pie. It was not surprising that the Chinese government tried to keep things as they were after gaining control from the British. The biggest question at the time was why the UK would give up control of such an asset.

They stood on the corner of a major intersection; very busy with all sorts of motor vehicles coming and going from the many businesses. The paved area along both sides of the street were filled with people going about their business; here and there street food traders sold their goods to the passing office workers who then ate it on the run. Everyone in Hong Kong seemed to be in a rush to be somewhere else; except Jonathan and Helen who appeared to be just watching the world go by.

"Where to now?" Jonathan was trying to remember the detail of the street layout from his last visit here, he soon gave up; the place had changed out of all recognition; some of the street names were familiar but the whole place had been built over several times since he was here in the Army.

"Close to here actually, it is an office complex that is our first port of call. One of the sales departments that produced and installed the equipment in Marion; at least they produced the labels. In this part of the world you can never take things at face value." Helen winked at Jonathan and set off down the street, seemingly against the flow of people that now appeared to be rushing in the opposite direction.

Only two blocks away from where they came out of the transit system they stood before a large gilded company sign that was attached to the wall about ten feet from the ground, in Chinese and English the word INDUSTRIAL were written in ten inch letters; on the top right corner a dragon was wrapped around the letter L, it was easily the biggest and brightest sign of any that were on the wall.

"Shall we see if they are in? It looks like they are open at least." Helen led the way into the entranceway through an automatic revolving door that started as Helen came close to it."

The reception looked like it would not be out of place in an upmarket hotel in the Middle East or here in the Far East; not the sort of thing you would find in the office of a business that supplied engineering equipment. A large circular area that was tiled with the most extravagant mural Jonathan had ever seen; it was on the floor and triple height domed ceiling; large colourful dragons that looped around each other, each dragon flecked with gold and silver with flecks of red and blue running through the design.

"Where is everybody?" Jonathan whispered. The large area was empty of people; around the outside were large gilded doors and an equally ornate elevator entrance. Opposite the door they had come through was a wide desk with only a computer monitor to clutter the surface that was gilded with the same dragon designs that were on the floor.

"Doctor Dudman, Mr Brown, it is so nice of you to come and visit; such a long way."

The voice came from behind them; The man must have come through a door that was about halfway round the circular room; the door had not made a sound either opening or closing so the man seemed to just be there. A medium sized man dressed in a suit was addressing them; about six feet tall and athletically slim. He carried himself with a confidence that was not seen often these days. The accent was indeterminate but was more like none regional English than anything else. It was difficult to determine his ethnic origin; maybe some Chinese and maybe some European. It was easier to say he wasn't African, but that was about it.

Helen was the first to respond. "Excuse me sir I don't think we have met."

"No, we have not but the two of you have been a point of interest for some time; you are both involved in matters that we have an interest in. Mr Brown has been at that point on many occasions but now you are both here, so, as I said we meet at last. Please follow me and we can go upstairs to be more comfortable."

The man turned and walked towards the elevator, Helen and Jonathan, slightly behind, followed. As they approached, the doors opened. Jonathan thought that the elevator probably had a proximity sensor that would open the doors when people approached if the car was available. Call buttons were unnecessary as why would someone stand outside an elevator if they didn't want one. The only signal needed is a direction indicator. All three got into the elevator. The man said "twelve" and the doors closed. The movement of the elevator was largely undetectable. Jonathan felt a slight pressure increase under his feet so he assumed that with the request for twelve that they were going up. He had been in buildings where there had been multiple floors underground as well as above; how the floor numbering system sometimes worked could be confusing. Inside the elevator there were no panels or buttons; no controls at all. Maybe the elevator will only respond to certain voices and not from everyone; quite a good initial security measure Jonathan thought. It would also mean that they might not be able to use the elevator without this chap.

The doors opened onto another large space, round and equally ornate, not dragons but flowers of all description. The elevator shaft was set off centre from the middle of the room and it appeared that you could walk all the way around it. Opposite the elevator was a large conference table that seemed to grow out of the floor; the legs and top were covered in the same design as the walls and floor; very expensively done. The wall behind the elevator and the wall behind the table were solid but the other two curves of the room were wall-to-ceiling glass, giving spectacular views over the surrounding area. Against one of the windows was a small circular table with three easy chairs set against it; all to the same design as the room.

"Can I offer the two of you anything to drink? It is already a warm day." The man smiled.

"Err... Yes, a mineral water would be nice." Helen said, still wandering what was going on here.

"And you Mr Brown?"

"Coffee, black would be nice, no sugar, thank you."

"Please sit down; we can discuss any requests that you have."

As they sat down a door opened in one of the solid walls and a woman, probably in her thirties, glided across the room with a large tray held high. She put the drinks down in front of Helen and Jonathan; their host had, what appeared to be, a small glass of beer; very cold with the condensation falling down the side even though the room was obviously air conditioned. Also on the table was a plate of digestive biscuits that seemed completely out of place.

The man saw Jonathan look at the biscuits. “Digestives Mr Brown, the English are obsessed with biscuits don’t you think? They seem to have them at all manner of occasions; particularly with tea or coffee.” Jonathan was more impressed with the woman who had brought the drinks in; from asking for a coffee to it being on the table couldn’t have been more than a minute and the man had only asked them what they wanted and then sat down; they were obviously being monitored.

“That is true but I’m not a great fan of biscuits; could you let us know what you require of us? We only came to talk about some of the machinery that your company can supply.”

“No matter; I am Henry and I think that I can service all of your needs during this visit to Hong Kong.”

“Henry? Can I ask your family name?” Helen said sipping her water.

“Just Henry, I have a family name of course but I do not use it so over the years I have been used to just using Henry; I hope it doesn’t concern you unduly Doctor.”

“No not at all, please forgive me for being rude Henry.”

42.

For Hector the rule nineteen enactments had caused him more problems than he had anticipated. The project had been put on hold as he and his team investigated the funding and control of the work that had been completed so far. The suspended principal had been unusually compliant with the investigation; Hector was now convinced that something serious was going within the organisation. It was no surprise that the principal had agreed to clause nineteen; he really did believe that he had lost control of the research and fielding involved with the project. All the historical information was found to be as expected but the continued funding and the most recent large injection of cash had shown many anomalies that were hard to explain. The organisation had been taking very large sums of from someone or something that was light on description. They knew hardly anything about the entity that was paying the bills. To Hector this was looking more and more like they had been tricked into taking all the risks and were to get only limited benefit from their endeavours.

The project was to have provided valuable information on some genetic anomalies that were to be found throughout the human population; this information would enable the project to predict and to manipulate these genetic differences; the possible value of such an ability was enormous; the organisation would make billions well into the foreseeable future; they would be able to control just about everything that involved human input.

The testing had gone to plan, and the results had been as predicted but the most recent enterprise in the small town of Marion and the water catchment area of Chicago was something else. Previously the testing had been against specific targets but the Marion test did not meet any of the criteria laid out in the plan.

Hector was getting very concerned; the organisation had been put out on a limb and had taken all the risks on this venture only to find out it had now moved out of their control. He was looking at the invoices for the sites around the country and in particular the hire of large buildings like the one in Marion. Only the Marion building had the extra expenditure spent on it. Large amounts had been paid to a sub-contractor that had its base in China of all places.

What are you up to?

Hector would call the meeting to lay out what he and his team had discovered; it was looking highly likely that they would have to close this project down and consign it all to the "didn't work" file. The organisation was far too exposed on this; even the contract to remove the two professors was now looking like a big mistake. Several agencies were now interested in what was going on; at first it was thought that only the large pharmaceutical companies would be spying, but that had not happened; the project had upset much larger fish than that. If they were not careful, the organisation itself would be in danger. Action had to be taken now. The Principal and his team had wasted vast sums of money for no gain except to put them all in danger. The very expensive research did appear to have gone well, but it was now apparent that the conclusions from it were vague and that something was being hidden. This organisation had lasted hundreds of years, acting and controlling wherever it was required, through wars and famine and had never come this close to being diverted before. Someone or something was in the process of taking over.

Hector pressed the call button on his desk. "David can you get the main group together tomorrow morning for ten; we are to close this rule nineteen down as soon as possible, there may be some work for you if the group decides that action has to be taken; please enable your team incase that is the case."

"Yes, Principal we will be ready for whatever you decide; I will inform the other members and ensure they are here tomorrow." The line clicked off.

Hector was already getting used to being addressed as Principal and he was very comfortable now he was back in New York; he would make sure the adolescent would not return anytime soon.

43.

Jonathan was confused by this man going by the single name of Henry. How did he know who they were and how long had he, or someone working for him, been watching the two of them, what had he said? "The two of you have been a point of interest for some time." Why? This was not what he was used to, it now appears that he had been watched or followed for the last months, it was not the way Jonathan operated, he hoped that no one would know where he was for a large part of the time, it had kept him alive.

Henry was sat with his back to the wall with the open space to his left; Helen and Jonathan faced him but had the whole expanse of the room behind them; this was not the ideal seating preference for either of them but here they were.

"How did you know of our arrival? We only decided to come here over the last couple of days." Jonathan didn't expect a blow by blow account as Henry had already said that the two had been monitored for some time.

"The two of you are trying to gather information on a project that we are involved with; you have been close to this meeting on a number of occasions but for some reason you have taken a step back so we let you go, so to speak."

Helen stirred in her seat; this was starting to feel weird and perhaps it was time to drink up and leave. "Why did you feel the need to monitor us for so long before showing your hand?" Did Henry know who she and Jonathan really were?

Henry was smiling again. "OK, you are Doctor Helen Dudman, real name Claire Steel but a Doctor all the same and you work primarily for the US government. You are Jonathan Brown, a hired assassin late of the British Army and you are well known to us. The two of you working together did surprise us but we can now see why you are here at the same time. It spiked our curiosity that you two now appear to be a team of sorts. Your employers, Mr Brown, are working for us, but they do not yet realise to what extent. Your employers Doctor do not seem to have a full grasp on what is going on. There are two powerful empires that are not performing as they should. No matter, we are pleased that we have been given a free hand whilst the opposition has been chasing shadows, and each other, from time to time.

"Well what is going on and why do you need to speak about it to the two of us? It seems that we are small fish in a very large sea." Helen held the gaze of Henry but it was difficult.

"The organisation, of which I am but a small part, has been working in the background for more than a thousand years; during this time the blood lines of the overseers can be traced without interruption. My own origin is from twelfth century rural England so I could be described as European; other overseers are from different parts of the globe but we all see ourselves and custodians of this planet, national origins do not affect our decision making; we are all the same. Nothing of any significance happens on Earth that we do not sanction or allow. We control the financial workings of the whole planet and have been doing so for many centuries. The research that you, Doctor, have been pursuing for these last years has been at our behest, the work that you and your colleagues have produced has been entirely for us. We have provided the finance and the oversight; despite what your employers, Mr Brown, have been led to believe. The reason the two of you are here is merely an indulgence on our part."

"But we have been mapping genetic differences that move through generations; we all, thought that it would be a massive money maker for whoever controlled the end result of the research, even some of the trials have confirmed that hereditary traits, in some cases, can be turned off. The potential profits for the organisation that can do this would be immense. It would be a licence to print money and would deliver mankind from some pretty awful diseases that are passed down through the generations."

Henry listened to Helen politely but was not being told anything he didn't already know; somewhat like an adult listening to a child that was explaining something they had just noticed; indulgent patience.

Helen hoped that she might be able to get Henry to tell, them what the bigger picture was. It seemed by the way this organisation was operating that they didn't actually need any more income. Perhaps it wasn't money but control.

"We thought that it was only fair to tell you what is going on with the project you have both been involved in. Admittedly Mr Brown has been following a somewhat different agenda but related to the main project all the same. Now the end is within grasp we agreed that some input was required for the two organisations that you work for; your masters Jonathan have already put two and two together but have, as predicted, come up with five. They have missed the point somewhat and assumed it was about their empire losing money from a project that they had lost control of."

Henry paused and smiled the same knowing smile that he had been using since the meeting started.

"First a small history lesson; Throughout the recent past, and by that, I mean the last thousand years or so, there have been groups or individuals that have gained power in many countries around the world; these groups vary from the political to the religious but they have all been driven by our input. The rise and decline of these groups has been under our control. I am sure you recall names such a Hitler, Napoleon, Pol Pot, etc. We have also manipulated large organisations to our own ends, very large financial groups and religious groups of different persuasions. We enabled the British Empire to be so successful. They were all, almost all, doing things at our behest. One or two over the years have caused problems for us but they have been dealt with as the need arose."

Helen was listening intently but Jonathan was beginning to think that Henry was a little mad.

"Why have you been doing this? To what end?" Helen wasn't sure whether Henry was telling them some fanciful story or was crazy.

"For control; these have all been exercises in control. The project you have been involved in was remarkably easy to instigate. I'm sure you have read in the popular media about the Illuminati, the Freemasons and more recently the Bilderberg Group." Henry paused for acknowledgment.

"You see all these groups, and others, actually exist but they have nowhere near the control that the popular media would like you to think. Groups of useful idiots, to be blunt After all who controls the popular media? In our experience half-truths work far better than whole truths."

"Why are we being given this information? Jonathan was getting a little bored with what he thought were ramblings. "Why did you leave the tokens lying around? What was the man doing at the airport?"

"Ah, the tokens; the one you found on the floor at the warehouse was a batch number and it was left there deliberately so that you might find it. We did have concerns that you may not notice it but you did prove to be very observant. It contained enough information to bring you here and the man at the airport was going to attempt to remove at least one of you. We knew, of course, that he would fail in that attempt but we thought that it would be you, Jonathan, who would intervene. He had the token in his pocket for two reasons; it identified him as an individual with certain genetic traits and, when you found it, identified him as connected to this organisation." Henry waved in the air to indicate where 'this organisation' was. "You may not be aware but that individual is no longer with us, he died shortly after your encounter Doctor Dudman."

"What? That is not possible he was alive and well when I left him; I checked for vitals and injury, he should have recovered in minutes."

Don't blame yourself Doctor he was one small part of an experiment to see if the agent actually worked in a real situation, and thanks to you it did. There have been one or two contradictions however but we hope that they are isolated from the main effort."

"Henry, if what you say is true; you and your organisation are involved in criminality on a global scale, ranging from murder to organised crime that spans the continents. I ask again; why are you giving us this information?" Helen was getting ready to leave; this was not going well and was turning out to be either an interview with the front man of an organisation that really did control the world or someone who was mentally unstable and had identified that she had been a party to someone's death at the airport. In either case this was not a good place to remain.

Henry was smiling gain; a smile that was beginning to irritate Jonathan.

“Doctor Dudman we have always been fair but firm in our endeavours; at this point in time we are no different. What we are doing is not, in the true sense of the word, a secret; the clues and information are there for all to determine. Your employees should have had a hold of the true meaning some time ago but were instead pursuing vested interest and were in conflict with Mr Brown’s employers. They failed to notice the wood because the trees were in the way. Since the two of you have direct access to the controlling parts of the system that pays you, we thought it might be fun to let you in on the true purpose of the genetic research.”

“Why the deception in the warehouse? Why not simply keep us out of it? The wide-open door and the false interior were interesting but didn’t fool us.”

“That was to attract your attention Mr Brown, and I must say it worked didn’t it. The fake interior was hiding nothing at that time, all the equipment that had been used to deliver the trigger had been removed the night before.”

Henry leaned forward and touched the table at the edge of the design that flowed from the table and onto the floor. The whole room shimmered, the ornate design of the floors and furniture disappeared and was replaced by a bare wall and floor; they were all sat in the warehouse in Marion, the roller door was closed, the sunshine shining in through the skylight. The desk and the chairs they were sat on were very simple and made of wood. Henry pressed the patch again, and the room was restored. “Nice toy, do you not think? Remember in this world hardly anything is as it first appears.”

“How did you do that?” Jonathan and Helen were more than impressed. The chairs now felt as if they were very well upholstered and soft to sit on. Helen closed her eyes and felt the chair, hard and made of rough cut wood. Henry was watching her with a smile.

“You see Doctor, your brain can be tricked into thinking that things are other than what they really are.

The meeting lasted for another twenty minutes during which Henry explained in rather loose terms what was going on and to what purpose. The two visitors were then invited to leave by the same way they had arrived.

44.

Helen was waiting in line to check in, the flight back to the UK would leave in about four hours, and Jonathan was right behind her. What they had learned from their meeting, with the man who called himself Henry, was rather too much to take in, let alone believe. The two had discussed what they had both heard well into the night. The meeting with Henry had lasted, perhaps, another two hours during which a very sumptuous lunch had been provided. It had been like the drinks; two members of staff this time, appearing from side doors and putting the meal up onto very ornate tables that neither Helen nor Jonathan had noticed before. The food choice was very extensive, and they both remarked that there was nothing on the table that they would not eat. It appeared that the food choices had been compiled after a long and exhaustive survey of their likes and dislikes.

"I'm sorry sir this item of luggage must go into the hold, it is too big to go with you into the cabin."

Jonathan was watching the rather large man in the line next to him; the item in question looked like a medium sized suitcase that most people would take on holiday and certainly too large and too heavy to manoeuvre into an overhead luggage compartment. The man was not at all happy and Jonathan thought that things might kick off but just as the man was about to ramp up the argument he folded and agreed with the lady behind the check-in; his suitcase went onto the conveyer and into the hold luggage. Jonathan had seen this sort of things many times; once when transiting through the Middle East he had watched a man argue about the same thing but that time the item of luggage was the size and shape of a washing machine; what it actually contained was unclear; the whole thing wrapped in cardboard and secured with cling film. On other occasions people had actually managed to get an unmanageable item of luggage into the cabin and had tried for some time to jam it into the overhead lockers before it was removed and put where it should have gone in the first place. Jonathan often wondered why some people tried to do the impossible but it was not uncommon.

"Yes sir?" The assistant behind the check in was talking to Jonathan; Helen had completed her checks and was waiting to one side looking at him. The incident with the suitcase had been distracting.

"Sorry I was miles away." Jonathan handed over his passport and put his very small case onto the conveyor.

Luggage weighed and passport checked the assistant handed Jonathan's passport to him. "Your flight will be notified in an hour, please check the boards and make sure you leave enough time to get to the gate. Have a pleasant flight Mr Brown."

Jonathan followed Helen as she set off down towards the departures. He was getting too old for this; he noted yet another passenger leaving the bag check in area with a very large piece of luggage that was destined for an argument at the aircraft door. He had been concerned that his concentration levels were on the decline for some time, although if he had to give a date for the start it would be around the time he first had dealings with Helen Dudman, more and more of his time was being taken up with thinking about her. The distraction with the passenger and the large baggage would not have happened previously; he would have noted it and moved on; his mind was not completely on the job. He was becoming too close to the good doctor, and he reminded himself that the job he was in did not allow for close relationships; not if he wanted to stay alive for very long.

The two were sat in departures watching the clock go around; it would be two hours now before the flight was called; like most large airport this one ran on a very tight schedule and any minor problem would generate delays all the way through the system. Their flight should have left by now but because of a mechanical problem they had been pushed back.

"What is the story behind the man dropping dead after you had stopped him? I didn't quite get the science." Jonathan had been thinking about all that the man Henry had been saying; it all seemed to be a little implausible and bordering on the edges of science fiction.

"Well, have you heard of the term flight response? Some animals have an automatic response when in danger to flee the scene. Horses, antelopes and many other species have it. When confronted with danger they don't stand their ground and fight they simply run away as fast as they can. It has been theorised for some time that not only do some species have this flight response but some actually have a death response. Did you know that some deer that are hit on the roads die when approached or are touched? No? If you do ever crash into one of these animals and it is not killed in the collision try holding your hand over its mouth and nostrils; it will more than often die. It will simply drop dead, the so-called death response. It has also been thought that in prehistoric times some now extinct species had a similar response. Detailed investigation of some ancient herd animals and the way they moved showed that when a large predator was in the vicinity one, or several, of the herd dropped dead. The predator was then misdirected to the dead animal, and the herd could move on. Of course, all this has been a supposition for some time but, if we can believe Henry and his gang, they have isolated this gene and have been able to introduce it into a human. Fantastically impossible if you ask me but that is what he was saying. The man at the airport died because he was unable to defend himself and I had touched him. Unlikely don't you think."

"Why has this not been noted before? It must have been around for some time in some people."

"Exactly Jonathan, but have you ever heard the saying he or she was frightened to death. So, you see, the idea has been known about but it could never be tied down. There is a cave painting in France, or is it Spain? No, it is in France. This shows a hunting scene that had had the scientific community puzzled for some time. It shows a group of hunters chasing numerous antelope; the hunters have yet to reach the herd but one animal has fallen over and the hunting party has not yet reached it. This has been theorised as an example of the death response but as the image was created so long-ago people have read into it what they wanted. Over the last decade much research has been going on into gene therapy and not all of it has been wisely directed; don't forget the financial rewards that spring from all this work. If this was the only route that was followed with the research that I was involved in I would be very surprised. Why introduce something into someone that would cause them to drop dead when frightened or cornered. Why not simply shoot them? The manipulation of genetic diseases would be far more beneficial and not to say much more lucrative. It could be the death response is simply a side effect from the therapy. Our man at the airport was just part of an investigation to see if this problem had been correctly identified. It could also explain why Professor Swift was spooked. Pity it caused his death Jonathan." Helen looked him in the eye; Jonathan was feeling very uncomfortable again. In the past he would have given no thought at all to the target but this woman was again making him think of other things.

"There is one other contradiction within this, however." Helen paused looking at Jonathan. "The former Director had an ongoing inherited medical problem that would have killed him within a few years. It was reported by his medical team that his illness was on the wane, something had been thought impossible. He then suddenly died as he was sat in a chair; no outside intervention, he wasn't attacked and as far as we know he was very content and calm at the time of death. So here we have the small contradiction to our death theory that Henry was speaking of."

"So, what are we going to do about all this vague information we have?" Jonathan wanted to get away from Swift and Catchpole, the man by the railway line and any other people that had met an untimely death.

"Well I have already flashed it up as have you I'm sure; we will just have to wait and see what pans out from this. In the mean time we get on this flight and go home. Oh, and I have been instructed to tell you not to attempt to kill anyone from now on, especially me. In the meantime, you are to accompany me to New York, there are some people we have to investigate, we are to go and poke a hornets' nest to see what comes out; might be interesting."

Jonathan had not reported any of the last day's activities to anyone, after all he was retired, and his two sets of bosses had told him such. Helen on the other hand was still working, so it didn't surprise Jonathan in the least that she was seeking direction from her masters in the United States. He was completely sure that he would not target Helen even if instructed to do so. Jonathan had hoped that when they were back in the UK, they could part company and he could go home; now they were to return to New York he wasn't convinced this would happen.

Henry's parting words came to mind when he was asked why he had disclosed all this information. "It is far too late for you or anybody else to do anything about it, as I told you this meeting has been an indulgence; we always like to let a little of the truth out." *Was Henry even real?*

45.

Hector had moved fast in the investigation; the outgoing principal would continue to be investigated and there was no chance of him or any of his supporters ever coming back. The failure at the high level had been a shock, even to Hector who had never rated the young upstart. Hector looked out of the window and the view of Central Park; the previous incumbent had made a good choice for his office and he intended to keep it. The normal rules of succession had been suspended, and he was now in the job until he tired of it.

It was soon discovered that the organisation had been taking vast sums of money from an unknown source to drive the genetic programme faster and further than was originally intended. The results of the research did appear to be far more than it was thought possible but they had lost control over it some months before. The main problem facing Hector was how would they regain control and maximise the benefits to them; it was not going to be easy.

"What is our man doing in Hong Kong with the doctor?" The small man was speaking across the office to Hector who remained looking out of the window. "He should have gone to ground and not be visible. He now appears to be a team with her. Is he working for the other side?"

"I don't know old friend but it has alerted us to the place in Hong Kong; if he hadn't been with the doctor, we would not have noticed that he was still active. He must be working with her as he has been far too close to be doing anything else. The question is why?"

"The company headquarters they have visited in Hong Kong was previously known to us; they supplied some of the engineering equipment but we now know it is also the likely source of the large sums of money we have been consuming."

Hector turned from the window and sat down at his desk. "Yes, my friend, the money has been coming from that company but the cash flow is way more than a large engineering company could supply; no, that is just a front, and having looked at the amount of money it appears to be something only a large country could supply. Again, the question is why?"

"You suspect a government has penetrated our organisation Hector?"

"No, not at all but it does give scale to the problem we have; an organisation with almost limitless financial resources that has targeted us and duped us into doing their work for them. They have been so clever that we don't even know for sure what we have been doing for them. We must try our very best to determine what we have been up to and then close it down; we have a large resource that is in the process of investigating the far eastern link but up to now it always comes back to the company in Hong Kong. That company cannot be the original source of the money."

Hector started to read the report that was on his desk for the third time. The Engineering company that had supplied some equipment for the project had now been identified as the source of the finance that they had been drawing on for three years. Total company assets were estimated to be two billion US. Compared to what the project had been consuming this was nothing; not even close to what had been spent. The Hong Kong company was still solvent with a very good working profit and all its assets intact. No, this company was a front just as they themselves were a front. It would require much more effort to determine who or what was paying the bills. Once this was determined they might be able to find out what was going on.

"For now, old friend, we will pursue the banking that supports this little engineering unit in the Far East and move against it if we are able. Two years ago, I would not imagine myself admitting that there may be people or groups of people that this organisation was powerless against. Let us hope that we are not too late in this endeavour."

Hector was a little irritated with himself that he had allowed the boy such freedom; the main point or error was that they allowed him to be elected to the chair in the first place; newer younger blood was the big cry at the time. Hector remembered it well, he should have stood his ground but been persuaded along with the rest that it would move the organisation along. There would be much soul searching once this little episode was put to bed.

The next job in a big list of jobs that Hector was to address was the storage buildings they had used and particularly the one in Marion. On paper they had all been just storage buildings that had been rented short term. Exactly what was stored for such a short time was a mystery.

The secure line on Hectors desk beeped once. “Yes, David what have you found?” The head of security had moved against some of the members, following instructions from the new principal; He liked the way the new boss operated; at least he made decisions and stuck with them, in all, five of the ruling committee had been removed and investigated, the former principal being one of them. David was unsure how much information could be extracted from the men but his team had processed them diligently.

“Principal, we have investigated the courier firm that delivered and retrieved items from the storage; all except the one in Marion seemed to be just a temporary storage with nothing being unpacked or used while they were sat on the floor. Marion was different, large amounts of chemicals that we could not identify the source were shipped into but not out of the building. There was also a large amount of expensive engineering equipment installed and then mostly removed. The power company has told us that the consumption in the building was raised for the time we had it but not by a huge amount; it certainly didn’t raise any questions with them, almost typical for a building that size which had some machinery in it.”

“What sort of chemicals were in use David? Did you manage to identify all that was put in there?”

“Yes Principal; all the items were the same type but of a greater amount as to the ones that were supplied to both research facilities towards the end of the project; the one in the UK and the one in France. Same types but far greater amounts but we have no record of any of it leaving the Marion building; it went in but as far as we can determine it did not leave. The only thing that came out was some of the engineering stuff they had been using.”

“Thank you, David, track down the equipment if you can and get our people to try and figure out what it was being used for and get back to that building and conduct an inch by inch survey, there might be something left that will give us a clue.” The line clicked off.

46.

Henry was briefing his equals, he had moved from Hong Kong to Japan, a journey that he used to do many times in the past but this was the first time here for many years; he thought that he would retire in Hong Kong and let the others get on with the job but he had been summoned one last time for the high meeting.

"All is on track and the people raised against us are of little threat; it is now inconceivable that they could have any adverse effect on our enterprises. We are past the third stage and all is now in place to conclude the operation. The US government agencies are completely unaware of the purpose and our willing fools in New York are chasing their tails. The two from both sides have been primed and released; this will further confuse those that could act against us if they so choose. Government accountability is a wonderful thing when someone is trying to hide something; they usually have to act within whatever law they have but we are better placed to do as we please, at least in the short term. The building hired in Marion in the US is still attracting their attention as we planned; the substance has been delivered and all traces should now be invisible to everything except the most stringent examination. The countdown has begun so we should see the first large scale results in seven days, coincidentally on the founder's birthday."

The meeting went on all day with all loose ends to the project being squared away. Henry smiled when he had announced that the first release would coincide with the day the founder had built this empire; always a day for quiet celebration and much pride by all the members.

"Thank you, Henry." the chairman said as the meeting was drawing to a close. "All members will thank and applaud Henry in the normal manner. The group clapped their hands once. The normal practice of clapping and standing ovations and the like had long been considered vulgar and actually served no useful purpose.

It would be several hours before Henry arrived in Hong Kong; he sat midway in the private aircraft that would take him home. He was the only passenger and he had spent most of the time in deep meditation thinking about the project and where it might lead. *Do not concern yourself with things that you cannot change or alter.* This had always been his philosophy; he had watched many opponents struggling to no avail.

The cabin crewmember came from the front carrying a small tray; it would contain very light lunch that Henry always had at this time. The young woman smiled as she approached the seat. "Henry, it is time for lunch, I hope this meets with your requirements."

Henry opened his eyes and made to take the food from the woman who just seemed to be frozen staring into space. The tray clattered to the floor as the woman fell sideways without uttering a sound.

He was out of his seat leaning over the woman; she was dead. He made a move towards the front of the aircraft, there should be another cabin crew and the pilot and the co-pilot. The aircraft was not big, he found the other steward sitting in the galley area, he had a half smile on his face with wide unseeing eyes.

The door to the flight deck was not locked on these flights; the security on this journey was way beyond what could be achieved in the usual commercial flights that filled the skies these days.

The StreamStar executive jet was on autopilot skimming along above the clouds at a cruising speed of five hundred miles per hour out over the South China Sea, staying away from any air defence assets that the Formosan government or China may have in the area. It is always better to stay away from any curious eyes. The route was taking them to the East of Formosa in a big loop; the closet they would be to land in this leg would be about two hundred miles. In around ten minutes the pilot was due to make a course change that would bring the aircraft to the South of the island of Formosa and towards Hong Kong. The course change would never be made.

Henry saw both the flight deck crew sitting looking forward, the pilot on the left still had a cup resting on his lap, half filled with coffee, both men were dead. There was no sign of what could have caused the two men to die; both had a relaxed look on their face and would have given the impression that they were both asleep, except both men had their eyes open. Death had taken the two men quickly.

Henry turned and went back into the main cabin. Sitting in his usual seat he thought that the time had come for his life to end; but why was he still alive when all on the aircraft were dead; was he not to die? He would die, of course, because he was on a jet aircraft that was flying over the South China Sea without anyone who could fly it.

Henry closed his eyes and thought for a while of his life and his early years with his brother. He was looking down a long road that sloped down to the sea in his home town in England; he and his brother would race up and down this road for hours during the holiday periods from school. They both would compete to get to the sea or back to the house in the shortest time. Henry couldn't remember ever walking on this road unless he was with his parents. In the dream he was walking on his own; there was no one else in sight; a bright sunny day but he was alone.

A lone figure stood at the water's edge; his father waved and called his name. "Henry, come on we haven't got all day, why are you so slow today?"

Henry would be missed greatly but soon be replaced. He had always known that his time on earth had an end point and that he would move on when the time came, the blood line would continue, he was not concerned.

The multi-million-dollar StreamStar executive jet continued out into the South China Sea; it would be two or three hours before it ran out of fuel; the further it went the less likely anyone would notice it. This part of the ocean was very empty. The overdue aircraft would be logged and eventually be reported as missing.

Henry smiled, he had never felt better; He was ready.

47.

Jonathan was standing on the corner of Central Park West and West 62nd; Helen was across the road in the park side waiting to cross at the intersection. The men they had come to investigate worked in a high rise overlooking the park; it was unlikely they would be able to gain access to the building so they would wait for the two men to emerge around this time and walk to favourite coffee shop they had started using. It would be a ten-minute walk for someone of average fitness but apparently one of the two men was particularly slow. Jonathan estimated from the description it would take them more than ten but less than twenty minutes to make to journey. The weather was good and the crowds light for this time of day so the likelihood of the two men appearing was high, perhaps five minutes and they would emerge from the building.

Helen saw the two as she crossed the main road; one large, almost lumbering, man and a much smaller and lighter individual. The smaller of the two was keeping the slow pace with the bigger man. Both turned the corner of 62nd and walked south towards the end of the park. Helen knew where they were going of course; a small coffee shop that served excellent coffee and small meals, mainly cakes and the like. They had both walked right past Jonathan; there was no reason they should have recognised him as it was unlikely they would have known he was in New York.

“Well we are on our way now; fancy a coffee Helen?” Jonathan said as Helen came up beside him; the two men were about thirty feet in front.

As expected the two men entered the coffee shop and went straight to the seat they nearly always occupied.

Hector eased himself into the wide chair he always used; from here he could see the door and the end of the Park across the road; the smaller man sat to one side also able to see the door.

“You know old friend I’m a getting to like this place over the other one we used down town; about the same level of custom but a lot more to look at outside.”

Standing in the doorway was Jonathan with Helen just behind him.

“Yes Hector it is always interesting to meet old friends in these unlikely places.” Both men stared at Jonathan who stared straight back.

Hector waved towards Jonathan and beckoned him to come closer. “Mr Brown, would you and Doctor Dudman please join us, I’m sure our meeting here in this fine coffee shop is not a coincidence. Jonathan turned and nodded to Helen, raising one eyebrow before turning to face the men in the corner.

Hector and the smaller man stood as they were joined by the two visitors. “Please have a seat Doctor.” Hector gave a slight bow as he indicated the seat that was opposite him. Jonathan sat in the seat next to her; absolutely the wrong position for him. He would never choose this seat if he had been given the choice.

Hector was the last to sit down, as he did so he attracted the waiter who had been hovering just out of earshot. What can we get you two travellers?"

"Coffee will do just fine for me." Helen said, still unsure as to where this was heading. Coffee is good for me, thanks, black no sugar." Jonathan needed a coffee this was getting well outside his comfort zone.

Hector made idle chit chat until the coffee had been served. "What brings you two to New York? I can possibly guess why you are here Doctor but you, Mr Brown are another matter; did we not terminate your employment on rather generous terms."

"Mr Brown is now in our employ but not in the position he held with you Hector. You don't mind that I call you Hector?"

"Not at all Doctor but I must admit we are somewhat wrong footed by your companion here, we did not expect to have dealings with him again and we are quite surprised that you are now *sleeping with the enemy*, so to speak"

The meeting in the coffee house lasted for more than two hours; Helen was surprised at the big man's candour just about everything Helen asked him was answered immediately, there didn't seem to be any attempt to hide what the ongoing situation with the gene research was.

"You see Doctor, the project that you were part of had very high aspirations; we did intend to finance and drive a radical change in the way defects in the human gene sequences would be treated. Quite apart from the wonderful results that could be attained with the modified treatment it would have put my organisation in the forefront of global profit return."

"But what about Jonathan here and Professor Swift? Catchpole?" Helen was intrigued as to how Hector was going to argue the rather extreme measures they had taken to keep the project secret; certainly, outside of normal business practice."

"Dear doctor I must admit that I have no knowledge of what you could possibly be refereeing too. Professor Swift was murdered whilst on holiday from the project and I believe that Professor Catchpole was murdered in London after he had left our employ. Are you suggesting that we had anything to do with these murders?" Hector was enjoying this; he had little concern about the assassin being directly or even indirectly connected to the organisation and more importantly to him. The mechanism that ran the empire would hide every contact that they ever had with Mr Brown quite easily. The government agency may know what had been going on but to prove it would be another matter entirely.

"Hector, we know for sure that Mr Brown has been a paid assassin and he has been working at your behest so you are in, potentially a lot of trouble that would, in all likelihood see you put away for the rest of your life."

Hector was still smiling. "No doctor that will not happen; today is the first time that Mr Brown and I have met; is that not true Mr Brown?" He paused to give Jonathan chance to say something; he didn't. "Besides if you feel that you hold evidence against individuals that are implicated in wrong doing then you must inform the authorities at the earliest opportunity; if I can provide any assistance as a good citizen then please do not hesitate to seek it."

Helen knew full well that there would little gain in pursuing this lot; their tracks would be well covered. The bigger picture on the aims of the research might be a different matter.

"Have you still full control of the research Hector?"

Hector's smile was still there but Helen thought it had faded slightly.

"To be honest Doctor we are in the process of closing it down; it has not been the overwhelming success that we had hoped. The cost has spiralled to the point where we cannot sustain it; we simply cannot afford the expenditure."

"So, you have lost control over it then; how has that affected the proposed outcome? Is if now under the control of someone else? Are you doing anything to retrieve the situation?"

“Doctor Dudman as much as I would like to sit here and answer questions from you regarding random subjects I’m afraid I and my colleague here have some considerable amount of work to process. I feel we have given you and Mr Brown sufficient time to come too whatever conclusion you have.”

The four sat staring at each other without any further conversation. Jonathan was the first to move; he saw no reason to remain sitting in this group; it was time to go.

“Let’s go Helen, we are done here.”

“Goodbye gentlemen it was nice to meet you.” Doctor Dudman held out her hand and shook the hand of both men in turn. Neither man said anything but smiled as she turned and left; Jonathan walking behind her.

48.

It was two days later that the media was filled with the incident in the Chicago area. A contaminant had been identified in the water supply that was proving fatal to large sections of the population. It seemed random as sometimes only one member of a family would be affected and the others in the same group showed no signs of illness at all. It was puzzling the Centre for Disease Control and was creating widespread panic. Large quarantine areas had been set up and after a ten-day operation it appeared that the pandemic had been contained.

Those that had been infected were dead; the agent that had triggered the event seemed to have had a one hundred per cent success rate. Those that were not infected appeared to be in the same health as before the infection started. The CDC knew that this was not possible but here it was. The main effort now was to point the finger of blame but evidence was not forthcoming, it appeared to even the most biased commentators that the large number of deaths might even have a natural explanation. As the episode in Chicago was winding down similar things were happening in other parts of the world. All the major powers had experienced something of the same as well as many small nations. It did present itself as completely random and the only thing that the theories linked was the water supply. The Chicago area was held up as an example; there were no fatalities outside of the area that was supplied by the water route that passed through the small town of Marion. The other outbreaks around the world were also contained by a specific area that supplied the water. How the mechanism worked to guarantee the one hundred per cent fatalities was not understood.

"Can I leave now and retire as was promised?"

Jonathan was sitting opposite Helen in small conference room in down town New York. They had both been out of the loop on the project and were waiting for Helen's boss to call it a day. The news from Chicago had filled the news channels almost without a pause; remarkably even the weather had taken a back seat. The information was scarce; large areas of the metropolitan area of Chicago had been shut down and the rumours of many casualties had been played down. Helen had checked in and tried to find out what was going on but the people on charge were in no mood to discuss the problems further north. The news channels largely agreed that the outbreak or whatever it was had been contained and the cordon would be raised within the week. A terrorist link had not been ruled out but it did seem that the event may even have a natural occurrence. How it all fell together was still a puzzle and an endless subject for discussion for all the news channels, both national and international. The media were already pushing for a decision on when the quarantine would be lifted and the East Coast could go back to normal.

"How did the West ever fight World War Two?" Jonathan had been watching the news feed on the monitor that was placed high on the wall. "These days' major events only last for a short time; maybe it's because of the short attention span of most people. Hundreds of people are dead and the main subject is how we can get back to normal and move on. Perhaps we will have a minute's silence and hold hands or have a group hug."

"Don't take this seriously Jonathan it is only the news feed for the masses, I assure you this episode in Chicago and the other incidents around the world are not being forgotten It will run and run; believe me there are some very big players engaging with this. If there is any good that has come out of this is the way various governments have stopped blaming each other; there seems to be a concerted effort from most to get to the bottom of this; there has been very little finger pointing and very few conspiracy theories; not at all usual."

"But I think our part many have come to an end; it has left us behind. I think it might be a good idea if we got away from this area and went somewhere for a bit of down town. What do you think Jonathan?" Helen looked at Jonathan who was still watching the TV.

"What do you mean we?"

Jonathan wasn't expecting to go anywhere with the Doctor ever again; he was only waiting to be let go and then he would vanish on his own; he had had enough of working for the government, eventually he knew it would trip him up.

"Jonathan the people looking after all this are of the opinion that the episode in Chicago is not a one off for the United States. They have already identified three other areas, besides the ones out in the world, that have produced similar, if much smaller, outbreaks, if that is what we should be calling them; I would have used the word attack but I am not in charge of much now. We, that is you and I, have to get away from this or it might not end well for us. We will get caught up in the shit storm that is about to appear. You are very used to being invisible so I think that you should come up with a plan to get us away for the short to medium term."

Jonathan continued looking out of the window but thought about the question; he had been planning to disappear anyway and now it looked like he would have the good doctor in tow.

"I was thinking the same but it was going to be a solo journey but since we are now getting on and are both unemployed why don't we make it an extended holiday; somewhere remote and away from any major population centres."

"Good but we must make a decision soon as the travel restrictions to and from the United States will not be relaxed anytime soon; they are about to get very tight and I suspect that if we leave it any longer we will be here for the duration; we leave now or not at all." Helen smiled. "Where are we going then Jonathan?"

"Iceland. I will get onto it straight away we should be able to get on one of the flights to Europe that transit through Keflavik. It may need our combined clout to get us on the flight. I have a small place not far away where we can stay out of the way for as long as we need to.

Once the flights into and out of the United States are shut down there will be very little international traffic through Iceland."

49.

It was not easy for the two to get a flight across the Atlantic; the quarantined area had been modified to conform to the water catchment area but the residual panic amongst the population was still causing major problems with transportation. Helen spent much time in getting the relevant authority to grant them passage but in the end, they managed to board a flight out of JFK that was going to Frankfurt via Keflavik in Iceland. The flight was about an hour from landing in Iceland when Helen stopped reading the report that she had been given as they had arrived at JFK. She was staring at the last page.

"What is it? All interesting stuff I hope." Jonathan wasn't really very interested in the stuff that Helen had been reading since they took off. It ran to about twenty A4 pages and had been printed double sided in quite a small font; unless their eyes were very good it was unlikely anyone could have peered over her shoulder to read it. Jonathan had given up after the first paragraph and had dozed off.

"I'm not sure; if this is correct we are in serious trouble and when I say we I do not mean you and I." Helen returned to the middle of the report and started to read it again, this time making notes on the margin with a pencil from her bag.

"How many times do you have to read that? It must be the tenth time you have worked backwards and forwards through it; it must be very interesting, perhaps you should get it published I'm sure it will be a best seller." Helen ignored Jonathan and concentrated on the text.

"Oh well never mind we will be landing shortly anyway, after that we have a seven-hour drive to contend with." Jonathan pulled his seat upright and began to collect his things from the seat pocket and from the floor. As he finished the seat belt sign flicked on and the cabin crew announced that they would soon be landing at Keflavik; the temperature on the ground would be around freezing but with a slight wind from the south. Helen folded the report and put it into her bag making sure the zipped compartment was fully closed; she then held her bag close to her as if she didn't want to let it go.

"I'm sorry madam but could you put your bag under your seat for landing please. If you like I could place it in the overhead locker." Helen looked like should put up a fight to keep a hold of her bag, Jonathan was puzzled.

"Yes of course." Helen snapped out of it and pushed the bag down onto the floor and rested just under the seat in front. "Thank you, madam." The steward carried on up the aisle checking that everything was ready for landing.

"What was that about Helen? I have not seen you like that before; I thought that we might have a situation developing here." Helen looked at him but didn't say anything.

Helen didn't speak to Jonathan until they were moving through the immigration control point. "How long before we can be at your place Jonathan?"

"As I said we have about a six or seven-hour drive; we will be up on the east coast between a notional park and the sea. It is an ideal place to keep out of harm's way. Why are you having second thoughts about this? Do we need to be somewhere else?"

"No, where you describe might be the best place in the world, certainly in the short term." Jonathan was starting to get a little nervy about the way Doctor Dudman was behaving and why she had suddenly become very quiet. Jonathan started paying more attention to his surroundings, noting and assessing every person that was near or who was walking past; something had changed and he was sure it would require action very soon.

Once through the immigration and baggage claim the two walked to a hire car desk. "You have a car for a mister Brown?"

"Yes, sir we have been expecting you, your usual preference has been brought around to the front of the building, and our agent will meet you at the door. Have a safe trip Mr Brown nice to see you again."

The agent was a woman in her late twenties and picked Jonathan out of the crowd immediately. "Mr Brown your car is here." Gesturing to a large Ford 4x4, she clicked the remote control to open the boot. "Can I help you with your luggage sir?"

"No, it's OK, thank you very much for your offer." The woman handed Jonathan the keys, turned on her heel and walked away. Jonathan threw his case and small bag into the boot and reached for the suitcase that Helen had.

Once in the car Jonathan looked at Helen. "What is going on Helen? Are we about to be compromised?" Helen was sitting in the front passenger seat but was still clutching her bag as if it held something very important that was about to be snatched away.

"Jonathan, I have to read this again to make sure I have understood it and then we can have a chat."

"OK I will just drive then; the scenery will be very nice and the views over the countryside and the ocean are quite spectacular this time of year."

Jonathan pushed the gear selector into drive and they left the small parking area that was reserved for VIP or reserved pickups. Soon they were out of the airport and driving down a very well-maintained exit road that would lead them south then east towards the coast.

50.

It was only an hour into the journey when Helen spoke. “What do you think has been going on Jonathan?”

“What? I thought that we had covered all this way back in our journey around the place. One organisation had been providing another organisation to carry out research into genetic modification, research that you yourself played a big part. Are you saying now that was not the case?” Jonathan was enjoying the drive, as he always did here. The scenery was second to none and the big empty spaces and very little traffic made this one of his favourite drives.

Helen waved the report she had been reading in the air. “This is the agency’s report on the coded notes that Professor Swift made, remember that we thought that it detailed the real direction the research was going and that it is likely he was removed by you to stop him passing any of it to a third party?”

“Well what have we got? Is it different from what everybody thought?”

“Jonathan professor Swift was well ahead of us all, he was recording not the direction the research was going but the likely consequences if the work progressed the way it seemed to be.” Helen paused.

“And?” Jonathan was wishing she would get to the point.

“The notes he left did not only set out the true purpose of the research but also listed what would happen if the end point was reached and implemented. The genetic modification that was originally envisaged was proven to be possible and was indeed trialled in several places. It would have generated vast wealth for whoever controlled it.”

“Yes, Helen we know that but what extra does Swift’s notes give us?”

They were now driving on the route one that took them up the East coast, sometimes moving inland to avoid the natural features; little or no traffic and clear, very blue skies.

“We have all been duped and Swift was the only one to notice it early on; why he didn’t flag it up immediately I cannot understand. The project was going badly wrong, not only were we able to complete the gene modification we also managed to introduce several changes into the sequence; these changes are not the type that can be corrected and, if Swift is right, they will soon be out into the wider population, there is no going back.”

“Well, Helen is that good or bad? I suspect that you are going to tell me it is bad, right?”

“Yes Jonathan, very, very bad. This little trick we have all been involved in is likely to kill many people on this planet, maybe millions, and the episode in the Chicago area was only a small indication of what is to come. I really don’t know where we stand on this now.”

"So, what exactly was Swift saying? Was he recording it for future work or what? I expect he was found out and his masters didn't like his thoughts on it; why else would I have been tasked to remove him. I expect that it was more serious than him asking for a pay rise."

"How long before we are there Jonathan?" Helen was looking out of the window at the pristine countryside and the sea as Jonathan kept the speed just below the limit on the road.

"Another two hours maybe a little less; do you want to stop and have a walk about? We can stop just down there, past that bend; there is quite a pleasant stopping place."

Jonathan pulled over and cut the engine, both got out of the car and looked out to sea; behind them the dark grey cliffs rose above them like a cloud. Just visible through some of the peaks was the snow that remained in the national park from the winter. The snow was unlikely to completely disappear during the summer and in the winter, it would increase dramatically when the temperature dropped well below freezing; temperatures of minus forty had been experienced in the national park on the high ground on many occasions. It was not an area for the faint hearted.

Helen leaned on the roof of the car. "Remember the bit that the man Henry told us about the flight response in some animals? Well Swift also noted that the work was moving in that direction; the death-response in some antelope is well known, as is the sudden death syndrome in humans. The mechanism in play that causes some to simply die and others not to is not fully understood. An awful lot of work has been carried out to identify if a genetic defect was responsible but no conclusive evidence has been identified; until now it seems."

"Professor Swift has indicated that, not only have we identified this death gene anomaly but we now have the ability to turn it on in people that would not normally be affected by it; we can kill even healthy adults whenever we feel like it. The Chicago thing was a large fielding experiment and as you know many lives were lost; the cause is not in the public domain but we are now sure that Swift was intending to put a stop to it and you, Jonathan, killed him."

"That was then, what are we going to do about it now?" Jonathan was always irritated when a person argued what might or might not have been; if it has happened then it has happened; time travel is not an option, it cannot be changed.

"I don't know Jonathan; I am of the mind that we, or anyone, cannot do anything about it now; it is too late."

51.

In less than two hours they had made the small house that had been owned by Jonathan for several years now; he had never used it as part of the job but had been there whenever he needed to be out of the loop; even his phone and contact mechanism didn't work out here; he could be completely off the grid for as long as he wanted.

The house was typical of the structures in this part of Iceland, primarily built of wood on a concrete platform and some brickwork that held the heating components of the house; a one-story house that had a moderately sized floor plan with a large kitchen, a lounge and two bedrooms. Jonathan had only ever used the larger of the two bedrooms; he had never had a guest in this place before. In an extension that pushed into the slope behind the house had been constructed several storage rooms that held a large row of energy efficient freezers. These required minimal power once they had been drawn do the operating temperature. The rest of the space was taken up with canned food, lots of it. A small workshop, with an enclosed diesel generator, was in a side room to the main area

The dwelling came to life fairly quickly; The heating was run from a geothermal device that had worked without fault for many years; it was the best thing that Jonathan could remember buying. Water was from a small stream that came down from the high ground in the National Park. Jonathan thought that it provided the best tasting water he had ever experienced.

This water supply never froze, even in the dark cold of the winter months because of the geothermal activity.

“Where do you get the power for lighting and the other things Jonathan?” Helen was amazed that he had all this set up and ready to go. The agency knew about his bolt hole in main land Europe but this was completely off the radar.

“Solar power mainly, but I have a backup generator out back if we need to use it. So far, I have only ever used it once, the power consumption of the kit in here is quite low; it takes twice as long to fire up the coffee machine but it does use about a third of the power a conventional boiling device would draw. Which reminds me, I must go up on the roof and clear any debris or dirt from the panels; the output is a little down.” Jonathan tapped a small gauge that was fixed to the wall in the kitchen.

Just over three hours after arriving Jonathan announced that they were now ready to relax; all the systems in the house were working and the heating was on; the house had come to life.

“I need to check in and find out what is happening; particularly with the two in New York.” Helen had just come from the bedroom and a shower; her hair was still wet as she wrapped a small towel around her head. Her hair colour had changed again and was now the same shade that Jonathan had noted on the instruction to kill her in France. “Hope you don’t mind but I have used your dressing gown.”

“Second question first; no, I don’t mind and as for the first request please feel free, the PC is in the office.” Jonathan indicated a small room that was off the kitchen.

“It’s all on and ready to go; anyone you call or connect to will not know where you are unless you tell them.” Jonathan looked at Helen waiting for a response; he didn’t get one except that she walked into the office and sat down at the computer.

“Give me a shout if you need anything; I am going to get cleaned up and then we can eat; most of the stuff will be defrosted by then.” Jonathan went into the bedroom and closed the door. He thought about the problems if she alerted her bosses to their location. Oh well I cannot be any more trapped than I already am and if they were going to kill me I would already be dead. He turned the shower on and set the dial towards hot.

Helen had made contact fairly easily; just a few codes and passwords and she was through to her boss; except her boss was no longer there, all she got was a technician that was working in the office that should have been in a very secure area but wasn’t.

“What are you doing there?” Helen was puzzled; all the secure protocol she had gone through should not have resulted in her talking to this person.

“I’m sorry but who are you?”

The system had identified Doctor Dudman as she has connected so the man on the other end knew who she was but Helen had never seen him before. The return from the system only indicated that she was through to the office of the Director.

"I am the technical supervisor, Doctor Dudman; we are closing down the facility so it can be relocated, we are very short staffed at the moment as I'm sure you know." The man continued to write on something out of view from the camera and didn't really show much interest in the conversation with the doctor.

"Where is the director? Is she available? I need to talk with her immediately." Helen was getting irritated with the man's disinterest.

The request to speak to the director stopped the man in mid flow. "I cannot get the director right now as "he" is not available; the department is somewhat busy at the moment. I could try and get a message to him if you really need me to, but I'm not sure it will get to him."

"What do you mean? Has the director been replaced? When did this happen?"

"It happened when the director you speak of died very suddenly, along with many others; surely you would have known this. I must remind you Doctor that protocol one is in place; goodbye Doctor, good luck." The connection ended and Helen was left staring at the screen.

"Protocol one? What the fuck is that?" Hele shouted at the blank screen.

Doctor Helen Dudman, or rather Claire Steele, did not know of Protocol One because it was way above her pay scale. The technician had only assumed that because she was active she must be in a position to understand and to act upon the protocols now in use. He was not to know that the whole agency was about to cease to operate in any meaningful manner; those days had now passed. The chaos that was about to be unleashed would largely pass her and Jonathan by but they would not be able to escape all the effects.

"What's up?" Jonathan felt much better after a shower and a shave; he was now thinking of eating and was going through ideas in his head.

"We are now to comply with Protocol One." Helen said, still staring at the blank screen.

"What's that when it's at home?" Jonathan was looking into the cupboards at the cans of food that filled the shelves.

"Beats me, but I am willing to bet it is not good."

52.

During the three weeks they had been in the house there had been only one incident that indicated anyone else was alive; a ship had moved close in shore and then had moved off following the coast. Jonathan had watched it through binoculars for as long as it was visible. *Cunard colours but quite small* it looked in poor shape and was making lots of smoke. *What are you doing here?* The news channels had been full when they arrived of the increasing number of fatalities in the US and then across Europe; after day four the news items trailed off and only reruns of the popular sitcoms were shown end to end. The local radio station only played music; there didn't seem to be any news items or news programmes on anything. There wasn't even any add breaks to change the tempo. The internet had kept pace for longer but it too was now giving less and less connectivity. The local servers had dropped out and for a while access to some of the satellite linked servers was available but after ten days there was nothing. Jonathan had managed to log into the normal route he used but it didn't put anything out the other side, there was no connection other than to the main server.

During the time spent together Helen and Jonathan had become firm friends, nothing serious and they still occupied their own rooms when sleeping. It seemed to Jonathan that Helen was not interested in him or anyone else in that way. He didn't lose any sleep over it, he had been on his own for quite some time; his life had depended on it at times. Jonathan spent the first week taking an inventory of everything that was in the house, particularly the food; he estimated that they had enough essentials for about six months; longer if they were careful. The rest of the days were spent monitoring the TV and radio channels to glean information. The problem was, there was less and less on both media. There didn't appear to be any live news channels operating. Jonathan had even tried the small shortwave radio he had stored in the workshop; after some time with the back off he had managed to get it working. Lots of static but he found a single transmitter that was working; a Tai broadcaster that was reciting religious texts over and over again. Johnathan didn't think it was a recording because the man speaking kept stopping and then starting again. He didn't speak the language that was in use very well but he could get the gist of what was being said; all doom and gloom and the end of the world is nigh sort of stuff. It would go on for hours at a time and then suddenly stop only to return with the same man hours later. *Does he ever get any sleep?*

"Someone outside Jonathan."

Helen was looking out of the window in the kitchen that gave a view down to the road. A large 4 x 4 had pulled up. Helen recognised it as one of the big Asian all terrain trucks that were popular in Europe. They had become more numerous because they were cheaper than the Western built ones and as good when the going was rough. Jonathan looked out to see that there were two people sitting in front with maybe one other in the back. The windows were steamed up so much that the rear was partly obscured by the condensation. The occupants didn't seem to be in a hurry to come up to the house.

“Better safe than sorry Helen, let us assume threat before it comes to bite us.” Jonathan opened a concealed draw under the counter; inside were two pistols and spare ammunition. One was an automatic Glock the other a short-barrelled magnum revolver made by Remington. Both very capable weapons as long as the target wasn’t too distant.

Jonathan passed the Glock to Helen and moved away into the rear of the room; Helen moved into the other room that had a view and stood back against the wall furthest from the window. The people in the truck did not move, but seemed to be talking about something.

Helen moved down the side of the wall to gain a better view up then down the road. “It looks like they are on their own, can’t see anything else close by. They could have come over the hill behind us if that is possible.”

“No, not very practicable, they would have to have all the right gear and be willing to walk for a couple of miles to get into that position. When I chose this place being out flanked was a consideration. I think these people are alone, at least for now.”

The nearside door of the SUV opened and woman got out and looked up the drive to the house. To Helen and Jonathan, it seemed she was looking directly at them but both would agree that they were not visible at the rear of the building. The woman removed her coat and threw it onto the seat she had just left, closing the door. She walked slowly up the drive towards the main entrance, as she neared the door she stopped and held her arms out from her side and then slowly turned around.

"Not armed then, unless she is very good at hiding it, could have a knife though." Jonathan had been looking at the car as well as the woman. Nothing was happening with the car, the one or maybe two people in it had not made a move.

The woman was now at the door and out of view of both Jonathan and Helen. A double knock was heard by both of them.

"Better see what she wants; you watch the truck and I will open the door; perhaps I have won something in a competition, or she's selling double glazing."

Jonathan moved towards the door, keeping to the rear of the room until he couldn't be seen through the front window. He released the door catch and let it swing open, at the same time stepping sideways to put the door frame and the open door in between him and the car. It would look like the door was open but he couldn't be seen from the road. The woman who had knocked could see him.

"Mr Brown, would it be possible to speak with Agent Steele? We have urgent business that she should be aware of." There was still no movement from the SUV on the road.

"Come in and close the door behind you." Jonathan waved the handgun in the direction of the room and stepped back, keeping space between then. "No taser this time then?"

The woman who had entered was the same woman who had taken him down at the door of his hotel room; he was not going to let that happen again. He kept the gun pointing directly at her.

"Sit down on the sofa with your hands underneath you." The woman did as she was told.

"Any movement outside?" Jonathan was still looking directly at the new arrival.

"No, not a thing, I suggest that you take over here and I will speak with our guest." Jonathan swapped places with Helen who went over and sat next to their captive.

"What's up Emily? Why have you come to see us out here in the wilds?"

Helen left her sitting on her hands; it would be unwise to trust even her former colleagues the way things had changed in recent weeks. There was no obvious reason that she should be here in Iceland looking for her.

"They won't come into the house unless I ask them to Mr Brown; they are very well trained to do as they are told; you can relax, what I have to say will probably interest you as much as Claire here. Can I retrieve my hands please, they are going to sleep? I assure you I am unarmed but if you need to, please feel free to search me. I would search you if the roles were reversed."

"Stand up fingers interlaced and on your head." Emily did as she was told and was impressed that her long-time friend stood well out of the way, she couldn't have had a go at her even if she wanted to; a professional to the last.

Helen placed her gun out of reach after making sure Jonathan was paying attention. She then put her left hand onto Emily's hands from behind and patted her down.

"She is unarmed and I think we can trust her, if they had wanted to harm us they could have turned up mob handed and shot the crap out of the house; we didn't know they were there until they pulled up outside."

"OK Emily, you can sit down again but what about your friends in the vehicle outside? I see they have switched off the engine so they might be feeling the cold." Jonathan was still keeping an eye on the SUV on the edge of the road; the people in it didn't seem to be doing anything at all.

"They will wait for me so don't concern yourself with them; they now work for me and I have told them to stay put, so they will." Emily smiled at Jonathan.

53.

Helen and Emily sat next to each other on the sofa, Jonathan stayed in the kitchen area and watched for any activity out on the road; nothing happened.

"So, what is going on? And why are you here with on this very quiet day in Iceland?" Jonathan handed the two a coffee and returned to the kitchen so he could see outside.

"We are here because we had nowhere else to go. When you left New York, and came here we knew where you were because of the tracker that you both have on you; the bog standard one that sits in the sole of your shoe Jonathan. By the time we were told to leave and come here things were getting a little tight. We had rather less comfortable transport but it was on time. We got here sixteen days after you on a military flight provided by the British, a C130 transport; cold, noisy and prone to vibrate a lot but beggars can't be choosers. I'm sure Jonathan would have liked the trip; it would have reminded him of happier times. It dropped us off at the end of the main runway and immediately turned around to take off. The problem with that was it didn't take off. It charged down the runway and just kept going into the sea; no attempt was made to get it into the air. Very strange but we have been seeing similar things all over these last weeks. It then took us until now to get to you; even here in Iceland things are not what they used to be." Emily paused and looked at Jonathan. "Have you two witnessed anything unusual since you have been here?"

"It is very quiet and there doesn't seem to be anything on the TV but other than that I chose this place for just that reason; nothing ever happens here and I don't get visitors, although we did see a cruise ship go sailing past the other day." Jonathan was not at all surprised they had seen no one although on previous visits there had been the odd car or truck go past the end of the property; Emily and her friends had been the first since they had arrived.

"The ship might be one of several that were going to be tasked to patrol remote areas, picking people up, at least those that want to be picked up; a bit trial and error but sometimes if people can be isolated they show no symptoms and do survive in the short term. There were many ships at sea when all this kicked off, it may have been one of those. We don't know about what happens after because we are still in the early days, I think that because the situation is now out of control the rescue ship idea will fail. We have known about you and this place since we first stated following your exploits some years ago and I must admit it is out of the way but at the moment there seems to be no one in the area at all, even the small village a few miles down the road is completely deserted." Emily paused to think. "We and by that, I mean everybody is in mortal danger; I am not even sure from what and if we can even do anything about it."

"A little melodramatic, don't you think; we have been here a few weeks and we have not seen any threat at all, unless you are saying that you and your friends are a threat to us." Jonathan was still watching the vehicle outside; the engine now running and there didn't seem to any movement from the person in the front. The one in the rear he could not distinguish.

"I would ask your friends in but I think they will be better left outside; it might be a little crowded in here if they joined us." Jonathan sat at the breakfast bar with a view to the two women and to the outside through the kitchen window.

"Never mind Jonathan we will be going shortly and I expect that we will never meet again; at least not in this life." Emily suddenly looked very drawn and exhausted.

Emily began to recount what had been going on from the moment she and Jonathan had first met outside the hotel room. She talked for another hour, answering questions that came from the two of them, before getting up to leave. "I have enjoyed our little chat and I hope you didn't find it too fantastical because I assure you that all possibilities have been looked at and there does not seem to be any way out of it. I'm sorry." Emily leaned forward and gave Helen a hug, holding on to her as if to steady herself. "Goodbye Claire."

"Goodbye Jonathan pity we didn't meet in other circumstances it might have been fun." Emily went to the door, opened it and left without a glance back. Jonathan watched her walk to the SUV. She got into the same seat she had left before and the vehicle drove off, following the coast road North.

"What do you think of that?" Jonathan had come to sit in an armchair facing Helen.

“Emily has backed up and given more detail to the report I had before we left New York. The report was almost the stuff of fantasy but it is nothing compared to what Emily just said.” They both sat in silence thinking about what they had just heard. Jonathan was already working on a plan to get them both away and out of the danger zone, if that was possible.

The brief from Emily had been thorough and was presented from memory without notes. Jonathan had been impressed with the detail that she could recall without thinking about it. Still in her game it would help if our mind worked in that way; she would not have been the leader of a team if she was only half good.

The situation in Chicago had not been contained; it was identified quite early on that the contaminant had been introduced through the water supply in the warehouse in Marion. This had led to the catchment area for the Chicago metropolitan area being affected. The puzzle was that it was first thought to be a poison of some kind but not all those that ingested the water became ill or were affected in any way. You were either unharmed by the agent or it killed you; you didn’t become ill, you simply died, there were no recoveries. Fatality rate was around eighty per cent.

The water trail did not prove to be the answer as very soon after the Chicago outbreak was declared as contained, other areas of the US started to present the same problem; shortly after the first international outbreaks started to occur.

The CDC with the help of the disease control agencies of other countries had seized all the available records from the original project in France and Wales. All the associates of Hector had been arrested and were held in a large prison complex, large teams had been interrogating them under powers granted by Presidential decree. The country had been put on a war footing and maximum effort had been applied but the rate the problem had spread was unmanageable, even the teams investigating had become casualties; one day a team would be working and the next they would all be dead.

Very soon the mechanism of the deaths had been established but the way the problem was now out in the real world was a mystery. Population centres that could not have had the water contaminated were succumbing to the disease, if that was what it was. The speed of the spread was astonishing, even the Black Death in the fourteenth century was nothing like this, either in scope or speed of infection. Because the agencies combating it were being infected themselves and only a week after the global effort was announced it ceased to be anything that was effective. The spread was not confined to humans but was also soon present in other primates, other mammals appeared to be unaffected. Protocol One was enacted because the whole government department was ceasing to function. Protocol One was a complete shutdown of the system to preserve information while they still could.

It was soon apparent that the gene modification had not just triggered the so-called death response but has started switching off parts of the genome in people and then other primates. It was not a plague in the normal sense but it was having the same effect. Emily didn't know but thought that the whole world was now in a state of absolute crises and that population numbers were plummeting. Disease unconnected to the gene modification had started to get out of control because of the number of unburied bodies that were accumulating in all the population centres across the globe.

Emily had recounted what the department had been doing; she and her team had been tasked to come after Helen and return her to the US; since she had been a scientist working on the original project her input was deemed essential. It was all too late Emily had lost contact with her control and there was no way that she could retrieve Helen and get her back. The team that had come decided that it would be better to get as far away from civilisation as possible. They would wait and see what happened. They were certainly not going to hang around near large population centres.

"But if it isn't an infection, in the normal sense, then what is it." Jonathan was still not convinced and thought this was far too fantastical to actually happening."

Helen remained silent and seemed to getting more drained by the minute; her lively matter of fact outlook was gone.

"What is it Oppenheimer said? *I am become death, the destroyer of worlds.*"

"A piece from Hindu scriptures." Jonathan had heard the phrase many times, he had worked with a bloke in the army who said it all the time.

"Don't you see Jonathan? I should have been able to stop this and you actually killed the one man who would have stopped it. We are both guilty."

"No, if I hadn't been there they would have found someone else, Swift was a dead man from the start and you didn't know what was going on anyway; if we were both removed from the equation it would still have the same answer. The pressing problem we have now is not what might have been, but what we are going to do about it. The past is gone and cannot be changed. For now, we must look to ourselves; the problem, if you can call Armageddon a problem, is that we are unaffected; Emily and her team are also unaffected, that indicates that we are removed from the source of the problem, I suggest that we keep it that way for now but we cannot survive here for years; we have limitless water but the food will last at tops another eight months."

"Yes, I suppose you are right but have you considered that if we are in danger here the first either of us will know about is when one of us drops dead?"

"A pleasant thought, Helen or should I call you Claire from now on? Look on the bright side neither of us is going to have a long and painful death, at least not from this gene thing."

"I suppose you are right; let's not dwell on what might be and concentrate on what is. I like Helen, I have gotten used to it. Right now, Jonathan, I need a hug."

54.

The next day Helen woke with a start, not immediately realising where she was; the light was shining through the window onto the bed so it was probably later than she normally woke. The sky was blue with no wind that Helen could determine from her viewpoint.

“Morning Helen.” Jonathan was propped up on one elbow lying next to her.”

The night before had passed in a daze for Helen; all she wanted now was to be away from all the problems that they both found themselves involved in. It might not be easy or even possible to survive what was happening. Jonathan had been surprisingly gentle the evening before; for someone who had killed and had been in the process of killing her he had become a friend and since last night he was more than that. She thought that they were going to see this through to the end together.

“Why didn’t you wake me? What time is it?” Helen starred at the ceiling wondering what had triggered the episode that had led them to the same bed.

“If we were paid to work we would be on a disciplinary for being very late. The time of day does not matter now, if what Emily told us is correct, and I think it is, we are out of gainful employment for ever; at least we are still here, I suspect we are the very lucky ones, at least for now.” Jonathan leant over and kissed her very lightly on the lips. Helen responded by pulling herself up and onto him, kissing him hard, her desire rising.

The two spent most of the day entwined in each other's arms; there seemed to no reason it should ever end.

"Fancy a coffee?" Jonathan was up and moving towards the door.

"Aren't you going to put some clothes on? You don't want to frighten the locals looking like that." Helen watched him as he left; for someone who she had known for some time now his build and athleticism surprised her; well-proportioned and no visible excess fat; a few scars across his back but otherwise he could have earned a living as a model. She smiled at the thought of Jonathan parading up and down the catwalk.

"We have to decide what we are going to do. We could stay here until the food runs out but I suspect that there may be others in the area that might want what we have. Emily said the place was deserted but you never know; if I was out there with not much I would be looking around for a better place to live and survive. Any visitors we receive might not be too friendly. One or two we can handle but more than that may be a problem" Jonathan had returned with the coffee, handing one to Hele then sitting on the side of the bed; he hadn't put any clothes on.

"I Suppose we could both do away with clothes and become naturists Jonathan but it might limit our time outside." Helen was happy and wished that this time would go on for ever but she knew that was not possible and they would have to make contingency plans for the near future.

“We should probably venture out and see what is around; further North from here gets a bit quiet with nothing much other than few tourist accommodation and some buildings that are used by the park rangers, that’s the way Emily and her friends headed. I don’t think the rangers are about because we would have encountered them by now. The other way is back from where we came from; the small village and then the town; I don’t think that we should venture in that direction, if the population has been reduced to ten per cent, that percentage could be quite a number of people down that way. Keflavik is small but still contained 15k or so inhabitants, that would mean that there could be a thousand plus, looking for an opening. I wonder if that ship we saw stopped there; I’m not sure it could dock but it could have stood off and sent a tender ashore. No, better to stay away from there.” Jonathan finished his coffee and got back into bed.

“OK Jonathan we can fill in the details later and move out to have a look tomorrow; in the meantime, I think we should make the most of our newfound friendship.”

55.

"We won't venture too far today but have a quick scout around and come back." Jonathan had moved the car out from the garage and was checking the oil.

Do you normally check things like that on nearly new hire cars? Helen was sitting on the step watching Jonathan.

"Yes, I do actually, we depend on this transport, at least for now; we may get something better on our drive around but for the present I will keep looking after what we have got. The spare fuel we have should keep us going for the time being I estimate that we have about a thousand miles of juice in the store but who knows when and if we will be able to get more. If anything, serious happens to this we will need other transport; perhaps we will get that today." Jonathan opened the passenger door and waved Helen into it."

"Thank you, kind sir but don't assume you will get anything for it." Helen laughed.

Jonathan drove down the drive and turned left onto the main road; this was the same way that Emily and her friends had gone, Jonathan hoped that they would not encounter them on the way and that that had got well away. It was not to be; two miles down the road they stopped next to a body that was lying by the side of the road, a man, bits of him had been chewed off by some animal. Jonathan thought it would probably have been a dog that had wandered from the small fishing settlement that could just be seen in the distance.

“Shouldn’t we have a look at him Jonathan, he might be one of the people that was with Emily.”

“No, he’s definitely dead and since we do not know how this thing is spread it would be unwise even to get out of the car let alone go and poke about. I would say that he is not local.” Jonathan pointed out the clothes and the fact he was wearing a shoulder holster minus the weapon. “If I had to guess I would say it was one of those that stayed in the SUV when Emily visited.”

They both looked at the unfortunate man lying by the road.

“I expect we will see more of that but I am a little puzzled as to why we have only seen him; where are all the locals? Perhaps it came on slowly and they are all at home. We will find out soon enough when we go past that place.” Jonathan indicated the small group of buildings about half a mile away”

Jonathan drove on; both keeping their eyes on the buildings that were getting closer.

“All quiet, no smoke or sign of life.” Jonathan looked through binoculars at the five or six wooden houses that were now close by. “No heating on and some windows are open; I don’t think anyone is at home; what do you think. Jonathan handed the binoculars to Helen.

They both knew that, in their current position, they were exposed. Anyone on this side of the settlement would have seen them come down the road from where they had stopped at the body; they could hardly avoid being seen if anyone was looking in their direction. The village was very picturesque; brightly coloured woodwork against a clear blue sky and a turquoise sea. From their position they couldn't see any boats except one that was broken into pieces and had been pulled onto the shore. There weren't even any vehicles that could be seen. The whole place looked deserted.

"Let's go and have a look then." Jonathan engaged drive and moved slowly towards the buildings. Nothing was happening and the settlement looked like it had been abandoned but not that long ago; the windows were clean and the paintwork on all the buildings was clean and bright. Jonathan turned the engine off and opened the windows, listening for anything that might indicate people were there; nothing but a slight sound of the wind coming off the sea.

"If we are not in need of anything specific do you think we need to go any further into this place?" Helen was not at all sure that they should be even this close; aside from the danger of infection there may be people who wanted what they had; transport!

"Over there, see that?" Helen looked in the direction that Jonathan was indicating. There was a small window set back into the porch area of one of the last buildings in the row; something seemed to be moved behind it and there was a light on in the window. Helen looked through the binoculars.

"Jesus! Someone is looking at us, a man I think, have a look." Helen handed the bino's to Jonathan.

Maybe but he is not moving, is he?" Jonathan watched for another minute and sure enough the figure did not move at all. "He is standing a little oddly though."

Jonathan retrieved the Glock from the glove compartment and got out of the car.

"Get into the driver's seat and be ready to go, the Magnum is in there." Jonathan pointed to the box that was in between the font seats. "Be ready Helen."

Jonathan moved to the left of the line of sight; whoever was looking out of the window could not see his approach. Once he had reached the building he went all the way around the back and came up to the window from the other side, still out of view. He adjusted his position until he could just see into the window and he figure that was still motionless behind it. He moved in front of the window and peered in, a momentary feeling of sadness passed over him. On his way back to the car Jonathan had a quick look around the area and down to the small jetty that the fishermen had landed the daily catch.

"Well what is it? Was it a man?" Helen was puzzled by Jonathan's sudden return.

"Yes, it is a man but he is a dead man. He is hanging from a large hook that is attached to the roof beams. Maybe out here was his favourite view. I would guess he has been dead a couple of days, any longer and he would have started to fall down and he hasn't been eaten by anything yet. Not many flies but it is getting colder these days. Anyway, there has been some activity on the jetty but not recently; quite a lot of bags and personal items lying around, some has blown off the wall into the water and is now washed up on the beach; a lot of paperwork that had the Cunard heading on. I didn't get too close but it was nearly all from that line."

"Let's go Helen there is nothing more for us here. According to the map there is another small inlet with a fishing community about four or five miles up the coast; we can have a look around but if there is nothing of interest we can call it a day and head back."

56.

It was five hours before the two arrived back at the house they had left in the morning. The two-mile journey north had not given them any more information than they had gained in the first fishing community. The second group of buildings had once been the home to around ten or twelve families who worked a living fishing just of shore. Fish in the area was plentiful and gave the families a relatively good and stable life. The fish were probably still there in abundance but the people had gone. The buildings were the usual Icelandic design; brightly coloured and set close together. The group of dwellings had been photographed on many occasions in the past; an ideal tourist image that looked very beautiful and tranquil. The two had stopped in the middle of the community and had looked into every building; everything was there except the people. In the last house a dog had surprised Jonathan; a large German Shepard had come running into the kitchen area from outside as he was about to leave; loud aggressive barking at first then the dog suddenly turned around and ran away as if frightened of Jonathan. Helen had come running with her gun ready but the dog was gone and didn't return.

"What do you think happened in the two settlements? They looked the same; no damage and lots of personal items lying around but nothing living there, except the dog of course." Helen was still trying to be more positive in a world that didn't seem to have any positives.

Jonathan smiled. “Yes, that dog did give me a bit of a fright; if it had attacked me I would have been in trouble. I think it was more surprised to see me than I was to see it. Not aggressive really, just startled like I was.”

“Helen, we are not seeing the whole picture here; if we can believe your brief from the document and the stuff that Emily told us why aren’t there any bodies lying around. The infection, or whatever it is, makes some people drop dead without warning, so, where are they? We have seen two; one, who I would say was not local to the area and the man hanging in the first village; I would say he had done it himself but you never know. The two groups of houses would have what? Fifty, a hundred occupants?”

“Fancy a coffee?” Helen was up and on her way to the kitchen as she spoke. “We are no nearer to understanding this than we were before Emily showed up but I would suggest the obvious Jonathan.” Helen paused, looking into the living room. “They have been taken off by someone, probably that ship we saw going past, Emily did say that was one of the plans that had been put in place.”

“Yes, but in any evacuation not everyone wants to go; particularly when there is not obvious danger for those that would stay. There were no dead people so therefore the sudden drop-dead syndrome, for want of a better description, has not happened here.” Jonathan thought that the single man on the road might be a casualty of it but he was the only one.

Helen sat down next to Jonathan and gave him a mug of coffee. “I don’t suppose we will ever find out but we have to decide what we are going to do. We could just sit here; we have water and heating that will last forever and the town in the other direction will have masses of food that we could make use of for years to come. The fishing is probably still and option. Perhaps the end of the world has passed us by.”

“That would be nice Helen, I cannot think of anyone I would rather spend the rest of my life with.”

“Is that a proposal Jonathan?” Helen smiled and looked out of the window.

57.

Jonathan was sat at the computer looking at the connection history to determine which of the routes was the last to drop out. Checking the dates, he had determined that one of the servers close by had been the last connection before only the satellites were operating; these had also dropped out a few days after the land based ones. What he found was that the land switch-off had been approaching from the US and then had jumped to Europe and further East. Iceland had been the last to show symptoms and had been the last to still hold some connectivity. Jonathan learned back in his chair staring at the list of connections on the screen. Her ran the software again to see if anything had changed; nothing different showed on the screen. There were a couple of satellites that responded to his transmission but there didn't seem to be anything being processed through them, nothing at all.

"It seems we are alone; at least in cyberspace. I wonder how the ship we saw is communicating?" Jonathan was puzzled, there should be something going through the grid but he certainly couldn't find anything with the equipment he had.

"What was that Jonathan? Perhaps we are indeed alone, have you considered that?" Helen was working through the TV channels looking for any activity, there was none.

As Jonathan leaned forward to turn the monitor off the screen displayed a brief flash of light; now the screen showed a small circular icon at the top right. Jonathan changed the screen resolution to make the image bigger. "This is strange, come and have a look at this Helen."

"Mmmm we have seen that before haven't we Jonathan?"

Now the image was bigger it was plain to see a representation of the circular disks they had encountered in the warehouse in Marion and the item in the pocket of the man at the airport. Jonathan checked what was active in the computer.

"The camera just came on so maybe someone is looking at us, the microphone is also live." He checked the connectivity from the software he had been using a minute before. "We are not connected to anything at the moment so perhaps this is some buried software in this machine."

The screen blinked again; this time the circular device was shown in the middle of the screen and about as twice as big. The image was now very clear; it was one of the discs that was found in the warehouse and on the man but with a slightly different form of letters going around the edge.

"Can you hear me Mr Brown, Doctor Dudman?" The voice was coming from the speaker that sat next to the screen that now presented a man's head and shoulders.

The man looked very like the Henry they had met in Hong Kong but was a lot lighter in build; he had less hair and it was darker; maybe a relation but not Henry.

"Yes, we can hear you; who are you and what can we do for you Mr…?"

"I am here with the offer of advice that will be useful for the two of you. As you know the current world order has taken a different direction from the one it was on. I am here to help but I must tell you that you are in a somewhat precarious position; you are not in any immediate danger but you cannot stay there and do nothing. As the days pass that idea will not be a good one and things will start to happen that will eventually kill you both."

The man paused as if to give them a chance to comment.

Jonathan was the first to speak. "At the moment we have no idea of what you are on about; we are quite self-sufficient here and certainly for the next six months at least we will do fine without any assistance either from you or anyone else, so what do you want?"

"As you may know the world population is in somewhat of a flux; the main population areas on all continents have been going through a change and by the end of next month, that is about six weeks away, the combined population of Europe and North America will number in the region of three million souls; a bit of a reduction from close to a billion, I think you will agree."

The man was smiling. “The rest of the world? Well that is somewhat of a work in Progress, at least for now.”

Jonathan and Helen just stared at the man on the screen. Both were thinking that this had to be a bad dream; mass murder on an industrial scale had been perpetrated and in less than a month the population had been reduced to a fraction of what it was; this was not possible.

“Who are you?” Helen sat down and peered at the screen, looking for anything in the background; the man appeared to be sat with his back against a painted wall with just the edge of a door or window frame visible at the edge of the screen.

“My name is not important but I can say that my brother, Henry, was quite taken with the two of you. You both showed promise and when we discovered that you were both in the zone that would escape we were quite pleased. You see Doctor Dudman you have been selected to survive, not by us or anyone but by your genetic makeup, the agent we introduced has passed through the both of you and has left you unaffected, better than one in a million.”

“Where is Henry? Can we speak to him?” Helen didn’t know what speaking to the other man would achieve but she was trying to guide the conversation in a direction she chose.

“Henry is dead.” The man’s announcement was matter of fact, giving no indication that he cared in the slightest that his brother was dead.

“OK, Henry’s brother, what do you want of us?” To Jonathan, this was now getting into science fiction, something that was just made up and didn’t really exist.

“The ship that you have seen going down the coast will return over the next day or so. You and Doctor Dudman are to embark on it. If you decide that you won’t you will have forfeited your last chance at any long-term survival. When your food runs out you will have few options, I suppose you could improve your fishing skills but believe me you will not survive for long on a diet from the ocean unless your skills in that area improve dramatically.”

All thee remained silent for several minutes. The man on the screen was the first to speak. “So, there we have it, the ship will be in your area before the end of the week, if you don’t get on it you will die, so the choice is yours. Goodbye Doctor, Mr Brown.”

“But why is all this happening? What is it all for? Helen knew that the research had enabled this organisation to kill millions of people but why were they doing it. All the mass murderers in history always had a reason even if it was crazy.

“Doctor Dudman, think of all the woes that currently have plagued the population of this planet; wars, famine, global warming and such like. What is the root cause of all of these?” The same smile was there.

“No? Well I will state the obvious; there are too many people here, too many by a considerable margin. If mankind had obeyed the rules of the rest of the animals here the total number of humans would number in the tens of millions, instead we are at the billions. We decided to act to resolve the problem."

The screen returned to the disk displayed in the centre then went blank. Jonathan checked what was operating and noted that there was no signal coming to or leaving the computer. He pinged the satellite; the response came back indicating the connection was still available; the satellite was working as expected.

"Well, what do you make of that nonsense Helen?" Jonathan was trying to figure why the man had even bothered to contact them. He had just told them that millions of people were gone, so what difference would the two of them make in this new world that had sprung up like some horror move or the story line from a post-apocalyptic story.

"I don't know Jonathan; do you think we should be following instructions from a group that are obviously crazy? Have they caused as much damage as they say?"

"Well there are two options before us; we can stay here and see what happens or we can move away and the only way to move is onto that ship. If we go anywhere else we may as well stay here." Jonathan was all for staying put but could see the argument to get away with others who are already onboard the vessel that may be headed somewhere a little hostile. This part of Iceland will get very cold and isolated once the winter arrives.

The two went over the pros and cons during the hours that followed the advice from the man who said he was Henry's brother. How did Henry die? If he was one of the group that was controlling this it would be safe to assume that he could avoid the infection; perhaps this organisation is what he said it was and they are all subject to the same threat.

It was two days before the ship made an appearance, heading south towards Keflavik; it wasn't moving fast but it would take Jonathan and Helen about six hours if they were to drive down the coast to meet it. There was a hamlet which was much closer but it was small and certainly nowhere near big enough for a vessel of that size; it did have an anchorage, so it would be possible to put a tender ashore if they chase to do so. The decision would have to be made in the next hour or they will miss the opportunity.

"The cruise ship it is then; I have always thought that cruising was for people that were much older and more sedentary than me but it seems we have an invitation that we cannot refuse." Helen had persuaded Jonathan that it was the only real option they had. The ship was evidently working to some sort of plan and if they stayed where they were there was no plan.

58.

It was a surprise to Jonathan that they didn't have to go far to contact the ship: after a short drive of just over an hour the ship came into view around the headland. It was anchored about five hundred metres offshore.

Once the decision had been made it only took them a couple of hours to close the house down; better to do it properly as they didn't know what the future would hold for them and they may have need of the bolt hole at a later date. They took the minimum with them; change of clothing and the two guns. Helen kept the Glock and Jonathan the revolver. They didn't have sufficient for a prolonged battle with anyone but they did have enough to get them out of trouble in the short term.

As they stopped at a small concrete landing stage that had seen better days, Jonathan wondered what and who was waiting for them on the ship. It was a small vessel, the design like so many small cruise ships that catered for the niche market of the better off. Part of the name could be seen on the side of the superstructure behind the bridge, something Sea? She was still making a lot of smoke, enough to get them fined in the continental United States in past days, it didn't matter today.

"Looks like we are expected." Helen gestured towards the ship from which a small vessel, one of the vessel's tenders, had left and was making its way towards them. Jonathan watched them through the binoculars.

“They do not appear to be armed and only two people in it. You go behind the truck and I will be over there.” Jonathan indicated a small wall that ran parallel with the beach that was next to the jetty.

“Better safe than sorry, it will give us time and space to react if they are intending us harm.”

The boat was now slowing down with the coxswain taking care not to damage the boat; once next to the concrete wall one man jumped out with a rope and made the boat fast to the jetty, the other remained in the boat at the controls. Both men looked in the direction of Jonathan and Helen, unmoving.

“Better do something Jonathan or we will stare at each other until it gets dark.” Helen moved from behind the vehicle that had brought them. As she started to walk towards the two men Jonathan followed close behind. Neither man at the quayside made any movement but continued to stare at the two approaching. Jonathan still held the handgun and was ready to react if the situation required it. Nothing happened; they were now within talking distance.

“Good day Doctor Dudman, Mr Brown, we have been waiting for you to decide that you should come with us, time is getting short. I assure you that you are not in any danger if you come with us but if you decide to stay things may be a lot different; this is the last opportunity for you to change things. If you come with us you do not need the weapons but if you want to keep them for self-reassurance please bring them with you.”

The man speaking was the one still in the boat; an English accent that Jonathan thought might be from the West Country. The man on the dockside said nothing but held onto the mooring rope ready to cast off. Both men looked fit and well, they were wearing what looked like a company uniform that was worn by the deck side of merchant ships. Plain but practical; the clothing had seen better days, it was relatively clean.

“Well they know who we are and they know who we are so it looks like we have been expected; shall we go for a cruise?”

Helen moved towards the boat and Jonathan followed. The man in the boat helped them both step from the concrete into the boat. Once they were both sitting, the man on the quayside threw the mooring line into the boat and jumped in after it. The engine revved and the boat reversed away from the small harbour, making a turn as it did so. Once clear the helmsman put the engine into forward and the boat gained speed as it left the small harbour and headed towards the waiting ship.

59.

“Welcome aboard, I am Captain Smith and command this vessel; we have been expecting you two for some time but you seem to have been trying to elude us.”

The man speaking was well over six feet and looked like he spent a lot of time in the gym. His handshake was firm but not over tight. He wasn’t wearing a uniform just an open neck shirt with a thick jumper over the top. Safety boots and blue combat trousers made him look like some sort of engineer that had been at work just before.

“Please follow me and I will fill you in on what is happening and what you can expect from us.”

Captain Smith turned on his heel and walked towards an open door that led into the superstructure of the vessel.

“I hope he doesn’t end up like the other Captain Smith of the Titanic.” Jonathan said to Helen as they followed.

A sign indicated that this route was for crew only and was a restricted area due to dangerous machinery. The corridor was long and dimly lit but they soon arrived at another door that was marked by a sign that said it was the main briefing room. Obviously, the layout of this vessel gad been changed from the original.

“Please be seated.”

The Captain waited for Jonathan and Helen to sit down and then sat opposite them across a large square table; there was nothing else in the room other than the table and eight chairs that were place around it. The walls of the space were completely bear, with only the ventilation outlets disturbing the plain off white. The floor was bare metal deck with no covering. The sound of some distant machinery could now be heard.

“We are now underway so I expect that you will not see Iceland again but never say never I suppose.”

“Why are we here?” Jonathan was the first to ask although they both were beginning to think that their futures were not in their sole control anymore.

“You have been given the chance to survive, there are no guarantees but I can assure you that you are both in a better place now you have joined us.”

“But what is going on.” Helen was still unsure about the need to leave what was, on the face of it, a secure place where they could have survived for a lengthy period; they were now into the unknown.

“All in good time Doctor, first we have to have something to eat and drink. There will be a very thorough explanation when the rest get here; should be in around ten or so minutes.”

There was a bang on the door which was immediately opened; one of the two men that had brought them from the shore came in with a tray that had coffee and sandwiches on it. He placed the tray onto the table and left without a word, closing the metal door behind him.

"Please help yourself, the briefing should not take too long, then you can take a look at the accommodation that will be your home for some weeks to come. That's if our plan comes to fruition that is."

The Captain stopped speaking, poured himself a cup of black coffee and sat back in his chair. Jonathan took the coffee and poured a cup for Helen.

Very talkative, this Captain. Jonathan thought to himself. Captain Smith was just staring into space and not looking at either of them.

"Sandwiches are good Captain, it makes a change from making them ourselves, doesn't it Jonathan."

The Captain smiled and looked at his watch. The door opened and two men and one woman came into the room; the woman carried a fold over folder that was bursting at the seams. All three sat down at the table without saying anything.

"Ladies and gentlemen, I think we can start now." The Captain nodded towards the woman with the file."

She had sorted some pages from the file and had laid them down in sequence in front of her. Jonathan was sat opposite but could make out what was written on them, one of the titles looked like it said Game Start or something Start anyway. The woman was probably in her late thirties, slim with her hair tied back; not a trace of makeup and her hair need in need a colour, badly.

"You two are here because you are both in category one of this emergency; that is to say you are both displaying some sort of immunity from the contagion that we face. In the true sense of the word it isn't a contagion but a widespread modification or change to the way we are all built. However, the spread of this problem at first sight does appear to some sort of disease that is passing from one person to another. The speed of transfer is so fast that under current medical thinking it is quite impossible; but none the less it is happening."

The woman looked at them both in turn as if waiting for a reply; Jonathan thought that she had much more to say so kept quiet.

"What is going to happen now?" Helen was still puzzled that they had taken the trouble to do this when the whole population was in dire trouble. If what they had leaned over the last couple of days was indeed true, this ship, and those in it were of no significance at all. Nothing on this ship mattered.

"As I said you two are unusual, in fact so unusual you should not be here at all, you should have been dead some time ago."

"And? What now?" Helen was starting to get irritated; what are they expecting from them.

"You are both now in this vessel as guests, we will be leaving the area once we have double checked the shoreline; we are then going South from here and then to Scotland to establish a centre for the continuation of the project that is now in place. I must admit the resources and the people we have available may not be enough and the project will fail. In a moment a guide will show you around the ship and allocate accommodation; the crew and people on here only number seventy-three."

60.

"Doesn't make sense Helen." Jonathan was getting concerned, the briefing had taken over an hour but they had not leaned anything of significance that was new to them; the lady had gone over what they had been doing and what had happened to the research once it had been used as a weapon. None of the detail surprised them and most of it had been filed in by Emily when she had appeared at the house in Iceland. When they had both asked questions, the answers were either vague or contradicted what they knew to be true.

After the briefing they had been led down a corridor that appeared to be a crew only route; bare steel walls and a red painted floor. It was at the end of the corridor that a large steel bulkhead door opened onto an open area that was brightly lit and furnished with what would be expected on a cruise ship that had a large number of passengers that wanted to be entertained. The only thing missing were the passengers except one or two that they encountered going through the space.

He large open area went through three floors and was topped by what appeared to be a large sectioned skylight that could be moved back to allow the outside sunshine into the space. The roof was closed and seemed to be opaque, very dirty or both. The centre piece was a large ornamental fountain that swept upwards to give a different view from each floor; the whole thing decorated in brightly coloured murals around each level. The only thing missing was water: the pools at each level were empty. The odd thing about the fountain was that the water could be heard cascading down from the top to the bottom.

"Why the sound effects mate?" Jonathan asked the man who was their guide. Jonathan could see no plausible reason to have a fountain that was turned off and take the trouble to have only the sound of running water; even someone who could not see would not be fooled for too long. They had been shown around part of the ship but had not met any people that they could speak too. Helen had tried with a woman who had walked past them in the opposite direction but it seemed her attempt at communication had not been heard.

"Your accommodation is just this way Mr Brown, you can have a look around when you are settled, food will be brought to you."

The man turned and was gone, Jonathan opened the door and went in; it was a medium sized cabin that provided the most typical holiday accommodation on a ship this size. Jonathan had been on a cruise only once in his life when working in one of his former jobs on the lookout for pirates in the Middle East. The room he was now in seemed very familiar, even the standard image on the wall, a scene from Sorrento or some other part of the Amalfi coast.

“Is this it? I expected to have a sea view at least, this must be one of the cheaper options for a cruise on this ship. I thought that this type of cabin had been phased out years ago.” Helen sat on the bed and looked around.

“You are right this size and type of cruise ship is a rarity but there are still many that do the shorter cheaper holidays. I expect this ship had had half a dozen different names and had operated under several flags.”

There was a knock at the door.

“Your bags Mr Brown, if there is anything else please ask. Your meals should be here in a moment. Sorry there was little choice but we are operating under a somewhat constrained budget at the moment, I’m sure you will understand.” The man smiled and closed the door.

“What did you think of that Helen?

“Think of what?”

“That bloke didn’t look at me once; the cabin could have been empty and I think he would have still said the same thing.”

“Perhaps he didn’t want to get into a conversation, perhaps he is busy.” Helen lay back on the bed and closed her eyes.

“Do you remember anyone asking what we wanted to eat after we came on board? Jonathan was still staring at the door.

“No Jonathan, they didn’t ask me. Why do you ask?”

“He said that he was sorry there was little choice. That implies that there was some choice does it not.”

“I suppose so but perhaps he just said that to fill out the conversation.”

“No Helen I was not asked about food either so I will be interesting to see what comes in the next few minutes.”

The knock at the door heralded the arrival of the food. Two large plates of sandwiches. Enough for ten never mind the two of them. The normal meeting type sandwiches; everything from beef to a three-cheese mixture. Even pork pies cut into four pieces. The man who had delivered the food left without a word.

“If you were thinking about some food that had been gathered on a budget that was tight on time and resources. What would expect it to be Helen?”

Helen was asleep and starting to quietly snore. Jonathan was in two minds; wake her up or let her sleep. He chose to let her sleep for an hour or so; the food could wait that long. He picked up the coffee pot that had arrived with the food. Still very hot even though the pot was not insulated. Things may be better after a decent coffee. He sat on the bed next to Helen and pondered what they were no getting into; perhaps nothing but he had never left anything to chance; he had no intention of starting now. Coffee first then he would wake Helen for something to eat then perhaps a little explore.

Jonathan sipped his coffee and considered were they were and how they had arrived at this place in time. The noise from the ship's machinery could be heard in the background but it had an odd tone every three and a half minutes; no mistaking it was regular and the same. To say the ship was in the North Atlantic it was very stable, Jonathan couldn't detect any movement at all. Very quiet for this time of year; where they even moving? Jonathan thought that they were not.

61.

Helen woke with a start, not fully knowing where she was. Jonathan was still sitting on the bed next to her.

"How long have I been asleep?"

"I'm not sure, my watch has stopped; I thought it best to let you sleep, it's not as if we have anything urgent to be getting on with is it?"

The watch Jonathan was wearing had been with him for a good twenty years and had been worn on all sorts of jobs, both for the military and more recently his civilian masters; it had never gained or lost more than a few seconds a week over that period. It was a very good watch and now it had stopped; perhaps it was an omen for what was to come.

"Have a coffee it will wake you up; we have a little exploring to do; if nothing else it will fill in the time; we may even meet people who are in a similar place to us."

"Have you noticed anything odd with the coffee Helen?"

Helen drank from her cup and thought about it.

"Very nice if a little strong for some people."

"Is it hot enough?"

"Yes, it is just right, why?"

"It came out of that pot which isn't insulated and has been here in this cabin since we arrived; over an hour at least; it should be cold by now and it isn't. Not the normal pot of coffee do you think?"

"Perhaps it is one of those new technology items that perform very well with minimal complexity."

"No, it is just an old fashioned ceramic coffee pot; it should be cold."

Jonathan handed Helen the plate of sandwiches then took one himself.

"Even this food looks like it was prepared ten minutes ago; I must admit that some sandwiches do tend to last longer than others but these are very fresh, almost like an image of what sandwiches should look like."

Helen looked at the sandwich in her hand and took a bite.

"Seems fine to me, very tasty and the butter is excellent."

"Perhaps you are right." Jonathan was still not convinced that something strange wasn't going on but when they have a look around the situation may explain itself. Jonathan noted that his watch was now working but was unsure if it was right. It was not anywhere near the time that it had stopped.

They both agreed that they should go and see if they could find other people and question them as to their own feelings about being on the ship.

62.

The hallway outside the cabin was empty in both directions; They were in the middle with the same distance either way.

“Which way? We came from down there so I think it might be useful to go the other way. By my reckoning the front end is down there so if we go this way we should eventually arrive at the stern.”

Jonathan nodded and started to walk towards the end of the corridor that he estimated to be about fifty metres at most. As they went, Helen tried some of the doors; none were unlocked. The decoration was typical cruise ship with random pictures on the wall and an edged carpet running through the whole space.

The door at the end was also locked but had a round window set in the top half; the view out was to a large deck area that had a structure that was probably a bar; the space also had several piles of sun loungers that had been stacked up and tired down. It all looked as though it was not in use. The sea could be seen moving away from the stern of the vessel.

“So, we are not going to get out this way, are we? I think we should go back the way we arrived and find our way up to the top deck and search around there.”

Jonathan didn't answer. He raised his arm so he could see his watch and continued to look at the sea.

"What are you doing?" Helen was all for leaving now and going to the opposite end of the corridor that only had doors that were locked.

"Helen, this is getting weirder by the minute. While you were having a doze, I timed the sound changes of the ships machinery by counting in my head; it was running like the sound was in a loop, that is a recording and not real sounds. I could be wrong of course but this image we are now looking at is doing the same. Look at the sea and the wake that is made as we travel through it."

"Wave sequences do seem to repeat themselves Jonathan I have seen it when I was on holiday with my parents; it is caused by the shape and speed of the ship that is pushing through the water that has a swell."

"Yes, I know but this is not like that, the sequence lasts two minutes and thirty seconds; about the same length as the noise from the engines; this time a visual loop rather than just sound."

Are you sure?" Helen certainly wasn't sure at all and thought that Jonathan was seeing things that were not really there.

"There is one thing that confirms it Helen." He looked at his watch.

"Over there by that stanchion in exactly fifteen seconds a seagull will appear and fly from right to left before it disappears behind the edge of the ship."

A large gull flew into view just as Jonathan said it would, before transiting from right left then disappearing behind the edge of the railing that was attached to a large part of the ship's superstructure.

"That is creepy Jonathan, how did you play that trick?"

"Not a trick Helen, at least not a trick that I could play. In the sequence there are four birds that appear then disappear, the one you saw was the second in the series and low and behold here is the next one." Another seagull could be briefly seen behind the ship before diving down and out of view.

"I think that we are looking at a similar projection that was in the warehouse and then in Hong Kong; the question is, why is it here? For that matter why are we here?"

They both stood for several minutes looking at the projected loop; now they knew what it was the falseness was obvious and would only fool a casual observer.

Jonathan tried the door again, there was no give but that was to be expected for a door of this type that led to the outside.

“Back the way we came, past our accommodation and see what is at the other end.

They both returned down the corridor; this time trying all the doors that they encountered; all were locked. The cabin they had come from was still as they had left it. Jonathan felt the coffee pot; it was still hot.

“This pot should be cold by now but it doesn’t seem to have cooled a bit.”

They tried every entrance door the other way and found the same; nothing open and no sound coming from any of the cabins at all; the background engine noise was the same.

The door at this end was one they had originally entered so they both expected it to be unlocked; it was and opened easily against the closing spring.

“One thing before we go further Helen.”

“What?”

“When we came aboard we were armed, were we not?”

Helen paused and looked back down the corridor.

"Yes, we were but now we are not, the two handguns are not in the cabin but I don't remember putting them down anywhere; did we leave them in the boat that brought us from the shore?"

"No, we didn't I would certainly have remembered a request to hand them over and I would not have simply put a gun down and forget that I had done it."

63.

The technician was watching the progress of the two; he had been assigned to monitor them and keep them inside the bounds of the programme so that their interaction could be tightly controlled. The part the two had played had been accurately predicted but they were now out of the normal constraints that the project required. He wasn't sure why the operation had progressed so quickly but he was now in a position to halt certain parts of it. The two he was now watching had to be segregated or the whole thing might leap off into a different direction.

"How are they doing?"

Another man was watching of the technician's shoulder.

"Are they anywhere near figuring out how to escape?"

"No, I can keep putting obstacles in their way for ever so I should be OK until the end is called; is that still today?"

The foreman looked at his watch; he was hoping that this was indeed the end of this particular project but he knew that it was likely they would simply run it again in a couple of days. It did pay the bills however so he was happy to do as required and take the quite substantial amounts of money.

"Yes, we are still on schedule, it has another six and a half hours before the plug is pulled. After that we have at least a week sorting out what went right and more importantly what went wrong. First impression that I have is that the model evolved far too quickly so the results cannot be relied upon to initiate it in the real world. It simply wouldn't work."

The technician looked back at the data that was displayed at the bottom of the live image that was on the second screen.

"It would be interesting to see what they could achieve if let out."

"We can't do that, this is a minuscule part of the project and it is coming to an end so we will contain them and have a debrief about them at the end." The second man turned and left the area to go and supervise others that were doing a similar job to the technician.

The technician was bored and started to have thoughts that he could amuse himself with a little harmless fun; the two subjects were contained so it wouldn't hurt to play with them but he also considered the repercussions if he was caught working outside the control. It would be unwise to put anything in the way of the main programme. No, he would just sit and watch for now; the end is in sight so he will be able to relax into something more interesting later today or at the latest tomorrow. The debrief would not start for some time as the amount of data to be assembled would be a mammoth task in itself.

64.

Jonathan and Helen paused at the door that would lead to the entrance they had arrived through; both now unsure as to what was to happen.

They were now both unarmed and very vulnerable. It was now obvious that they were being held in the part of the ship with only one way out.

Why all this as going on was a mystery; why hadn't they simply been left on the shore; they could not affect anything outside of their very small area of Iceland.

The corridor was as empty as the one they had left. From memory Jonathan thought that there was a water tight door just beyond the end of the carpeted area. There were no doors until they reached the end. This part had no pictures on the wall which were bare panted steel. They were now into the crew only area of the ship. The sound of the machinery running far below was the same, including the cycle that indicated that it was ether a reciprocating machine or it was a recording loop.

"Well here goes, let's see what the rest of the vessel has to show us."

Jonathan pushed open the door to the stairway, up which they had come from the boat earlier.

“Why have we not seen anyone else since the man left the food and coffee?”

Helen said the same that Jonathan was thinking; the place should have at least someone going about the business of running a vessel this size. The entranceway led to a set of plain steel stairs that went up as well as down, everything was painted the same off white on steel.

“Upwards and onwards I think.”

Jonathan led the way taking the steps two at a time; he was now in the mindset that prepared him for violent confrontation. Helen two steps behind was now also prepared for conflict. They had to get out of this; the house on the shore in Iceland was suddenly a very attractive proposition. They should never have agreed to come here. The place was all wrong.

“What’s the bet that the door will be locked?”

The sign over the door said “Bridge Deck”.

“Not sure this can be the bridge deck as we entered down at water level came up one deck into the cabin area. Here we are two decks above that but, from what I saw of the ship from the outside the bridge deck should be another two maybe three decks above us.”

“None the less that is what it says, not the bridge but the bridge deck.”

Jonathan was not convinced. “I have never seen it labelled like that, on passenger ships decks are always given a name for the punters and a letter for the crew, usually “A” Deck would be the deck under the bridge. So, the bridge would be accessed from “A” Deck.”

“Very interesting Jonathan.” Helen moved the handle and pushed on the door. It opened very easily to reveal another corridor, much shorter that the one they had left below; it had two doors on one side and a door at the far end; all were closed.

“Does this remind you of anything Jonathan?”

“No but it is quickly becoming a pain in the arse.”

“Well you will remember, as I’m sure you are old enough, the early computer games that were text only. Some of them were text only maze games. Do you remember the line “You are standing in a corridor that has two doors on the right and one at the far end?”

“Vaguely but what are you saying? We are in a maze?”

“Sort of, we cannot go anywhere other than the direction they are guiding us, every other option is denied because the doors are locked. Why would all the doors on an empty ship be locked? Do they have a problem with petty theft?"

"If that is the case then only one of theses doors will be open and the other two locked."

"OK we will short cut this and try the last door first." Jonathan strode to the door at the end of the corridor and ignored the two that led to the side."

The door was unlocked and opened with little effort despite having the appearance of a large, self-closing barrier. Jonathan stepped through and found himself on the bridge; the whole space was empty of people. The view out to the forward part of the ship gave a stunning image of the sun just closing with the horizon. It looked like it would be dark within twenty minutes or so. The sea was flat calm with only the occasional white top to the swell that was moving towards them.

"Funny that a ship of this size and complexity and under way is sailing along without anyone here. I know the world has changed a lot over the last couple of months but this is foolhardy to say the least." Helen had stepped onto the bridge area behind Jonathan. Both looked around and walked to each of the bridge wings. All the navigational equipment was working, the main radar was showing nothing close to them; not land or any other vessels.

Jonathan stood behind the main compass and looked towards the horizon.

"Not real; this is another simulation or projection of some kind. I assume we are actually on a real ship because we saw it come insure before we boarded. I think we are experiencing another Honk Kong moment but this is impressive."

Helen was staring at the bulkhead that held the door through which they had just come.

"Jonathan, I think you better look at this."

The entrance door to the bridge they had used was gone; only a blank wall with a notice detailing emergency procedures was there. There was no other way off the bridge unless the doors to the two bridge wings would open and let them outside, but that wouldn't get them far.

65.

The technician smiled as he removed the door through which they had entered the bridge; the two subjects could now be contained until the project either progressed or ended; either way these two had come to their useful limit. He was surprised that it had been so easy to contain them; he thought they were cleverer than this.

A Message flashed up on the main screen; it indicated that the final phase had now begun and the close down would start in ten minutes. *Excellent! An early knock off.*

He began running the routine checks to enable him to make a quick exit once this had drawn down. He knew that it would all start again in a couple of weeks and he might even have the same subjects to monitor but it would be slightly different; it always was. He supposed that, in time, they would play all this for real but until then the simulation would be run over and over again to make sure it would work in the real world.

He watched the two subjects; he was itching to introduce a little fun into this ending but was still prevented by the strict controls that had been set.

It wouldn't hurt though would it? This part was now separated from the main effort and these two could not affect any outcome.

"OK what we are seeing cannot be real so we are being fooled by what we see." Jonathan was stating the obvious but he couldn't think of anything else to say. The situation had to be resolved.

"We could go over every inch of this place and ignore what we can see. Feel our way around to see if any of this is real. The deception is big so there might be other fake stuff going on."

Helen began moving along the rear wall feeling along the wall and pushing against the blank spaces. It was all as it looked. A bare wall with odd attachments and the emergency sign. The door should have been there but she couldn't feel it.

"Sod this, I'm going to have a little fun."

The technician smiled and typed in a string of commands. There was a pause before an image stood on the bridge.

"Have you worked this out yet Mr Brown, Doctor Dudman?"

Standing just in front of Jonathan was Professor Swift. Helen could only stare at the image that had just appeared.

"Nice to meet you again Professor Swift; slightly better circumstances this time." Jonathan was as shocked as Helen at this thing that had suddenly presented itself. Jonathan knew that it could not be real as he would have bet considerable amounts of money that he had indeed killed Swift; there was no arguing that so, this image must be just that; an image and only part of an elaborate deception. The image changed to Hector, on his own this time.

"Very funny, where is your small friend today?" Jonathan was interested in how this could possibly work; he had never heard of the science that could be doing this. The man looked real and had been talking to him, or was it at him.

"Mr Brown, I see you are not too overwhelmed by my sudden appearance, perhaps it's your training that lets you keep so calm."

"No, I just don't particularly enjoy games that have been put upon me; this is obviously some sort of game and I'm not willing to play it. What do you, or whoever is driving this want?"

Jonathan was irritated that he was indeed talking to this apparition.

Helen walked over and around the image that was facing Jonathan.

"Looks real; doesn't seem to be projected from anywhere."

She gave Hector a prod in the back; she felt resistance; this image had form that was not possible. Hector was real.

"Creepy."

The technician was amused by the small alteration he had made to the programme but he couldn't push it any further as his boss would be in the room any time soon. He typed a short command.

Hector disappeared and the two were left alone on the bridge.

"What do you make of that?"

Helen was looking at the finger that had podded Hector.

"He felt very real but as we both know he couldn't have been. Whoever is in control of this has technology available that is the stuff of science fiction."

“Remember that they have wiped out a large part of the worlds’ population in a very short time, that is the stuff of science fiction, this is just a curiosity that we must bottom.”

Helen was still looking at her finger.

“What’s wrong with your hand Helen?”

Helen turned her hand over and looked at the whole length of her first finger on her right hand.

He is still attached to me, or at least part of his suit is, look.

She held out her hand for Jonathan to look at, sure enough there was a piece of the suit material attached to her finger about the size of a small postage stamp. Jonathan moved to touch it but as he got close it faded from her finger leaving her skin and finger nail unmarked.

“Shit, that was close.”

The technician decided that he would now leave this module alone until he was told to do something. *Do as you are told.* He should report this anomaly but if he did he would deep in it for carrying out an unscheduled intervention. No, he would forget it.

Helen was still puzzled by what had happened. Some of the clothing that she had touched seemed to stick to her; more than that it was as if the material was bonded to her skin. It then slowly moved forward and was gone.

"Well that was weird Jonathan."

"It sure was, I think this whole thing is one big projection but with a complexity that shouldn't be possible." Jonathan had no idea what they should do. They couldn't stay here although it did not appear they were in any danger.

"What do you want from us." Jonathan shouted into the air; perhaps whoever was doing this was watching or listening.

The technician heard the question from the system; he would have to do something before the supervisor came back because the subject would attract some attention if he kept this up. The project was very near the end and all would have gone well if he hadn't tried to be smart and interfered. He typed in a few lines of code, hopefully this will be the end. Back to the plan, he would just contain them as instructed.

On the bridge the door reappeared.

"They are letting us go Helen."

“Or wanting to let us to go somewhere else. Why were we here? Doesn’t make sense. Swift then the large bloke sent to speak to us and actually say nothing of any significance, all a bit random.”

Helen walked over to the door and pulled it open. The door moved without much effort and she stepped through, Jonathan close behind her. The corridor was the same and the door at the end led to the same stairs. It wasn’t long before they were back in the cabin with the coffee and the food.

“I need to find out how this coffee pot works, it is still hot, do you want some?” Jonathan poured two cups from the still very full and hot pot, redirecting his panic.

66.

The technician had received the close down routine; it did surprise him that the project was not to end entirely. It was odd that some of the Autonomous Elements or ELs would be separated and used in separate runs. These two had been working together for the whole run but were now to be divided and used in two different tests. One of the tests was a rerun and the other would be a continuation of this one; most unusual.

A whole series of code changes had been given to him for implementation later on in the day. The Doctor would be retained on the project and Brown would start again in a separate but related project. How many times they would have to run this scenario before it was real could be determined by this or the next hundred simulations. He was far too low in the food chain to be privy to the expected outcome and the plan that was driving it all forward.

"OK my friends, let's get the show on the road, or should I say shows." He smiled as he entered the command for the software modification to begin loading. Nothing would be apparent to the two for a couple of hours at least. It all depended on the other areas that were to be modified or stopped. The two would be unaware of the changes until they found themselves playing the new parts. He often wondered if some of the memories from one scenario would be retained for the next.

"I vote that we stay here until they come and tell us what is going on." Helen was laid on the bed. "We have plenty to eat and drink, the shower works and it is quite cosy in here. As we cannot get out it would be the simplest thing to do."

"You are right, we have run up and down the spaces that we are allowed to enter and ended up back here. Rats in a trap springs to mind."

The software began loading, major parts of the simulation began to change immediately. The run had been suspended until the control elements had initialized but now things started to happen all over the parts that were outside this one. It would be a few minutes before the technician could start the changes for these two. He was looking forward to the challenge.

67.

Helen, laying on the bed, thought that she might even go to sleep for a while. She was unsure as to why she was now so relaxed; the situation had got worse by the day. It would have been great to stay at the house in Iceland; why had they decided to leave.

Jonathan was getting wound up; the opposite to the way that Helen was feeling. He felt that something was going to happen and soon, he often felt like this just before a job started.

The room was dark; light came from the edge of the door that wasn't completely shut; it was difficult to figure if the light was natural or from the corridor lighting. Helen stirred and was almost overwhelmed by the pain in her head; it came in waves and threatened the structure of her skull; she lay back and waited for the pain to subside.

Helen could see well in the darkened room; not all that big; a single bed she was lying on and a small chest of drawers or cabinet of some sort was the only furniture. A TV monitor on the wall at the end of the bed; a large floor to roof mirror was on the wall next to the door. This was not the room she had fallen asleep in. Jonathan was not here. She took stock of herself; apart from the mother of all headaches she seemed to be complete, with no damage. She moved her limbs one by one and flexed her toes and fingers; OK so far.

As the pain in her head subsided she noticed an awful smell that seemed to fill the room. It took a few minutes for her to realise that the smell was coming from her and the bed she was lying on.

"God, how long have I been in here?" She wasn't all that sure where "here" was but she must have spent several days in this position. The bed smelled as if she had emptied her bowels and bladder several times at the least.

"I have got to get out of here." Helen said under her breath. She rolled sideways intending to swing here legs over the side and sit up. The swinging went OK but some bedding wrapped around her so all it achieved was to drag her sideways from the bed and crash onto the floor. The pain in her head had reached maximum and now her joints joined the assault. She gasped as she tried to manoeuvre in to a sitting position.

"Move and we will get up; no problem." Helen was feeling a little better; she stayed on the floor for what seemed like an hour but was less than a quarter of that. The pain was now manageable.

Helen got to her feet hanging onto the end of the bed; confident she wasn't going to topple over, she made for the light shining in from the corridor. She reached the door and hung onto the handle, steadying herself with the other hand on the wall.

The door moved as she pulled at it; as the light came in from the outside she saw an apparition so awful that she couldn't understand what she was even looking at. It was minutes before she realised she was looking at herself in the large mirror by the door.

Her hair hung down in grimy knots and appeared as if unwashed her entire life. Dressed in what looked like a hospital gown that had seen better days with large multi coloured stains all over it. The face staring back out at her was not one she recognised; gaunt would not even be an approximate description. Helens sunken eyes and the flesh on her face with the skin stretched over the bones in her face; she thought she must have been ill for some time or she had been deliberately starved. Helen pondered the image for a few seconds; she didn't feel hungry and now the pain in her head was receding she didn't feel all that unwell. She looked down the length of her body; her arms and legs were emaciated and very dirty; her finger nails and toe nails were black but not with the dirt. She held up her hand to get a closer look; her nails were dark; as if they had been painted; she looked back to the mirror and opened her mouth, her gums and teeth were also black.

"What the hell has been happening? I've got to get out!"

Helen stepped through the door and found that she wasn't in a corridor at all but a large open space. The room she had been in was one of five, set at one side of what looked like a ballroom; the floor appeared as if made of wood with a large circle in the middle with some company motif etched into it. There was a large amount of paperwork scattered as if thrown down at random. One complete side was windows allowing the bright sunshine to flood the interior space; a stage or raised orchestra platform was at one end, it too covered in discarded paperwork and files. Higher up there seemed to be a view gallery or a walkway that went around the whole room.

As she stepped onto the dance floor she realised that it wasn't level but tilted towards the room she had just left.

A movement at the edge of her vision caught her attention; a very large rat, sat on the stage watching her, its nostrils twitching but otherwise unmoving as if it was trying to gauge any threat that Helen might pose.

"Good morning ratty." Helen didn't like rats one bit but she was way too tired and weak to pay any attention.

A large box file was in her way as she stepped across the centre; she looked at it trying to read what was on the front cover; LAST OPTION. Helen tried to bend to pick it up but instead fell to her knees. She moved sideways and sat next to the box file. It held a few hundred sheets of paper that had names listed in alphabetical order; against each name were three tick boxes; Yes, No and ? She leafed through looking at names she didn't recognise. There were several Dudman but only one Helen; the No box, ticked. The pile of paperwork didn't explain why the vast majority of names had Yes against them or give any clue what any of the marks against each name meant.

68.

Jonathan Brown didn't attract much attention; just over six feet tall with an athletic build and short greying hair; he looked like many of his age group who looked after themselves. At forty-three, a man who came across as very serious and not prone to wasting time in idle chit chat. Today, he was just another man walking with the flow of people that filled the streets at this time of day in this part of Nottingham; the shoppers were out in force; many with children in tow because of the school holiday that had started the day before. The crowds had been swelled by the large number of office workers that had come out to get a takeaway lunch or to sit for forty minutes with their friends in one of the many cafeterias and eateries that are on every street corner in big cities these days.

He slowed his pace; he didn't want to arrive at the meeting a second too soon; someone hanging around would attract attention and he didn't want to be noticed. The target would be on the corner of Tolbert Street and Goldsmith's Street just outside the large shopping complex that occupied a whole city block. They would be waiting for someone who had asked him over to this part of the city for lunch. Jonathan didn't know the person he was to kill and had only the briefest idea of whom or what they were; a Doctor by all accounts but not a medical Doctor but some sort of scientist. Didn't matter to Jonathan the only information he ever wanted was enough to do the job. Jonathan was nearly at the crossing and there was no sign of the person who was to die.

Jonathan stopped at the crossing that led to the shopping centre; he saw them across the road looking down the length of the street; obviously looking for someone; *shame they would never meet them. Jonathan pondered why he hadn't seen the target sooner; perhaps they were hidden from view by the crowd as the angle changed when Jonathan had approached the crossing.*

Standing in the second rank of people waiting for the lights to change, Jonathan made a final assessment; the target was wearing a light blue, long sleeve shirt over which they had a leather jacket that was opened; the shirt sleeves peeping out of the cuffs. Excellent, Jonathan thought as the lights changed. Jonathan closed the distance. Jonathan moved to one side as he walked towards the target; he could see inside the jacket to the shirt that had a packet of cigarettes or something similar sticking out of it; might be a phone so he would avoid that.

Going well so far Jonathan said under his breath as the distance closed. He would pass to the left of the target on his right side and then continue into the shopping centre.

The man was startled as Jonathan brushed past him, moving backwards to get out of Jonathan's way. The moment had passed, Jonathan carried on into the shopping centre. That was very amateurish, he had missed the target, there was nothing to do except get away and consider his tasking for another opportunity.

Professor Catchpole continued to wait for his contact to arrive. She was only two minutes late but here she was.

“Emily how nice to meet you, perhaps we can get away from here and have a coffee.”

Have you ever entered a room and thought that you had been there before? Or looked for someone in a crowd who suddenly comes into view.

There have been several explanations of the Déjà vu. The image that is immediately forgotten then suddenly remembered. Does the brain store it incorrectly then let it surface at the same time as the correct memory is stored?

Much has been written regarding the possibility of parallel realities that offer a million different outcomes for every incident. What if all possible variations are played out before one is chosen to represent reality.

What if nothing in our world is real?

Printed in Great Britain
by Amazon

37277353R10210